ACCIDENTAL
LAWYER

KIM HAMILTON

TouchPoint
Press

ACCIDENTAL LAWYER by Kim Hamilton
Published by TouchPoint Press
Jonesboro, AR 72401
www.touchpointpress.com

ISBN-10: 1946920150
ISBN-13: 978-1-946920-15-7

Editor: Melody Miller
Cover: 99designs.com, Alfred Obare (Alfie™)

Visit the author's website at KimHamiltonBooks.com

First Edition

Printed in the United States of America.

To my supportive husband, Peter; and my daughters, Megan and Kelly who make me proud every day.

CHAPTER ONE

Some lawyers demonstrate their legal prowess in courtrooms with a cool confidence, examining witnesses and charming the jury. Others hunker down in law libraries dissecting case law and writing brilliant legal memorandums. They're all armed with fancy words, legal precedents, and an air of self-importance. But not me. I wasn't that kind of lawyer. I was armed with a cell phone camera, a large advertising budget, and a few shreds of remaining dignity.

My name is Jessica Snow. I work for the law offices of Dawson Garner. It was mid-August. My elevated professional status had me standing alone at the intersection of North Avenue and Smallwood, an area that cried out for urban renewal. The summer heat shimmered like a hellish vapor off the asphalt. My mouth was dry, but the rest of me was cloaked in a layer of sweat. Worst of all, the humidity had ravaged my hair. What wasn't matted with perspiration was frizzed out like a science-fair project gone wrong. I was there to take photos of the intersection where my client had been hit, but my investigation was interrupted by the assaulting screech of the worn brakes on a Baltimore City transit bus. I involuntarily cringed knowing that when I turned toward the bus I would likely see my face across its entire girth with the words, *Dawson Garner & Associates, Have You Been Injured? We can help. Call 555-WANNA SU.*

I angled my head in that direction, and there it was. A colossal, roaming display of shameless self-promotion. I was still gaping at it when I heard feet shuffling toward me. Someone tapped me on the shoulder.

"Hey lady, isn't that you?"

I turned toward the voice. A shirtless guy wearing an Orioles baseball cap pointed across the street toward the bus. Standing beside him were three other shirtless men, all in their early twenties, passing around a joint.

Their eyes darted from me to the bus and back again. They were waiting for me to confirm that it was, in fact, my face on the bus, but I couldn't speak the words. It was hard for me to admit that I was an ambulance chaser.

When Dawson hired me six months ago, I was fresh out of law school, had passed the Maryland Bar exam, and was among the many young grads looking for work. It was no secret that I was hired, not because of my superior legal mind, but because Dawson wanted a young, female lawyer for his advertising campaign. I wasn't proud, but I took the job. I was desperate to move out of my parents' house. I considered my current employment a temporary holding place until something else turned up. I was competing for legal jobs with thousands of other recent law-school graduates. My problem was that I was not at the top of my class. I hovered closer to average and I had no connections. Zero. So, until that recruiter called with my dream job, I was determined to be the best rookie ambulance chaser in the city and prove to Dawson that I was more than just a pretty face. Despite my inexperience and misgivings, I'd become an integral part of Dawson Garner's legal machine, which pained my mother greatly. It could be a dirty business.

The four guys continued to look from me to the bus as it pulled away.

"Sure does look like you," the one in the Oriole's cap continued. "Except for the hair. Hair's different."

They stared at my hair. Some of them grimaced. The image on the bus was a testimony to the miracle of Photoshop. It transformed my eyes from ordinary blue to a deep, purple-tinged blue. My mousy brown hair appeared shiny, smooth, and so brown it looked almost black. The bus-me was stunning. In contrast, the person they saw before them resembled a young Sandra Bullock having just rolled out of bed.

"Yeah, that's me. Any of you need a lawyer?" I squared my shoulders with false bravado and forced eye contact.

They nodded, I suspected, in collective approval of my profession. Another guy, whose cargo shorts hung so low I could see the fly of his boxer shorts, said, "We got a lawyer, lady, but he ain't as fine as you."

This brought laughter and more head bobbing from his companions. They inched closer. The air had thickened with heat and the pungent smell of pot. I hugged my messenger bag into my chest.

"Yo. Give little miss attorney some space—you freakin' her out." This came from a guy who had tattoos mapping both arms, over his shoulders, and at the base of his neck. The others took a step back and Tattoo Guy turned to me. "I know Dawson Garner. Handled a case for me once. Got me a lot of money." He tilted his head toward the others. "They don't mean no harm. Having some fun is all. You lost?"

"I'm not lost. I wanted to see the intersection. I have a client who was struck by a car here last week."

"You mean Melinda?" Tattoo Guy asked.

What luck. I hadn't expected to find a witness, but that would sure seal this case for me.

"Yeah, Melinda Taylor. Did any of you see what happened?"

They glared at me in disbelief.

Orioles Hat spoke up. "Lady, Melinda don't get hit. She don't ever get hit. She walks into cars when they turn and she falls on the ground. Melinda's a phony." He took a hit off the joint.

And there it was. The ugly truth about this business—some clients lied. Melinda's credibility had been tossed to the curb, yet I had to support her story until I had conclusive evidence to the contrary.

"How do you know she didn't get hit if you didn't see it happen?"

Orioles Hat tilted his head to the side and studied me. "Are you for real, lady? How could I see something that didn't happen?"

He was right. Their revelation about Melinda had thrown me off my game. It was time for me to leave. I reached into my messenger bag and handed each of them a business card. "I'm Jessica Snow. Call me if you need a lawyer."

My new pot-smoking friends each pocketed my card and ambled off to reposition themselves on their street corner. I waited for the walk signal, crossed the street to my car, cranked the air conditioner, and shot out in the direction of my office.

It's a big jump from a law school classroom to a real legal environment with actual clients. The first thing I learned about personal injury law was there's a shitload of money to be made if you have the stomach for it. The second thing I learned is that I don't quite have the stomach for it. My colleague, Marty Ferguson, he's got a stomach made of steel. He'll start a file for anyone with a pulse. Last week he signed up a guy who drove his car straight into a mailbox. The client claimed he was distracted by a billboard of a woman with a generous cleavage. Marty plans to sue the billboard company. Or maybe the woman with the cleavage. Probably both.

I cruised south on Charles toward the office and passed a variety of row homes, some newly renovated, some worse for wear, and numerous retail spaces: hair salons, tattoo parlors, food vendors. Our office, which once housed a doughnut shop on the first floor, was a traditional row home flanked by Uncle Mo's Subs and Sundries on the south side and Top Notch Tax Service on the other. The interior of my car was beginning to cool when I parked in one of our designated spaces behind the building. I walked in the back door and through the kitchen to our reception area.

"What the hell happened to your hair?" Kari Cruz asked.

Kari managed our front office. She had ten years on me age-wise and, despite my legal training, was savvier than me in many ways. Kari knew the nuts and bolts of the personal injury business and possessed a bold and brassy manner that I envied.

"It's the humidity," I said, trying to smooth down the sides with my hands.

"That is one bad case of the frizzies." She laughed. "I should hook you up with my girl, Paulette, at the House of Hair. She could tame that monster down."

"I don't have time for that right now. You know that new pedestrian case? Melinda Taylor? She's a phony. I ran into some guys on the corner where it happened. They claim she has a history of scamming for insurance money."

"You went to that intersection by yourself? Jess, you can't be doing that. Not in that kinda neighborhood. You got book smarts, not street smarts. Let me ride shotgun with you when you do that investigating stuff." Kari exuded inner-city-girl confidence, having grown up one of three children raised by a single mom in West Baltimore.

Dawson emerged from his office holding a cigar in the corner of his mouth. He never lit it inside but liked to play with it. "What's wrong with your hair?"

"It's the humidity. It's awful out there. I should get hazard pay." I tried to run my fingers through the strands, but they got caught in the tangles.

"Did you get the photos?" Dawson asked.

"I got some great photos. But I also talked to four guys who say Melinda's a phony. She has a habit of walking into cars."

Dawson pulled the cigar out of his mouth and pointed it at me. It was time for another lesson. "Did the insurance company say she's a fake?"

"Not yet."

"Then she's not a fake now, is she?" he said with a crooked, disapproving smile.

"Right, got it."

"That's my girl. But just in case, call Dr. Khann's office. Let them know we may have a liability issue. Have him keep her treatment short."

Dr. Khann was one of many medical providers to whom we refer clients. It's a competitive industry. Dozens of doctors in the area woo us for our referrals. They'll show up with doughnuts in the morning or arrange a catered lunch. Food is a great motivator. I referred a new client to Dr. Shon on Pratt Street last week, not because of his stellar medical credentials, but because he'd delivered a tray of homemade cheese ravioli and tiramisu from Sabatino's. We don't prostitute ourselves for food alone, though—there are other incentives. Dawson used Drs. Leighton & Loade near the Belvedere Hotel because they show up with an occasional box of Stradivarius cigars. Other popular incentives include local event tickets, and there are many: The Ravens, the Orioles, shows at the Hippodrome, anything at the Arena, the Preakness...Baltimore's a great city for doling out bribes.

"Can you meet with Delroy Johnson? He's expected any minute," Dawson said. "I need you to get his new file started."

"Delroy? I settled a case for him last month. What's he got now?"

"It's another bus case. He said the bus made a sudden stop and was rear-ended. Delroy banged his head and has some neck pain. You know—the usual."

"Argh. I hate bus cases. And Delroy's cheap cologne makes my eyes water."

"Yes, but at least it helps mask his bad breath."

I nodded my agreement.

"He's a loyal client, Jessica. Give him the VIP treatment."

Dawson retreated to his office as the front door opened. Delroy Johnson walked in. "It's so hot out there. This guy on the corner has a sign that says 'will work for air conditioning'."

Delroy was in his early seventies. Until his recent semi-retirement, he worked long hours at the pawn shop he owned on Holliday Street, The Pawn Palace. His son runs the shop most of the time, with occasional assistance from Delroy.

Today he sported a lime-green collared golf shirt and madras pants in yellow, green, orange, and pink. His ankle-high white socks peeked out over a pair of pale-yellow Sperry's. I guessed he took his last settlement check and hit the men's department at Macy's. He proudly marched toward Kari and me. An invisible cloud of cheap cologne engulfed my breathable space.

"Dawson said I need to meet with you to get my new bus case going. What do ya think it's worth this time? I'm looking to upgrade my entire wardrobe, maybe even get one of them monogrammed bathrobes and start smoking a pipe."

Delroy was a man with a clear vision.

"Too soon to tell, Delroy. Let's start with the accident. What happened?"

"I was on the number seven bus leaving Mondawmin Mall heading to the Pawn Palace. Just before St. Paul Street, Marva—that's the bus driver—slammed on the brakes, and then the van behind the bus rear-ended us. I flew out of my seat and hit the one in front of me. That's how I got this." He pointed to the center of his forehead, which looked normal to me. "Then I fell back again and my head nearly came off my neck." He rubbed his neck with both hands and winced. "I need to go back to see Doc Cohen."

"Sure, Delroy, I'll get you over there. But first, did you see what caused the bus driver to make the sudden stop?"

"No. But there was people talking about it. Seems Marva saw her husband on that street corner getting chummy with a local... uhhh... a local business woman, if you know what I mean. Marva was so honking mad, she slammed the brakes, threw the bus into park, and launched herself out the door after her husband. Poor guy. I hope for his sake he outran her."

"What about the van that hit the bus?"

"I don't know anything about that van. Mind you, I was in a great deal of pain," he said, rubbing his neck again and wincing.

What a pro.

"Okay, Delroy. Here're some papers I need you to sign. This one is our retainer agree—"

"Oh yeah, Jess. I know the drill. I seen these before. Gimme a pen and I'll sign away." Delroy seemed pleased to be a regular, like part of the family.

I handed Delroy a pen, and as he signed the paperwork, I got on the phone with the receptionist at Dr. Cohen's office. Cohen was a chiropractor with a private practice a few blocks from our office. There's a framed chiropractic license on the wall near his desk, so I'm pretty sure he's legitimate. He treated many of our clients with neck and back pain. It's a simple arrangement. He provides us with medical records and bills documenting our client's painful injuries, and we send him a fat check to cover those bills as soon as the claim is resolved. If we're unable to resolve a claim, he eats the bills and doesn't charge the client. This is business as usual in the world of personal injury law.

I arranged for Dr. Cohen to see Delroy knowing it would score us a catered lunch sometime next week, courtesy of Dr. Cohen's marketing manager.

I stood to escort Delroy to the door. As we reached the middle of the reception area, he stopped. "You know, Jess. I like you. You're easier on the eyes than old Dawson there," he said tilting his head toward Dawson's office and wincing once again at the effort. "I'm gonna share my little secret with you."

"Secret? Oh, I don't know, Delroy. You should share those with your wife or you're drinking buddies—not me."

"I'm not married, and my drinking buddies aren't good listeners on account of their advanced inebriation. No, Jess, you gonna like this. You see, I got to thinking after my first bus case that these accidents happen kinda regular in the city. Folks are always riding buses and buses are always having accidents. Get where I'm going with this? I ride the buses a lot and now that I'm retired, I can ride them even more to increase my odds of being on one when that next accident..."

"Nah nah nah..." I slapped my hands to my ears. He smiled at me and nodded his head. I continued to chant as I walked away from him, returned to my office, and shut the door. I heard Kari exchange a few words with him. The front door closed.

Kari hollered through my door, "That Delroy sure is clever."

#

Dawson stood in the reception area waiting for me when I returned from the bathroom. "Jess, would you come into my office?" I knew he was in there with Sal Seidelbaum, the firm's marketing guy. They were discussing a new advertising campaign. My stomach turned at the thought of more transit buses and billboards bearing my face.

I found the two of them sitting opposite each other in matching faux-leather wingback chairs. I took a seat on the faux-leather sofa and was joined by Bailiff, Dawson's beloved orange tabby cat. He had ten pounds of excess fat and the propensity for shedding mountains of fur. He snuggled in and nudged me with his nose, requesting a gentle petting. I complied.

"Jess, we've got to work on increasing our incoming business. We need to capture more of the market, make more money. So, I've got some good news for you. Sal is going to produce our first television commercial." Both men were on the edges of their seats with silly schoolboy grins, barely able to contain their excitement. A numbing chill passed through me. I felt a little nauseous and saw black spots dance before my eyes. Bailiff sensed something was wrong and tried to leap from the couch. It was more of a waddle, then a fall.

"What's wrong, Jess? You look a little pale," Dawson said.

I had to be careful here. We all knew that I was hired as a prop for the firm's advertising. Until I could prove that I was a capable attorney and able to bring in clients and generate loads of money on my own, I was pretty much at his mercy. I couldn't refuse to do the commercial. But I didn't have to be enthusiastic about it, either. Maybe I could talk him out of it.

"Commercials are so expensive. We've got plenty of business coming in. Have you seen the stack of files on my desk? And Kari took two more accident claims this morning. Why bother with a commercial when we have steady business?"

"Because, Jessica, this is how the game is played. More clients, more money. I ran into Stuart Milligan last week, and he told me he bought a place in Hilton Head, right on the water—five master suites and a Koi pond."

Stuart Milligan's office was located across the street. He was a personal injury attorney who saturated the airwaves with TV and radio advertising. He was a little more high-profile than Dawson Garner & Associates, but no more reputable. Dawson always measured his success against Stuart Milligan's.

"You already have a place in Hilton Head," I said.

"That's the point. Now I need a bigger place in Hilton Head—six master suites and a shark tank."

Good grief.

Sal nodded. I guessed he was mentally tallying his production fee, which would include a week at Dawson's new place in Hilton Head.

"Are you sure you want to spend all that money on commercial advertising for the purpose of one-upping a weeny like Stuart Milligan? Besides, you got the better of him when Jolynn Wright left him and brought her medical malpractice case to you."

Jolynn Wright was the victim of a botched boob job that left her breasts misshapen and lumpy. They were later repaired to a spectacular double D cup. Jolynn claimed she couldn't have Stuart represent her any longer because his sexual advances toward her had become tiresome. She trucked her double Ds and her file across the street to our offices, where Dawson paid her the utmost respect and almost never looked at her boobs. He settled last week for six figures.

"That's a huge settlement you ripped from Stuart's greedy paws. Wave that in his face if you want to be on top of the scoreboard."

"Yeah, he was pretty pissed off about that. He'd counted on that fee to buy another Mercedes to add to his collection. Still, I'd like to stick it to him. We're doing the commercial."

He stood and Sal rose, too. I took it as a sign that I was dismissed.

I stopped at Kari's desk to use her lint roller to get Bailiff's long, orange fur off my suit. Kari looked at me, bright-eyed and expectant. "Well?"

"Well, what?" I asked. She grabbed the lint roller from me and motioned for me to turn so she could do my back.

"You're gonna be on TV, girl!"

14

She always eavesdropped.

"I don't want to be on TV."

"Why not? That would be so cool. How many people get to have their face on the TV? You'd be a local celebrity. And that would make me a local celebrity by association."

"That kind of advertising demeans the profession. It seems desperate."

"Well, if we don't advertise, how will clients find us? They'll end up with someone like Stuart Milligan." She turned me around by my shoulders, put her face close to mine, and looked me in the eye. "Dawson will go broke, the firm will shut down, and we'll all be sleeping on the streets." She tossed the roller onto her desk and bobbed her head at me. Pursing her lips, she said, "Is that what you want?"

Her performance was a bit over the top, but she had an interesting perspective that I hadn't considered. If we didn't represent these people, some other attorney would.

"I don't see why you wouldn't want to be famous is all."

#

I settled in behind my desk to make the easy money. Shifting into negotiating mode, I rummaged through my snack drawer and pulled out a bag of Sun Chips.

Here's how the negotiation dance goes. Let's say I had a routine soft-tissue injury claim, and let's say I thought it was worth about $15,000 to settle it. I call the adjuster, make a ridiculous demand of $20,000, and artfully state my rationale for why my client deserves this sum, what with all the pain and suffering, inconvenience, and emotional trauma caused by the irrefutable negligence of the insured driver. In a perfect world, the adjuster would acknowledge my savvy appraisal of the claim, thank me for being so reasonable, and write me a $20,000 check. Sadly, this never happens. What the adjuster does is point out the minimal nature of any injury, the excessive amount of treatment, and the overall crappiness of the claim, blah, blah, blah. They usually offer something closer to $10,000. After a few phone calls back and forth and more posturing by both of us, we wind up agreeing to something around $15,000, which is where we both knew it should be in the first place. It's a colossal waste of time, but the meaningless volley makes us both feel victorious.

The file at the top of the stack was Tyler Martin. Tyler was one of our regular clients. Litigious and loyal. I liked him because he had a steady job at Walmart. He was bright and respectful, easy to work with. Tyler never hounded me about moving his case faster. I'd already reviewed his file and knew this was another typical rear end, soft-tissue case worth about $5,000. I picked up the phone and called Brenda Ballister, or Brenda Ballbreaker as Dawson calls her.

I got her voicemail. "Hi Brenda, it's Jess at Dawson Garner calling on Tyler Martin, case number 3475ASDF2898474-2012. I'm hoping we can settle this one. Give me a call, 555-926-6278."

I hung up and moved onto the next one—Sharlyn Monroe. This one had some meat on it. Sharlyn held a soft spot in my heart. She was a young woman without guidance, trapped in the dead-end world of her drug-dealing boyfriend, Darnell Black. I could tell she was smart and I knew she could improve her circumstances. She was off to a solid start. Dawson had lined up a job for her around the corner at Hal's Bar and Grill. She was a prep cook. Hal said she had mad skills.

Sharlyn had the misfortune of being a passenger in Darnell's car when he made the ill-fated decision to text a customer and arrange for a delivery of whatever street drug he was dealing at the time. While texting, he failed to maintain control of his vehicle, causing it to cross over the center line into an oncoming minivan. Fortunately, the sole occupant of the minivan was its driver, who turned hard to the right to avoid a direct impact and instead took a hit to his passenger side. Sharlyn was not so lucky. Darnell also turned hard to the right, causing a direct impact to Sharlyn. She was left with a concussion, a broken arm, several lacerations, and multiple soft-tissue injuries. She recovered after a few months of treatment and was back to work at Hal's. Meanwhile, she was still living with Darnell, who was anxious to get his hands on her cash. Darnell had called me every day the past week.

I'd begun negotiations with the adjuster on her claim, Art Miller, to the tune of five actual phone conversations, thirteen voicemail messages back and forth, and three unanswered emails. I don't like negotiating via email. It's cowardly. I dialed Art's number, expecting to leave another voicemail message. He surprised me by answering the phone on the third ring. "Jess," he said after the perfunctory niceties, "I got you more money on this one and hope we can settle it. I've got $28,000. See if you can sell that to your client."

Wow. I would have taken $25,000. "Come on, Art, get me $30,000 and we can close this up. She broke her right arm for Christ's sake, and your insured does not make a sympathetic defendant. He's was texting, Art—texting."

"All right, Jess, calm down. Let me talk to my manager, see if I can get some movement on this. I'll call you in a couple of days."

I thanked him and hung up, marking my calendar to call him in two days. I confess that a huge part of me, like 49 percent of me, wanted to take the $28,000 so I could get the file off my desk. But the other 51 percent knew that it was my job to get as much for my client as I could, regardless of how many dance steps I had to perform. I was bothered by the fact that Darnell was so anxious to get his hands on Sharlyn's money. I knew Sharlyn could do better than a drug-dealing loser and I was determined to help her continue down a better path. The job at Hal's was a good start.

I continued going through my stack of files, making phone calls, playing the negotiation game. In about two hours, I was able to call on all seventeen files and managed to settle three. Just another day at the mill.

I was about to move on to my other pile of claims for review when Kari put a call into me. It was Brenda Ballister.

"Hi Brenda, thanks for calling back. Did you get my demand package?" The demand package consists of copies of all the medical records and bills, as well as any claim for lost wages. Rarely do I send an actual "demand."

"Yeah, I got it," she said with a slight chuckle. The chuckle worried me. I'd said nothing funny. "He's racked up $1,800 in meds and claims $400 in lost wages. Is that right?"

Her tone riled me. She had me on the defensive and I needed to play offense. "Right, the medical records indicate he had swelling and muscle spasms in the neck and back. He was in a great deal of pain initially and had to miss three days of work. I'd like to settle for $8,000."

I heard snickering again from her end. "Jess, this guy's claim is a joke. Your client has had five accident claims in the last five consecutive years. There was no damage to his car and minimal damage to my insured's vehicle. The medical expenses of $1,800 are excessive, and the lost wage claim of $400 is laughable."

She pissed me off. It's a known fact that injuries can be sustained even with minor damage to a vehicle. Our practice practically depended on this. "Look Brenda, my guy has documentable, objective injuries. You and I have settled dozens of similar claims reasonably and amicably. What's with the attitude today?"

"Tyler's a phony, Jess. With all his priors, we put an investigator on him..."

Oh, shit, this can't be good. I hate this job.

"... and we discovered that while Tyler was supposed to be home resting, he found his way with some friends to the laser tag park, where he played two successful forty-minute games, running, ducking, and hiding with his painful neck and back injury."

"You're wrong. It must have been someone else. Do you have photos? Send me photos." This was a lost cause, and I knew it, but I couldn't give up. I was an advocate after all. "It's possible that your investigator followed the wrong guy into the laser tag park. Or even if it was Tyler who walked into the park, it's so dark in those places. How could your investigator know it was Tyler actually playing? He might have been hanging out in the lounge area playing pinball or texting his girlfriend..." I couldn't believe the BS coming out of my mouth.

"I'll stop you there before you further embarrass yourself. Yes, I have photos and I'll send them to you. Meanwhile, to get this piece of crap claim off my desk, I'll give you $1,500 to make it go away."

"It's worth $5,000 until I see the photos."

"I'll email them to you. Goodbye, Jess." She hung up.

I was going to strangle Tyler.

I went to tell Kari about the incriminating photos and found her with a death grip on the office phone. Her eyes were wide with disbelief. "Jesus, Mary, and Joe. You're sure?" Kari said into the phone.

Apparently, the caller answered in the affirmative. Her jaw dropped. She disconnected without a goodbye and stared up at me. Her mouth started to form words, but she remained silent as the color drained from her face.

"What is it? What's wrong?"

"Something awful happened."

"What is it?"

"It's Harvey Metzger. They found him..."

"I didn't know he was missing."

"No, you don't understand. They found him… dead."

Harvey Metzger was an independent financial advisor. His office was two doors down from ours, but he wasn't there much. I didn't know Harvey personally, but I knew he and Dawson were buddies. Dawson had invested some money with him.

"What happened? How'd he die?"

"All I know is they found him dead at home, and it was no accident. Li'l Ham told me they called in the homicide unit." Li'l Ham was Kari's industrious cousin. He stopped by on occasion to sell knock-off handbags and watches from the trunk of his Cadillac sedan.

Kari's eyes were still on me. "You've gotta tell Dawson."

"Tell me what?" Dawson said, looking confident and robust as he emerged from his power meeting with Sal. Sal walked right passed us staring at the screen on his iPhone. Dawson must have noticed the distressed look on our faces. "Oh no, this can't be good. Jess? What is it? Did we lose another client to Stuart?"

I stood with my mouth hanging open, trying to find the words. Kari spoke them for me.

"It's Harvey. He's dead."

"What do you mean he's dead? He can't be dead. I saw him last night."

"Oh, he's dead all right," said Kari. "Word is he was shot in the head and died in his desk chair."

Dawson put one hand on Kari's desk and stared down at the floor. I couldn't read his expression.

"Who would want to kill Harvey?" I asked.

"A lot of people." Dawson turned and, with a rigid gait, reentered his office and closed the door.

CHAPTER TWO

Kari and I stood, wide-eyed, mouths gaping. After a few beats, she walked to Dawson's door and tried the handle. "It's locked. He never locks the door."

Sal still lingered in the corner of the reception area thumbing his iPhone, seemingly oblivious to what had just transpired. He put the phone in his breast pocket, picked up his briefcase, and walked out the front door as Marty walked in. They exchanged brief greetings as they passed each other.

"What was Sal doing here?" Marty asked. He carried his gray suit jacket in his hand, exposing a short sleeve, collared shirt that was partially untucked. The maroon tie he wore was pulled loose at the neck and hung at an awkward angle. His brown hair fell in disheveled strands across his face. This look was common for Marty. I called it 'post-mugging.'

"Dawson's having him produce a TV commercial," Kari said. "And he wants Jess to be the star." She beamed at me like a proud mother.

Marty shrugged, unimpressed. "That's what we hired her for."

Ouch. Marty didn't like me. Or maybe he was having a hard time warming up to me. Kari said he and Dawson had interviewed a lot of young lawyers, and I didn't even make Marty's top five. He wanted someone older with more experience, and maybe a penis, Kari said. He may not look all put together, but the truth was, as a lawyer, Marty was sharp, cunning, and tenacious. I could have learned a lot from him, but he showed no interest in teaching me.

I changed the subject. "Did you hear Harvey Metzger was killed?"

He looked up at Kari for verification. "It's true, but we don't have any details. Li'l Ham heard it from the guy who cleans Metzger's pool. All we know is that he was found dead in his house."

"Dawson locked himself in his office when he found out," I added.

Marty walked over to Dawson's door and gave it a two-knuckle rap. "Dawson, it's Marty. Can I come in?" There was no response. Marty waited a few seconds then spoke to the door again. "Why don't I pick us up some lunch?"

Silence.

He tried again, "How about a cheesesteak sub from Uncle Mo's?"

"With peppers and onions," Dawson yelled through the door. "And a Coke."

Within fifteen minutes, we had lunch in hand. Marty rapped on Dawson's door again. Dawson flung the door open and marched past us toward the kitchen. He held a manila folder in one hand. We followed in silence.

The four of us took seats around the kitchen table and Kari distributed the sandwiches. I dug out the napkins and stuck straws in everyone's drinks. There'd never been this much dead air among the four of us for this long. Kari broke the silence. "Why have you been hiding in your office?"

"I wasn't hiding. You knew where I was." Dawson hinged his mouth open and took a giant bite out of his sub. This kept him from speaking for a bit, which I suspect was his intention.

I tried another approach. "It's sad news about Harvey..."

"Harvey Metzger can rot in hell," Dawson said and took another bite of his sub. While he chewed, he opened the folder he had carried into the kitchen and spread the papers across the center of the desk.

Marty, Kari, and I examined them. The document's letterhead read *Harvey Metzger Financial Services.* They looked like financial statements. The account was in Dawson's name and had several hundred thousand dollars in it, distributed among fifteen or twenty different stocks.

Marty put his reading glasses on to get a better look. "Looks like a lot of money. Harvey made you a nice little profit last quarter."

"No, there's nothing there. Those are phony figures. I saw him last night. He lost it all. It was a Ponzi scheme." Dawson took another bite.

I was stunned by Dawson's nonchalance as he delivered this news. Perhaps he was still in denial. Perhaps he's tougher than his slender frame would suggest.

"You saw Harvey last night?" Marty asked.

Dawson nodded, mouth full.

"And you discovered then that he had lost all your money?"

Dawson nodded again.

"And this morning he was found dead?"

Dawson started to nod again, then swallowed hard. His eyes widened. "Oh my God. I may have been the last person to see him alive."

"Other than the killer," Kari clarified.

"I'll be a suspect. I'm a lawyer for Christ's sake. They'll want to hang this on me. The press will lynch me."

#

I spent the rest of the day distracted by the implications of Harvey's death. Marty ran off to a deposition and Kari tried to busy herself at her desk. Dawson shut himself back in his office but didn't lock the door this time.

At five o'clock, Kari put the answering service on and we peeked in on Dawson to make sure he was all right. He was putting golf balls into a coffee mug.

"How're you doing?" Kari asked.

"Not good. I'm only sinking three out of five."

"Not your golf game. We're wondering how *you're* doing."

"I'm fine. Damn." He missed another putt. "Thanks for your concern though. You two go on home."

We headed out to the parking lot and got into our cars. The firm's private lot had enough spaces for eight cars. This time of year, it was still light when we left. In the winter, the lot was dark and foreboding at this hour. Dawson had security lighting installed, but that illuminated the lot, not the alley leading up to the lot or the dumpster that sat at the end.

I drove an old Honda Civic that I'd owned since college. It was a dull maroon color with a dent in the rear bumper from when I backed into the dumpster—(it came out of nowhere)—and several dings and scratches of unknown origin. It wasn't a looker, but it was reliable and paid for so it would have to do until I saved up for a new one.

I cruised down St. Paul Street toward my Fells Point neighborhood, passing the Inner Harbor, Baltimore's crown jewel. It was home to a variety of restaurants, retail spots, and many unique attractions—The National Aquarium, the Science Center, four ships that are National Historic Landmarks, and much more. This part of town crackles with energy and life.

I worked my way down President Street to Aliceanna and found a parking spot just a short block from my home. I lived in a classic, old Baltimore row home I rented from a vintage Italian woman named Mrs. Bianco. I was not aware of her first name. Everyone called her Mrs. Bianco. All of four feet, eight inches tall with an athletic frame for a 75-year-old, she had the energy of a Hopkins lacrosse player. She's also my next-door neighbor. In the pocket of her housecoat, she carried a nine-millimeter Smith & Wesson and was known to use it to scare away teenagers returning from the waterfront bars who had the poor judgment to urinate on our block. Her deceased husband had bought three distressed row homes back in the 60s and renovated them. They raised a family in the middle one and have always rented the adjacent two. Rumor was that the late Mr. Bianco was a "made man"—part of the Luciano Family out of New Jersey. He had earned a fortune in the casino business before he died under suspicious circumstances. On nice evenings, Mrs. Bianco sat on her front porch, wearing one of three housecoats, smoking a Tiparillo and sipping port. Tonight, however, she sat on my porch.

"Hi, Mrs. B," I said, putting down my messenger bag and taking a seat on the step next to her.

"Jessica," she said in her Italian accent. "You are smart lawyer, so I come to you." Her pack of Tiparillos sat on top of a file folder spilling over with paperwork. She reached for the pack, lit up, and offered me one, which I politely declined. Then she handed me the folder and said, "It is small part of what Mr. Bianco left to me, but it is gone. All gone."

I opened the file. It contained statements like the ones Dawson had showed us. Phony financial statements from Harvey Metzger's firm. There were a lot of zeros. My stomach turned with outrage, my anger ignited. How could Harvey do this? How could anyone do this? My incredulity aside, the more practical side of me wondered if Mrs. B could still afford to upgrade my appliances as we had agreed when I signed the lease.

"The papers are phony, Jessica. The money is gone."

"I know. Dawson had money invested with Metzger, too. I'm not sure there's anything I can do for you right now. We have to let the investigators follow the money trail and see what's left. I bet there's a lot of people like you and Dawson who are victims. Metzger was a crook."

"That bastard," she said. "I'd shoot him myself if he wasn't already dead."

I had no doubt of this.

She reached into her housecoat, caressed her handgun, and gazed ahead.

"The world is full of bad people." She pointed her Tiparillo at me. "Have you got a gun like I told you?"

"No. You know guns make me nervous. I need some training, but I don't have time for that. How about you let me get a dog for protection instead?" Mrs. Bianco had a no-pet policy written into my lease.

"No dog. I teach you to shoot, no problem. My friend, Estelle, she has a shooting range out in the county. We go there. How about Saturday?"

That put me on the spot. I wasn't sure I wanted to learn to shoot from a 75-year-old Italian mob widow. Or maybe I did.

"I'll think about it, Mrs. Bianco. Thank you for the offer."

I said goodbye and stepped inside my house. Crossing through the living room, I glanced out the large double window and noticed Mrs. B had vacated my porch. I passed by the powder room, took the long hallway leading to the kitchen, and climbed the stairs to my second-floor bedroom. It was a cozy home. I was still working on the décor. It was mostly IKEA Swiss-modern with a splash of yard sale and consignment treasures.

I did a quick change into my running clothes, grabbed a bottle of water, and headed back out to get some exercise. My approach to exercise was to get moving and stay moving until all the distasteful aspects of the workday were replaced by happy thoughts, or until my hair was matted with sweat. Whichever came first. I set out to walk the ten blocks to the waterfront pier where I liked to begin my run.

Heading down Caroline Street, I stopped at Aliceanna and waited for the traffic signal to turn. The number nine bus approached and slowed to a stop across the street. Looking up, I saw Delroy Johnson through the bus window. He smiled and waved at me with an abundance of enthusiasm. He mouthed something to me and pointed to another man sitting next to him who also smiled and waved at me, but appeared confused. I replied with a befuddled wave of my own. As the bus resumed its route, Delroy put his pinky finger to his mouth and his thumb to his ear—the universal sign for "call me."

CHAPTER THREE

I was the first to arrive at the office the next day. Bailiff greeted me with a purr and a full-body stretch. He extended his front paws next to my feet, stuck his abundant butt in the air, and assumed the feline version of yoga's downward-facing dog.

"Good morning, fatso. Let's get you some breakfast." He waddled behind me as I filled his bowl with a double dose of light cat food and freshened his water. I made a single serving of coffee and checked my email on my cell phone. There was a message from one of the adjusters I'd been trying to reach. Marty, Dawson, and Kari came through the back door before I could read it.

"Hey, where are the doughnuts?" Kari asked.

We were supposed to get doughnuts delivered from Dr. Pomeroy, the new doctor on Biddle Street who had stopped by a few days ago to introduce himself. "I guess he forgot."

"Well, he sure isn't getting off to a good start. How could he forget our doughnuts? I was all jazzed up for some icing and sprinkles. He's one of those holistic, alternative-medicine-type docs. Seems ironic that he would be sending doughnuts instead of green smoothies and tofu, or some other healthy crap, but I didn't want to turn him down."

"'Never turn down a doughnut.' Those are words to live by,"

Dawson said.

We nodded our agreement. Kari pulled a box of granola bars out of the cupboard and sat it in the middle of the table. After everyone was set up with cups of coffee, we took seats around the kitchen table and grabbed granola bars.

Dawson knew the importance of regular meetings and good communication, but he hated the formality of the conference room. It had become our custom to sit around the kitchen table and share our plans and expectations for the day. It often went something like:

Dawson: Whatcha got going on today, Jess?

Me: I'm gonna make some more money for you, Dawson. Settle a few claims, lie to an adjuster, bribe a witness, you know, the usual.

Dawson: That's my girl. What about you, Marty. What's going on?

Marty: I've got a deposition this morning, viewing a crime scene this afternoon, and having drinks with the Mayor this evening.

Dawson: Rock and roll. What a team! Sounds like you all have everything covered. Maybe I'll play a few holes today...

But today was different. Today the mood was somber given the death of Harvey Metzger, the loss of Dawson's fortune, and the disappointment over the doughnuts.

"All right gang, we've suffered a hit. A big hit. But we need to move on and keep doing what we do best. We've still got enough money in the bank to continue our ad campaigns and produce the new commercial Sal talked about yesterday. It should be business as usual."

As he spoke, Dawson dug his right hand into his pocket and pulled out a cigar. He lit it and started toking on it, blowing rancid plumes of smoke into our faces.

"Dawson!" Kari said. "That's disgusting. Put that thing out. You aren't supposed to smoke in the office."

I stood up, grabbed the cigar right out of his mouth, headed out the back door across the parking lot, and tossed it into the dumpster. When I returned, Kari lit a vanilla candle, Marty turned on the fan, and Dawson sat slumped in his chair.

"Sorry," he said. "I've been smoking nonstop since yesterday. I guess the stress of all that's happened is weighing on me more than I want to admit."

"We're with you, Dawson. We'll get through this together," Marty said.

"It's a minor setback. We're bigger than this," I said.

"Freakin' A," said Kari.

Our chat was interrupted by a pounding on the front door. It was locked. We typically didn't open for business until eight-thirty. We adjourned, and Kari went to open the door. Lingering by her desk, I saw a pair of suits walk through the door. They adjusted their jackets, so we were sure to notice their holstered guns.

"We're with homicide. Looking for Dawson Garner," said the older one with salt-and-pepper-hair. He was tall, with a solid build and dark brown eyes that gave away nothing. The younger one was also tall, but skinny with red hair and freckles, like Howdy Doody in a suit.

Dawson appeared in his doorway. "I'm Dawson Garner."

"I'm Detective O'Mallory, and this is Detective Jones," he said pointing to Howdy Doody. "We'd like to speak with you about Harvey Metzger."

Kari and I drew in breaths and looked at Dawson, who appeared nonchalant. "Sure detectives. Come on into my office. Would you like some coffee?"

They both declined.

"How about a cigar?" I heard him ask as they disappeared into Dawson's office and closed the door.

Marty leaned in and lowered his voice. "Do you know who that is?"

"Who? Which one?" Kari asked.

"O'Mallory. He's the vice cop who headed up the East Side drug bust, alongside the DEA."

"I heard about that," Kari said. "It was all over the news a couple of months ago."

Why was a vice cop working a homicide case?

#

I heard sirens. Sirens are like background noise. It's Baltimore City after all. But this time the sirens didn't fade away. Kari and I hustled to the front door. Sure enough, there was a fire truck stopped in front of our building. It was outfitted with canvas hoses, axes, extension ladders, medical emergency equipment, and four exceptionally hot firefighters. One was a girl, but let's give credit where credit is due.

The firefighters leaped off the truck and got busy. Each was dressed in the requisite black jacket and pants with fluorescent yellow stripes. The girl and one of the male firefighters wore sky-blue helmets that matched the oxygen tanks they carried. The third's helmet was yellow, and the fourth's was black. Black Helmet took the nozzle off the giant hose and ran beside our building through the narrow alley, followed by Yellow Helmet, who gathered the slack in the hose and pulled it along. The Blue Helmet girl talked on the radio. Kari and I were giddy with excitement.

"Jess, did you see them? They're some smokin' hot civil servants."

"Hard not to notice. Come on, let's check out back." We ran through the kitchen. When we reached the back door, I stopped dead in my tracks. The cigar. The dumpster. The fire.

"Kari, I threw Dawson's cigar in that dumpster. It might've still been lit. Do you think that's why they're here?"

"I got no doubt about that, Jess. You think you need a lawyer?" Kari laughed and opened the door. I stood behind her and watched as the calendar-worthy firefighters doused the fire I'd created. It was not long before the flames were gone.

Meanwhile, the locals had gathered to see what the excitement was all about.

"What do you say, Mark? Do you think it's another dead body?" Yellow Helmet said to Black Helmet.

"I don't smell burning flesh. It's your turn to look in. You tell me."

Yellow Helmet pulled his muscled body up to the top of the dumpster and looked inside.

"Looks like the usual, bags of trash, some boxes and a lot of shredded paper—most of it burned. We'll have to call it in. See if the chief wants to send over an investigator."

"Is it a dead body?" someone from the crowd called out.

"Not human if it is," said Yellow Helmet. "You want to take a look? I'll give you a boost."

No reply from the anonymous voice.

Kari nudged me toward the dumpster. I was torn between confessing and keeping my mouth shut. They hadn't asked if anyone knew what happened, so why should I volunteer an answer? Don't ask; don't tell. The fire's out. No one's hurt. Let's get on with our day.

"Anybody see what happened?" It was the one named Mark in the black helmet. Darn him for being so thorough. Isn't that the investigator's job?

Kari shoved me forward. "She saw what happened."

She kept shoving me until I was face to face with Mark. He had classic good looks—high cheekbones and a square jaw, a tan, flawless complexion, and blue eyes that danced as he smiled down at me. I was compelled against all my legal training to confess.

"I threw a lit cigar in there."

He smiled. "Do you often smoke cigars in the morning?"

"Not usually. No."

"Is there any reason why you didn't extinguish it before you threw it on top of a pile of shredded documents?"

"Yes."

"Would you like to share that with me?"

"Oh, right. What was the question?" What the hell was wrong with me? Mark had turned my mind to mush with his intoxicating smile and beckoning eyes. I needed to get a grip. Focus.

"I'm sorry officer..."

"I'm not an officer." Still smiling, now with amusement.

"What should I call you?"

"You can call me Mark."

"Okay... Mark. It was stupid, I know, but my boss was smoking during our morning meeting. He's been under a lot of stress lately what with the Ponzi scheme and murder and all, so he's taken to smoking more than usual, which I totally understand, but it's still gross. It made me nauseous, so I took the cigar and threw it in there. I wasn't thinking. I'm so sorry," I said without taking a breath.

"Have you done this kind of thing before?" Still amused, he stepped even closer to me, so I had to look up into his perfect face.

"No. Of course not."

"She set fire to the kitchen last week," Kari chimed in. "Burnt the bejesus outta a bagel. It was a bagel blaze. Ruined the toaster." She nodded her head toward the door to our law firm.

I gave Kari the wide-eyed, tilted head, *what-are-you-doing-to-me–shut-your-mouth* look.

"Not much of a cook, are you?" Mark asked.

"I'm a hellava good cook. It's Kari's fault that the toaster caught fire. She's supposed to clean the crumb tray."

Marked glanced behind us at our building. "Do you work for Dawson Garner?"

"Maybe."

"Don't worry, I'm not interrogating you. Just curious."

"Mark, we need to get going," Yellow Helmet called out from the corner of the building.

"All right. I'm right behind you." Mark gave me another smile as the fire truck's siren revved up. He sprang into action, gathered his gear, and poof, he was gone.

"Jess, I'm sorry I mentioned the bagel blaze," Kari said.

"I'm sorry I blamed it on you."

"I was trying to keep the conversation going. I think that one, Mark, has a little crush on you."

We went back inside and found Dawson, Marty, and the two detectives standing near the kitchen window.

"What the hell happened out there?" Dawson asked.

"Your cigar started a dumpster fire," I said.

"You mean, you started a dumpster fire," he replied. "I didn't take my cigar anywhere near that dumpster."

"It was all worthwhile because one of the firefighters has a crush on Jess," Kari said.

I shoved Kari with my elbow and gave her the wide-eyed look again.

Marty said, "Are you starting fires just to find a date?"

"No!" Desperate to change the subject, I turned toward the detectives. "Do you know who killed Harvey Metzger?"

"We've got a few suspects. Nothing solid yet," O'Mallory said.

As they turned to leave, Detective O'Mallory said to Dawson, "Don't leave town."

CHAPTER FOUR

My cell phone rang. The display showed Sharlyn's number, but it was her boyfriend, Darnell, whose voice I heard.

"Yo. Snake wants to know what's taking you so long on the case?" Darnell's street name was Snake, and he had a habit of referring to himself in the third person. It was an annoying reminder of his arrogance. "When's Snake gonna get his money?"

"It's not your money. It's Sharlyn's money. And I won't talk to you about her claim."

"You been talking to her about other shit, like getting a job. And she won't even get high no more!" Clearly, I was a terrible influence.

I refused to let Darnell bait me.

"Put her on the phone."

"Bitch."

Then I heard Sharlyn's voice. "Don't call her that. She's my attorney. Why would you want to piss her off?" This was followed by the sound of an open palm against a cheek, a sharp intake of air, and a cry of pain. I heard the phone drop to the floor.

"I'm tired of you mouthin' back at me," I heard Darnell say. Footsteps retreated and a door slammed. Sharlyn was back on the phone. "Jess?"

"Are you okay? Did he hit you?"

"I'm fine." Her voice was shaky and her breathing was quick and shallow. "Can I come see you tomorrow?"

She hadn't responded to my second question, but she didn't have to. I knew he had slapped her. I wondered how often that happened.

"Are you safe there?" I had to ask.

"I'll be alright."

"Are you working at Hal's tomorrow morning? I can come by first thing."

"Yeah, I start at nine. Give me time to get things started and come by around ten if you can."

"I'll see you then."

She disconnected.

Sharlyn was a year older than me, but I felt protective of her like she was my little sister. She was in a bad place and I wanted to help her get away from Darnell whether he liked it or not.

#

I took a call from my mother. She called me a few times a week to make sure I hadn't become a Baltimore crime statistic. She imagined that all strange men who wandered within my personal space were armed with duct tape and chloroform. When I moved to Fells Point, she gave me a can of mace which doubled as a key chain and a fake lipstick that concealed a two-inch, double-sided blade. And a whistle. My parents, happily married for 45 years, still live in historic Mount Washington, the northernmost part of Baltimore City. Even though the area is safer than downtown, most homes, including ours, had a security system, a large dog, and a baseball bat at the ready.

"Hi, Mom."

"Jessica, I heard on the news last night that a Red Sox fan at the Orioles' game was hit in the face by a foil-wrapped hot dog thrown into the stands by the Orioles' mascot. He wants to sue the Orioles for public humiliation and foil-induced abrasions. It's upset your father. It could cost the team millions." She took a deep breath as if trying to steel herself. "You're not representing that Red Sox fan are you?"

Good grief.

It turns out my parents' biggest fear was not my imminent abduction or assault. It was that their own daughter might have a hand in suing their favorite baseball team. They'd have to pack up the old minivan and leave town in the cloak of darkness. There was reason for concern though. Kari had taken a call earlier. She'd repeated the words "hot dog" and "Orioles," then passed the call to Marty. So, more than likely, Marty had agreed to represent the unfortunate Red Sox fan, but Mom was asking if *I* represented him.

"No, Mom. I wouldn't represent anyone against the Orioles."

"Good, because your father would stop speaking to you."

Since taking the job, I was always on the brink of disappointing my parents. They loved me, yet they couldn't help but compare me to my sister, Julia. Julia was 28, two years older than me. She was a registered nurse at Union Memorial Hospital and a rising star in the medical community, bright, successful, and compassionate. She spent her days healing the sick and spreading good health throughout the city. If she weren't such a lovely person, I'd hate her.

"So how's your job search going?"

"Mom. I have a job."

I could hear her disappointment.

We chatted for a while, agreed to try to get together for a family dinner soon, and disconnected.

Kari appeared in my doorway. "Jess, you want to stop by Brenner's with me on the way home? They're having a sale on tuna steaks. I thought I'd pick some up for dinner."

"Sure, I'll tag along."

"Let me give Dawson his messages. Then we can head out."

I followed Kari into Dawson's office. He was standing near the window wearing boxer shorts and hovering over an ironing board, pressing his khakis. The soundtrack from *Mamma Mia* played on his Bose system. He sang along to "Money, Money, Money" under his breath.

"Dawson," Kari said, "how many times have I told you not to stand in front of the window with your pants off? It's not professional."

"No one's looking. Besides, natural light is great for finding Bailiff's hair." He reached for a lint roller and started to roll the next section of his khakis before taking the hot iron to it.

Dawson was a brilliant business man with a few quirks. One of them was his penchant for neatly pressed clothing. It was not unusual to see him like this. He claimed to find the rhythm of ironing mentally soothing. He'd been ironing a lot lately.

"Any word from the detectives about the murder?" I asked.

"Or your money?" Kari added.

"Not a word. O'Mallory and Jones are working the murder. There's a forensic unit trying to trace the money trail. I don't expect they'll find much."

"Jess and I are heading out. I have two messages for you. Do you want to hear them, or should I leave them on your desk?"

"Can you read them to me? I'd like to finish these pants."

"Sure," Kari said, reading from the top pink slip. "Sal said to tell you, 'everything's a go.' He said you'd know what that means."

I knew what it meant. It meant the commercial was a go. It was happening. A quiet dread rose around me.

Kari continued. "And the starter at your country club called. He said they were able to get your pitching wedge out of the tree, but your putter's still up there."

Dawson put on his pants. "Darn, that was my favorite putter. Maybe a good wind will knock it loose."

#

Brenner's Market was a small grocery store located around the corner from our office. We often picked up lunch there from the deli counter and stopped by for dinner items on the way home.

It was a warm evening. The setting sun produced shadows that provided some comfort from the heat as we strolled down Charles Street past the row houses and retail spaces that were all fairly well kept in this part of town. Baltimore had its seedier sections, but our block and the few surrounding blocks were well maintained and had an old

Baltimore, traditional feel. Polished brass plates identified street numbers, brick was crisply pointed, windows had thick panes with leaded glass, and roof lines were adorned with deep and detailed molding. The occasional boarded-up building and scurrying rat were sad reminders that our city had its flaws.

We arrived at Brenner's and grabbed a couple of handbaskets. I walked through the produce section and picked up some salad mix, bananas, and apples. Kari chose some tomatoes and lime for the salsa to go along with her tuna steaks. Together, we headed toward the seafood section. There was no line at the counter. A nice-looking guy in skin-tight jeans was walking ahead of us, also heading toward the seafood counter. As he passed in front of the lobster tank, his legs went out from under him. His feet flew up in the air. His right arm reached up to grasp at anything to stop his fall. He found the front of the lobster tank, grabbed the top, and hung on to the rim, until, slowly, the rim bent and the Plexiglas tank split open.

He hit the cold, tiled floor and was laid out flat. Water erupted from the tank like a tsunami. Lobsters scurried for freedom with their giant rubber-band clad claws in the air. Several of them ran right on top of the tight-jeans guy who laid, unmoving, on the cold tile floor.

Kari and I tiptoed forward, aware of the stream of water and swarming lobsters. Other shoppers were staring on from a safe distance. Dodging lobsters, I reached the man's side and bent down to help. He was not moving. I reached for his neck and checked for his pulse like you see in the movies, but I couldn't find it.

I looked around for help. Kari was angling for pictures of the scene and gathering a water sample.

"Let me take a look," said a familiar voice. I looked up and saw my sister, Julia. She sprung into emergency-response mode, dropping to her knees beside the young man's head.

"I can't find his pulse. Hurry." I told her.

She placed her trained fingertips onto his neck, and said, "He's alive but unconscious. Has someone called for an ambulance?"

"I did," Kari said. "They're on their way."

"We need to keep him still until they arrive."

I looked at Julia. "He's lucky you showed up when you did."

"They've got a great deal on tuna steaks today. I'm picking some up for dinner."

Tight-jeans guy started to move and flicked his eyes open.

"You are one lucky guy," Kari said. "You've got both a trained nurse and a brilliant lawyer by your side in your moment of need. This here," she said, pointing to me, "is attorney Jessica Snow. She can turn this unfortunate and arguably embarrassing incident into big dollars for you."

"Kari, not now," I said. "He's hurt."

"That's the whole point, Jess, right?"

"I understand, but let's get him to the hospital first."

"Hey, what's your name?" my sister asked.

"Anthony. My name is Anthony. What the hell happened? Why is there a lobster in your lap?" he asked.

Sure enough, I looked down and there was a two-pound lobster in my lap. One of his rubber-band shackles was missing. His giant claw clamped onto my skirt hem. I jumped up in alarm and then froze. The giant puddle of lobster water impeded my panicked escape.

"Kari, help me. Get him off me."

By now the store manager had arrived. He addressed the crowd with a loud, firm voice. "Everyone must move away slowly and be mindful of the slippery floor. I repeat, be mindful of the slippery floor. The floor is slippery. You've been warned. Should anyone else fall, it will be solely because of your own negligence. I repeat, if you fall, you will be negligent, not me, because I have warned you of the dangerous condition."

It was clear to me that this manager had been slapped with a few slip-and-fall lawsuits and had learned the value of issuing warnings. He was no dummy.

He instructed two employees to start gathering lobsters, a third to bring several large pots of water to a boil, and all the others to grab mops and buckets and start cleaning. I stood over Anthony with the lobster hanging off my hem while Kari tried to remove it with the compassionate tone of her voice.

"Okay, little guy, let go of Jess's hem. Go join your buddies in aisle twelve."

The manager reached toward my lobster, smacked it with a ballpoint pen, and threw him into a bucket.

"I suppose you've called 911," the manager said to Julia as he continued to survey the damage. There was a distinct lack of concern in his voice.

"They're on their way."

"Thank you," Anthony said. "My head hurts. So do my butt and my back."

"Of course you're hurting," said Kari. "You took a hell of a fall. Real nasty fall and you're hurt. Hurt real bad. You're entitled to compensation, you know. Ever heard of Dawson Garner & Associates?"

"DGA? Yeah, I've seen their ads all over the city."

"Darn right you have. And this here is one of their best personal injury lawyers." She pointed to me again and handed him my card.

"Anthony," I said, "I'm Jess. This is my very efficient and enthusiastic assistant, Kari. "The most important thing right now is for you to get proper medical care. This incident does have legal implications. You may be entitled to compensation, but that can wait until after you're feeling better."

Sirens came from the front of the store. Brenner's staff mopped up the water and put up caution signs. It looked like most of the lobsters had been recovered. Two EMTs assessed the scene and approached Anthony, who still had Julia by his side. Julia briefed them while Kari and I stood out of earshot. Anthony was in good hands. It was time for us to leave. "Take care, Anthony. Hope you feel better soon," I said. "Call us tomorrow. We open at 8:30 a.m.," Kari said.

She grabbed some prepackaged tuna steaks from the fish section and we proceeded through the checkout. As we exited through the automatic doors, the store announced a new special:

"Attention shoppers. We have fresh steamed lobster for sale. For a limited time only $3.99 per pound."

CHAPTER FIVE

The next morning, I dashed around the corner to Hal's Bar and Grill to meet up with Sharlyn. The place was empty except for a table of two sitting by the window. The owner, Hal, was behind the bar rooting through some papers.

"Hi, Hal." Hal Horton was an old friend of Dawson's. They had gone to high school together. As a favor to Dawson, he agreed to take a chance on Sharlyn and hired her with no experience. Hal was a good man. "How's business?"

"Same old, same old. Can't complain."

"Mind if I sneak back to the kitchen to talk to Sharlyn? I won't keep her long."

"Sure. Go on back."

I found Sharlyn sitting on a metal bar stool, elbow deep in a mountain of cooked chicken breast. She was shredding it with a pair of forks. The tranquil smile on her face suggested she was at peace in this kitchen. Her smile widened when she saw me. "Thanks for coming by."

"Want a hand with that?" I pointed to the mountain of chicken.

"Sure. Pull up a seat. I need to shred all this before we open." While I scooted a bar stool next to her, she grabbed a box of disposable gloves and two forks and handed them to me. I put on the gloves and took the forks. "Pull it apart and put the shredded pieces in that bin." She pointed to a stainless steel tub.

I snapped the gloves on and commenced shredding. "What's the chicken for?"

Her eyes brightened. "Lots of things: chicken salad, chicken fajitas, hot chicken dip. And Hal is going to let me experiment on him. Later, when we're slow, I'm going to make him my twice baked potato with barbecue chicken and coleslaw!" She was animated, confident and happier than I'd ever seen her.

"Sounds yummy. Maybe Hal will make it a special."

"He's been so kind to me." Her hands stopped mauling the chicken, and she looked up at me. "You've been kind to me, too. You helped me get this job. You're taking care of my case. It's like I can trust you."

"Of course you can trust me. I'm a lawyer!"

We got a good laugh out of that and continued torturing the chicken. She was too polite to ask, so I volunteered the update on her case.

"There's an offer on your case, but I didn't want to say anything to Darnell."

At the mention of his name, her lower jaw pushed forward, her smiled faded, and her hands worked the chicken like it had personally insulted her. "I'm glad you didn't. He thinks he's getting half the money, but he's wrong. I need to get away from him, and I need that money to get started on my own. What's the offer?"

"He's at $28,000, but I think I can get more."

Her eyes went wide and her smile returned. "That's a lot of money."

"It is, but if we sit tight another day or so, I think we can get it up to $30,000."

"Sure, I guess I can wait."

Her situation with Darnell had been weighing on me particularly hard since I learned he was violent toward her. I had to get her out from under Darnell's roof.

"Look, I know he hit you last night. You can't stay there."

"I'm not staying. He's been angry ever since his arrest."

"His arrest?"

"Yeah. He's out on bail. The trial's coming up and he's real edgy. I know I can't stay there. My cousin's coming over tomorrow to help me move my stuff."

"I can help if you need me."

"Thanks, but I don't have a lot of stuff. Just my clothes, my cookbooks, and the notebooks I write my recipes in."

We were down to the last four chicken breasts when Hal walked in. He looked at me with my gloved hands and winked, "You do good work, but don't expect me to pay you."

"You couldn't afford me."

"Smart-ass lawyer."

I peeled off my rubber gloves, and Sharlyn did the same. She retrieved her purse from a row of lockers and pulled out her cell phone.

"I'd like you to listen to this. It's a voicemail from some guy at the State's Attorney's office." She pressed the touch screen on the phone and let the message play through her speaker.

I recognized the voice immediately. It was warm, yet businesslike and still managed to send a tingle through me. The voice belonged to Chip Woodward. I went to law school with Chip. We took the same Domestic Law class. I managed to weasel my way into his study group. We dissected the issues surrounding several bitter and brutal divorces cases, and I developed a crush on him. It was a one-sided romance that existed only in my head. In the message, he identified himself as Charles Woodward, Assistant State's Attorney, and said he wanted to speak with Sharlyn about Darnell Black.

I told Sharlyn not to worry about it. I would call the ASA to find out what he wanted.

#

Kari and I sat at her desk, elbow deep in files, when Delroy burst through the front door. His breathing was loud yet shallow. He collapsed onto the couch and asked Kari for a glass of water. "The bus had no air conditioning. It crapped out eight blocks ago and went from hot as blazes to suffocating in a matter of minutes."

Kari handed him a bottle of water. He downed half of it, put the lid on, and rubbed the bottle on his neck. "Thank you. I'm starting to feel better."

"What's up?" I asked. "What're you doing here?"

"I was on my way to see my brother-in-law. I only stopped in here because I was about to pass out on that bus. I'm gonna rest here a minute and then call this hack I know. He's got air conditioning." He reached down to examine the contents of the plastic bag he brought in. "I got this here stuff for my brother-in-law. He's recuperating from an accident."

Kari and I both picked up on the word 'accident' and looked at each other. Kari didn't miss a beat. "What kind of accident?"

"I was gonna talk to you about it, but he's kind of embarrassed."

"Maybe we can help," Kari said.

I thought if he's embarrassed it was some bonehead move on his part like shoving a knife in a wall socket. I wasn't inclined to be pushy. Kari pressed on. "Maybe we can get him some money. You know we're pretty good at that."

"That I do know," Delroy said. "You two like beef jerky?" He pulled a bag of beef jerky out of the plastic bag and started to open it. He struggled with the sealed plastic bag.

"I like beef jerky," Kari said and sat down beside him.

Delroy, still trying to open the plastic pouch, said, "Well, since I'm here, I might as well tell you." He lifted the bag to his mouth and tried to gnaw it open with his teeth.

"Delroy, don't. You'll ruin your teeth," I said, reaching my hand out for the bag. "Hand it to me I'll use a pair of scissors."

As I walked to Kari's desk to grab the scissors, Delroy continued. "Marshall, that's my brother-in-law. He's married to my sister Lucy. He was in his bathroom. When he flushed the toilet, it exploded!"

"What do you mean, it exploded? Like the water came gushing out?" I opened the beef jerky and handed it to him. He offered it to Kari, who dug in and pulled out a piece.

"No, I mean it exploded. Like it had a bomb inside and *kaboom*. The whole bowl broke into pieces. Sharp pieces of solid porcelain shot out and one of them nearly cut Marshall in half."

I had never heard of an exploding toilet, so I wasn't sure Delroy had the story straight. "What kind of injuries does he have?"

"Lucy said he's got stitches up and down his left side. He's gonna miss a couple of weeks of work. That's all I know." He reached back in the plastic bag and started pulling out items. "He's feeling a little low. I got him a couple of bags of this beef jerky, some Skittles, a few Tootsie Pops, and this here men's magazine." He smiled and wiggled his eyebrows up and down, holding up a copy of *Juggs*. Kari worked on a piece of beef jerky. The effort was keeping her quiet.

"I'll look into this exploding toilet thing to see if other incidents have been reported."

"Okay. Promise not to mention this to anyone. Marshall won't like that I told you. But if you can help, I'll get him to sign up."

Delroy offered to let Kari keep the open bag of beef jerky. She declined, working her tongue between her teeth to dislodge the stubborn beefy fibers.

After he left, we finished running through our caseload— categorizing, prioritizing, and making sure everything was up to date. I took a stack of files that were ready for settlement. Kari took the ones that wouldn't settle to Marty. He would have to file suit.

Before starting in on the files, I googled "exploding toilets." The results were surprising. 'Toilet explosion leaves residents afraid to Flush," "Toilet explosion - YouTube," "Friendly Flush II Recall," "More Exploding Toilets," "Professor escapes unhurt in toilet Explosion." I needed to keep a closer eye on the news. I had never heard of any of this. I spent the next hour reading the results of my search. About three months ago, there was a recall on all toilets containing a flushing system called "Friendly Flush II." It was manufactured by Sagetech, a company outside of Corning, New York. The flushing system had been used in toilets manufactured by K.L. Meglan, a company in Reading, Pennsylvania. Those toilets had been distributed to and sold by retailers such as Hardware Discount Warehouse, Home Suppliers Inc., and Baltimore's family-owned

Deckles Home Outlet. There was no doubt that this was a legitimate issue. Recalls are not issued lightly.

So what went wrong with the Friendly Flush II? Why was it no longer friendly? I continued reading through articles and what I found made my pulse quicken. Unlike traditional toilets that use gravity to produce an effective flush, the Friendly Flush II uses forty to eighty pounds of water pressure to purge the unwanted waste. This requires a vessel that traps the air. As the vessel fills with water, it creates pressure and compresses the trapped air. The system can burst at or near the weld seam and cause the tank to shatter with outward trajectory.

This posed an impact hazard. Marshall couldn't be the only person injured in this manner. There had to be more victims. My brain processed the potential and registered dollar signs.

"Jess, I've got Delroy on the phone," Kari called.

"Let me talk to him." She put the call in. "Hey, Delroy, how's Marshall doing?"

"He's aching pretty bad. They gave him some potent pain meds, so that's helping some."

"Listen, I've been researching this toilet explosion thing. I think he had a defective toilet part. Can you go in his bathroom and see if there's a part called the Friendly Flush II?"

"I'm in the bathroom now. It looks like a bomb went off. Let's see, what's this? Hold on a minute. I need my glasses." I heard him put the phone down. Seconds later, he picked it up and said. "Yup. It's busted up, but there's a chunk with a sticker on it. It says Friendly Flush II."

"Delroy, that's it! Leave that piece there. This is important. I think Marshall's got a case. That part was known to be defective and is now being recalled. Do you think you can get Marshall to agree to meet with me tomorrow?"

"I'm sure gonna try. Let me call you back."

We disconnected and Kari appeared in my doorway. "What's up with Delroy?"

"He's about to get us the first Friendly Flush II case in Baltimore."

#

Around midday, I stepped out of my office. Kari was on the phone, and there was a middle-aged man sitting on the couch. He had a patch over his left eye and was wearing a Red Sox jersey. My mother had called this one right.

"Can I help you?" I asked.

"I've got a meeting with Marty Ferguson. I'm a little early," he said.

Before I had the chance to determine whether or not he was the Red Sox fan my mother had called me about, I was distracted by Kari who was holding the phone to her ear with one hand and waving at me like a crazed fan with the other. Her eyes were wide, and she had a big smile on her face.

"Yes, Ms. Snow is in. How are you feeling? That was a nasty fall you took yesterday."

While she listened for the response, she put her hand over the receiver and said, "It's Anthony. He's in the hospital. This is great." She freed that hand and motioned me toward my office. "Please hold for a moment and I'll get Ms. Snow on the line."

I bounded into my office and picked up the phone. "Jessica Snow."

"Hello Ms. Snow, this is Tony Graham. We met yesterday at Brenner's. I was lying on the floor while you were chasing off lobsters. Remember me?"

"Of course I remember you. How are you feeling?"

"I've got a killer headache and I kind of ache all over. They've got me on painkillers. The doctor is worried about a spinal injury, so they're going to run some more tests today. I was hoping you could come see me to discuss my case. I have health insurance to cover these bills, but I'm missing work and might miss some classes, too. I'd like to know what I might be entitled to. You know, dollar-wise."

"Sure, Tony. I'm a few minutes away. Should I head over there now?"

"That's fine. I'm not going anywhere."

"What's your room number?"

"It's 456 on the fourth floor."

"Okay. See you soon."

Kari stood in my doorway, ignoring the phone ringing at her desk. She had her handbag, a file folder, a camera, and a big grin on her face. "Come on, Jess, let's get moving."

While I was speaking with Kari, I noticed the Red Sox fan leave through the front door. Curiosity getting the better of me, I went to see Marty. He sat behind his desk, a pair of reading glasses resting on his nose. He was staring through them into a file folder. I wrapped on the doorframe, and his head shot up. He removed his glasses, focused on me, and sighed.

"What do you want?"

"Was that they guy who got hit with the hot dog at Camden Yards yesterday?"

"Yeah. Why?"

"I'm curious. Did you take his case?"

He tilted his head to one side and raised his eyebrows in that did-you-really-just-ask-me-that-question look. "Of course I took his case. Haven't you learned that simple lesson yet? Always take the case. We can dump it later if it's a loser." He harrumphed and leaned back into his chair.

"How bad is his eye?"

"He's got a scratched cornea that will bother him for a few days. He's a truck driver, so they'll be lost wages. Also, he was publicly humiliated so I can milk that angle."

Eager to assure him that I was pulling my weight, I told him that I was on my way to sign up a new client. "The guy's in the hospital. I'm heading there to see him now."

"Good injury?"

"Let's hope so," I said. And then it struck me hard. Was I hoping Tony was badly hurt? I struggled with the concept of 'a good injury.' It meant that we could make some easy money off of someone's suffering. That was the sad reality.

It was also what paid my rent.

CHAPTER SIX

We took my car and drove up Charles Street toward the hospital. It was a typical summer day in Baltimore. Sweat beaded on my forehead and Kari stuck her face in the air conditioning vent. Traffic crawled. Pedestrians weaved in between the cars stopped for traffic signals. We entered the parking garage and wound our way up to the fifth level before we found a parking spot. It was a tight squeeze. A massive SUV had parked right on top of the white line. Not to be deterred by a tight situation, I threaded my Honda into the spot.

Kari looked through the passenger window and said, "There's no way I'm gonna squeeze out of this car without scratching up both these vehicles."

Kari was not a big woman, but she was no willow, either. Her proudest and most prominent feature was her backyard. A full, well-rounded gluteus maximus. Out of respect for her derriere and the two vehicles involved, I restarted the car and backed out so she could open her door and exit. Then I resumed my tight parking spot, leaving Kari's dignity intact and the SUV unscathed. We proceeded to the elevator, which smelled like burnt cabbage, down to the covered walkway, and into the main hospital.

"What room is he in?" Kari asked.

"Oh, shit, I forget. Four something. I guess he's on the fourth floor."

"You're not good with details are you, Jess? Didn't he give you the room number?"

"Yes, he gave me the room number, but I didn't write it down. All I can remember is the first number was a four. Or maybe it ended in a four. It doesn't matter. Let's go to the information desk and ask."

"I feel like an amateur," Kari complained.

"We are amateurs. But let's pretend we know what we're doing."

"Hello, Jessica. Kari." It was a familiar and vaguely irritating voice. We turned toward it to find Stuart Milligan approaching. I cringed. At six foot three, he used his height to his perceived advantage, closing in and peering down at us. He smiled in a manner that suggested he wasn't at all happy to see us.

"Stuart," we replied in a manner that suggested we were not at all happy to see him, either.

"Trying to scare up some business, are you?" he said.

"We don't troll the halls like you, Stuart," Kari said.

"We're meeting a client. What are you doing here?" I asked.

"Trolling the halls for new business, naturally. There was a family in a minivan who got side-swiped by a Dodge Ram on the beltway. Really good injuries, maybe even permanent disability. I'm working the dad now. You hear about Harvey Metzger?"

"We heard that he's dead. What else do you know?"

"There's rumor that he was running a Ponzi scheme and lost millions. Didn't Dawson have his money with Harvey?"

"I wouldn't know." The lie slipped off my tongue with surprising ease.

Kari pulled me by the elbow. "Goodbye Stuart, we've got more important people to talk to." Out of earshot, she said, "I want to smack that sonofabitch."

"Me, too."

"Imagine him getting all excited about that minivan family's pain and suffering, and taking the dad's attention away from them while they're in crisis. That man is a disgrace to the legal profession."

I wasn't sure how what Stuart was doing to the minivan family was any different from the way we managed to get Anthony as a client yesterday. I was sure there was a distinction. I didn't feel dirty, but Stuart sure was.

We found our way to the information desk. Two women wearing hospital staff badges sat behind the counter, chatting away. We stood patiently for a few seconds, hoping to be acknowledged, but they were more interested in discussing where to order lunch than in helping us.

"Excuse me," I said.

One of them turned toward me without making eye contact and said, "I'll be right with you." Then she turned back to her coworker to continue the conversation. A minute ticked by. Kari's jaw clenched, and she stepped from side to side, struggling to stay patient. When she could take it no more, she slammed her hand on the reception desk. The two women snapped their heads in our direction.

"The sign over this desk says 'information,' and we are looking for information. Now. Not after you finish deciding on your lunch order. Now," said Kari.

I saw that we had attracted some attention from other's in the lobby, including a uniformed security guard who put down the sports page and headed toward us. I decided to play nice.

"Ladies. I'm sorry we startled you. We're in a hurry and need to find a patient."

"Well if you need something, you should ask nicely. I won't be disrespected. I won't have some crazy lady," she said, looking at Kari, "banging on my desk and hollering that she wants something from me now. That's no way to go about asking for help. Right, Marlene?"

I knew this type. She was the master of the hospital's database, and information was power. She was drunk with power. Arguing with her would get us nowhere. I glanced at her employee I.D.

"Linda, you're right. We're sorry for interrupting your conversation. We're looking for Anthony Graham's room."

The two women turned to each other and shared a knowing look. Marlene tried to suppress a smile and started typing into her computer.

Linda, whose tone went from pissy to pleasant, said, "How do you two know Tony G-String?"

"Who?" Kari and I asked in unison.

Both women giggled, and Linda said, "Tony G-String. That's Anthony Graham's stage name."

"Stage name? 'G-String'?" I looked at Kari, who was now giggling along with Marlene and Linda.

"Jess," Kari said, "we got ourselves a stripper!"

We took the elevator up to the fourth floor. The nurses' station was deserted. The frenzy of phones ringing and buzzers buzzing was hardly conducive to a patient's rest. We found room 456. Anthony lay in a hospital bed surrounded by three young female nurses and a slender male nurse. One of the female nurses sat on the side of his bed feeding him a Jell-O cup.

"There's nothing wrong with my arms. I can feed myself," Anthony said.

"I know, but you shouldn't have to," the nurse who was feeding him said. His admirers giggled in agreement.

"Excuse me, Anthony," I said from the doorway.

His four devotees shot daggers at me for interrupting their little fan fest.

"Oh hi, Ms. Snow, come on in. Everyone, this is Jessica Snow and her assistant, Kari. They may be representing me for my injuries."

The four of them sized up Kari and me.

"Well it looks like you're in good hands Anthony," I said.

"Looks like too many hands," Kari said. "You mind giving us some privacy? We have important legal matters to discuss with Mr. Graham."

The four gave Tony a final sympathetic gesture on their way out. One brushed his hair from his face, one fluffed his pillow, one laid a blanket over him, and the male nurse kissed his forehead. They glided out, promising to return later.

We pulled up a chair alongside Anthony's bed. He looked quite different from when we saw him flat out on the cold, tiled floor of Brenner's Market. His face was less pained. He had good color and shoulder-length brown hair that framed his face.

"Should we call you Anthony or Tony?" I asked.

"Call me Tony."

"Are you really a stripper?" Kari asked.

I gave her a quick kick and a wide-eyed stare.

"What? We need to know his occupation, don't we? For the lost-wage claim."

Tony managed a laugh and said, "It's Okay. I'm a male dancer. Not a stripper."

"What's the difference?" Kari asked

"It's a fine line. Basically, a male dancer keeps his junk under wrap."

Kari made a note in the file.

"Tony, I need to ask you a few questions about the accident so I can determine whether or not there is a liability issue."

"Liability?"

"Yes. We have to establish that Brenner's Market was negligent. In other words, we need to prove that Brenner's knew, or should have known, that there was water on the floor which created a dangerous condition. The way that tank collapsed when you grabbed it suggests that it was already cracked and leaking, so I think their negligence can be established. But we also need to prove that you were not contributorily negligent."

Kari yawned and picked at a hangnail. Tony's eyes glazed over. I suspected all they were hearing was, "Blah, blah, blah..." I forged ahead.

"That means that if they had posted warnings about the water on the floor and you ignored those warnings, you may have contributed to your own accident. Or if the danger was otherwise obvious and you weren't paying attention to where you were going, they would argue that you should have seen the danger and avoided it."

"Oh, I get it. Well, you guys were there. There were no signs or barriers around the water. Nothing. And it's water. It wasn't visible. I was watching where I was going and I did not see that water."

"That's what I thought. I just had to hear it from you. This means you have the basis for a claim against Brenner's Market. If you want to proceed with it, I'd like to represent you."

"What's the deal? What's it gonna cost me?"

"Our fee structure is standard for the industry. You pay nothing unless we recover. We take one-third of any settlement, and forty percent if it goes trial. Plus, we'll deduct any expenses we incur along the way."

"Yeah, that's what the other guy told me, too."

"What other guy?" Kari demanded.

"I called Stuart Milligan. I saw one of his TV ads last week. The guy looks like a schmuck. I called to make sure your fee was standard."

"That guy is a schmuck," Kari agreed. "A blood-sucking schmuck."

"Kari, we shouldn't bash the competition," I said.

Tony laughed. "That's all right, Ms. Snow, I don't need convincing. I'm going to go with you guys."

Before he finished his sentence, Kari had our retainer agreement and the medical authorization forms on his tray table. I explained the details. Kari handed him a pen. As he finished signing, we heard a loud, demanding voice from outside the door:

"Where's Anthony Graham?"

"Room 456," was the reply in a mildly effeminate male voice.

Kari snatched up the papers and shoved them in her bag.

We looked toward the door as two men of intimidating proportions and confidence walked through, followed by a smaller man who maintained an authoritative position between the two. They were all wearing dark suits and stern expressions.

"Who're you?" The one in the middle asked. His eyes were deep-set and serious. He was wearing an impeccable silk suit with a blood-red tie and comically large cuff links. His hair was a thick and luscious black. It was perfectly coiffed. He had the aura of Tony Soprano, and I guessed he had similar tendencies toward getting what he wanted.

The two men flanking him were distinguishable. One was

significantly taller than the other and had long, thick sideburns and jet black hair. The shorter one was bald. Both had their feet firmly planted, arms across their chests, suit jackets pulled back to reveal the guns holstered to their right hips. I saw Kari taking in these guys. She saw the guns, too.

I looked at Tony and whispered, "You know these guys?"

He shook his head.

A wave of intimidation flowed into the room and almost took my breath away, but I had to break through it. I couldn't show weakness. "I'm Jessica Snow," I said, masking my timidity with the assurance of a seasoned attorney. "Who are you?"

"I'm Franco Giovanni." He looked at Tony. "You the guy who fell in my store?" His tone challenged anyone to give an answer other than the one he expected.

I held my hand up to Tony and forced myself to speak. "This is Anthony Graham. He fell at Brenner's Market yesterday. I'm his attorney. You'll need to speak to me." The clipped, robotic tone of my words provided a rhythm that kept my voice from trembling.

I looked to Kari for reassurance. Her eyes locked on Giovanni. Her mouth hung open, but no words spilled out.

"Your services won't be necessary," Giovanni said with a dismissive wave of his hand. "I'll give him ten grand in cash, right now."

"I'll take it," Tony said.

"You can't agree to take the money until we know what's wrong with you."

"Okay, fifteen grand."

"I'll take it," Tony said.

"I'm recommending against it," I said.

"But that money would pay for the rest of my college tuition. I could graduate on time."

I hadn't realized Tony was putting himself through college. In fact, I didn't know much about him. I was pleased that he had purposeful plans for the money, but I still couldn't let him settle without knowing the extent of his injuries.

"I understand you're anxious to settle, but what if you need surgery or extensive rehab? What if you have a permanent disability? Fifteen grand won't cover your medical expenses, not to mention lost wages in that event. There's too much we don't know yet." I turned to Franco. "I'm not a fan of fast and shady back-room deals. I'm afraid we have to decline your offer, right, Tony?"

He reached for another Jell-O cup. "I guess."

"I'm not used to being turned down. Right, Elvis?" He turned to the guy with the sideburns.

"Right, boss."

Franco's eyes bore into mine. I could hear my heart pounding in my ears. My legs went wobbly. "We'll talk again in a couple of days," he said. "You got a card?"

Kari, who had been uncharacteristically quiet during this exchange, said, "Here, I have one." Her hands were shaking as she pulled one from her bag.

"Give it to Paulie," Franco said. The bald guy stepped forward, took the card, and handed it to Franco. He looked down at it, then back up at me. "I thought I recognized you. I've seen your face on a few buses. You seem like a smart lady. You be smart about our future transaction here, and all parties will be happy. If you're not smart, well then, I don't know. Things could end unfavorably." He sounded out each syllable of this last word and looked into each of our eyes as he spoke. Then his eyes rested on me. "Be smart and don't do anything until you hear from me."

"I'll have to notify the insurance company."

Franco gave a small laugh. He looked at Elvis and Paulie and they laughed on cue.

"Insurance company?" His tone was mocking. "You're looking at the insurance company."

They turned to leave. We could hear them laughing all the way to the elevator.

#

Kari and I were just settling in back at the office when we were interrupted by the sound of sirens. We fell silent and tilted our heads toward the front of the building. It was a familiar sound that we ignored, as is the habit of most city inhabitants. But today my pulse quickened. The image of Mark, the firefighter from yesterday, popped into my head. Kari and I elbowed each other in an effort to get to the door first. Kari beat me by a hair. We peered out the glass door together, listening to the sound of the siren. It faded away into the distance, leaving me with an idle sadness.

"We gotta get those firefighter guys back here. I could use the excitement and you sure as hell could use a date. That Mark, he was a looker. He took a liking to you right off the bat, even though you presented yourself as a thin-brained, cigar-smoking pyromaniac."

I didn't care for the way she characterized my first impression with Mark, but I had no defense. She was right. "How about I start another fire in the dumpster," I joked.

"Nah. We need to be more creative. I was thinking more along the lines of an electrical fire. Change things up a bit."

"I appreciate your concern for my love life, but it might be unwise to risk burning down the law firm. We should find a safer way."

Kari looked disappointed, but her brain was still working. I could tell by the way she ignored the ringing phone. "Let the machine get it," she said.

Then a hopeful smile appeared on her face. "I know. I'll fake a heart attack. That will get them here fast."

"No, Kari, that will get the paramedics here. Not the firefighters. Thanks anyway."

I returned to my desk and tried to push all thoughts of Mark to the back of my mind. Brenda had sent me the photos of Tyler playing laser tag. There was no denying that he was not only there, he was also demonstrating some impressive physical combative skills. I felt dirty handling his file. To my surprise, Brenda was still offering $1,500 to be done with it. I was obliged to take it on behalf of my client, even though the possibility that he was an unscrupulous scammer was pretty high.

It was not for me to judge. My job was to get him some money. He was lucky to be getting a dime. I emailed Brenda and asked her to send the check.

The next couple of hours were spent reviewing files and calling adjusters to squeeze more money out of them. I managed to settle a handful of cases, which served to justify my salary for the week. I also signed up a new client who was a passenger in a car that got hit head-on. He broke his wrist and sprained his back. He was passed out in the back of the car at the time, so he was unable to provide me with even the slightest detail about who may have been at fault for the accident. I ordered the police report and referred him to Dr. Leighton, figuring Dawson must be running low on cigars.

It was closing in on one o'clock. I started to think about lunch... and Mark. There was a bagel shop a block past the fire station. A ham-and-Swiss sesame bagel was what I needed. It was a few blocks from here and I didn't want to go alone.

"Hey Kari, I'll buy you a bagel sandwich if you walk with me to the bagel shop."

"What bagel shop?"

"The one near the fire station," I said with a conspiring smile.

"Atta girl, Jess. Now you're thinking."

It was overcast with a slight breeze, a nice break from the heat wave of the last couple of days. Kari and I walked to the bagel shop in a roundabout way so that we passed the fire station. I had a serious talk with her about not embarrassing me. I was more than capable of embarrassing myself.

"Thanks for tagging along, Kari. I don't want to do anything overt to get Mark's attention—that is, if he's even there. My plan is to walk by on our way to lunch and walk by on our way back and if he happens to see us, then maybe he'll wave, and we'll wave back. If that's all that happens, that's fine."

She rolled her eyes at me as if I was a complete idiot.

"You have some very low expectations. What if he's there, but he's too busy polishing the truck or sharpening the axes to notice pedestrian traffic?"

"Then we'll try it again tomorrow."

She harrumphed. I could tell by her pursed lips that she didn't like my passive approach. The streetlight in front of the station flashed yellow. I started to feel self-conscious. Maybe this was a bad idea.

"Why are you slowing down? We're almost there. Just keep walking. You look great. Your hair's not even frizzed."

We were about to cross the intersection at the corner of the fire station when the firehouse sirens started to blast. The flashing yellow lights turned to solid red with adorning flashing yellows. I was sure this didn't bode well for our plan to get noticed. Traffic came to a stop all around us. We heard a tire screech and then the unmistakable sound of metal hitting metal. We turned around to see a black pickup truck had rear-ended a baby-blue Miata. Kari walked briskly toward the Miata while rooting through her purse and handed the driver a business card. She pointed at me, and the driver gave me a tentative wave. They exchanged a few words and Kari joined me back at the corner. "Think I got us a new case."

An ambulance pulled out of the fire station and turned in our direction, then headed up north, followed closely by a fire truck. I noticed Mark in the back cabin of the truck. Our eyes locked. I was at a loss for the proper etiquette in this situation. Do I wave? Do I smile? A smile seemed inappropriate. He was heading to an emergency situation after all. However, Mark seemed to know protocol. He flashed his perfect smile at me before the fire truck pulled away.

I turned to Kari and said, "I'm not sure I smiled back. Did you see me smile back?"

Kari pursed her lips and gave me a disapproving frown. "No, I don't think you smiled back. I think you had that same confused look you have on your face right now."

I sighed. "I wasn't prepared for how this went down."

"No worries, Jess. We still got plan B. The electrical fire. Now let's go get that bagel sandwich."

My appetite returned upon entering Charm City Bagels. The smell of freshly baked bread embraced me like a soft blanket. All thoughts of embarrassing encounters with a gorgeous firefighter and demeaning TV commercials fled my mind. Charm City Bagels was a small shop with rustic wood tables that were scrubbed clean to reveal a glossy finish.

There were a few people in line in front of us, so we had time to consider our selections. A large display case housed an assortment of bagels, meats, cheeses, and salads. We inched forward as other patrons placed their orders. The flow of patrons moved to the right toward the cashier, then waited in the holding area until their names were called.

"Channel," a woman with bright red hair called from behind the counter. No one moved forward.

"Channel!" this time a little louder. Still, nobody stepped forward to claim the brown bag of goodness.

Same voice, with a bit of an edge, "Is there a Channel waiting on two tuna salad bagel sandwiches?"

A full-figured woman in her mid-twenties stepped forward. It was Chantel Devista. I went to high school with Chantel. Our parents still lived in the same neighborhood in Mount Washington. We had a few classes together along the way, but we weren't friends. I was into sports, and she hung with the drama crowd. Our paths rarely crossed back then. But now she was employed by our nemesis, Stuart Milligan, and I saw her more than I cared to.

She pushed her way toward the counter and snatched the bag from the red-haired woman. "It's Chantel, not Channel." With her nose in the air, she turned too fast and stumbled right into me. I grabbed her elbow to steady her. Recognition registered in her eyes as she looked up at me. "Get off me, Jess." She shook herself free of my grasp, did a head jab in Kari's direction, and made a clumsy exit.

"Stuart deserves that bitch," Kari said.

It was our turn to order.

"I'll have a sesame bagel with ham, Swiss, lettuce, and tomato," I said to a guy wearing a paper hat who couldn't muster the strength to fake a cordial greeting. "For here or to go?"

"For here." I gestured to Kari to place her order.

"I'll have a plain bagel with corned beef, sauerkraut, and melted Swiss. And a pickle. A big pickle." We side stepped to the right, past the prepackaged salads and yogurts, and grabbed some chips and two jumbo-sized peanut-butter cookies on our way to the cashier. I paid with my debit card, and we proceeded to the holding area.

When our order was ready, Kari and I found a table on the opposite wall. We tore into our sandwiches, exchanging full-mouth comments about the level of deliciousness. There's nothing like a fresh bagel to amplify a simple deli sandwich.

Kari took a bite of her pickle which squirted pickle juice in my direction and barely missed my jacket. "So what do we do next?"

I took the last bite of my peanut-butter cookie before saying, "I've got to get back to the office and settle some claims."

"I'm not talking about work. I'm talking about Mark. What's our next move?"

I wasn't sure how to feel about Kari's unwavering interest in hooking me up with Mark. On the one hand, it was nice to know she cared. On the other, it made me seem desperate. Was I desperate for a man? I didn't think so. I had my career to focus on.

I consolidated the remains of my lunch into a manageable trash pile. "I think for now, I'll let things take their natural course."

Kari sighed. "Where's the fun in that?"

CHAPTER SEVEN

Returning from the bagel shop, we noticed a news van parked in front of our office. The white van bore the *Nine News Now* logo. Two leggy blondes with ample cleavage spilled out of it. One adjusted her tripod and camera while the other checked her makeup in a hand mirror.

We slowed our pace to take in what was happening. From across the street, Stuart Milligan approached the media duo. Chantel Devista strutted along at his side. The blondes flashed toothy smiles at our rivals as they exchanged handshakes. Stuart pointed to our office door, and the news team turned their probing eyes in that direction. A nefarious grin formed on Stuart's ugly mug.

"This can't be good." Kari and I quickened our pace. We closed in on them in time to hear the reporter with the hand mirror say, "Thanks for the tip, Stewie."

Stuart blushed like a schoolboy. His rare moment of acknowledgment by an attractive female was interrupted when Kari stepped in front of him, her face mere inches away from his. "What the hell's going on, *Stewie*?"

Stuart backed away as Chantel stepped forward and planted her nose in Kari's face. "You two better go check up on your man, Dawson." She turned and raced to catch up to Stuart, who was heading to the safety of his office across the street.

A second news van arrived and pulled in behind the News Nine clan. They were followed by a third van and a fourth. Bodies and equipment swarmed the streets, all angling for position.

The female reporter saw the competition arriving. She swapped out her mirror for a microphone, signaled to her partner to get the camera rolling, and started speaking to the lens. "We're here with an exclusive on the arrest of attorney Dawson Garner. Behind me is his office where he formulated the plan to kill finance expert Harvey Metzger..."

Kari's body tensed. Her eyes shot daggers at the reporter.

"... a cold and calculated plan to take down..."

Kari rushed the reporter, snatched the microphone, turned to the camera, and said, "None of that's true." She raised the microphone to the height of the reporter's face and dropped it at her feet. The newsy beauties stood open-mouthed and silent, staring at Kari. Before they could protest the affront to their exclusive news story, I grabbed Kari's wrist and pulled her along with me in the direction of our office.

Two uniformed cops stood like sentries at our door.

"Sorry ladies, you can't go in there."

"Of course we can, we work here." I reached into my bag for a business card, but it wasn't necessary. The guy was staring at me like I was a celebrity.

"I recognize you. You're the bus lawyer."

"She's more than a bus lawyer. She's the best damn accident lawyer in town. You need a lawyer? You call her." Kari whipped the card out of my hand and gave it to him.

"Can we please go in?" I asked.

He stepped aside and whispered something to his partner as we passed. They both snickered.

We found Dawson, Marty, Detectives O'Mallory, and his faithful sidekick, Howdy Doody inside. Dawson sat on the sofa petting Bailiff. He stared up at the detectives, who stood side by side with their arms crossed against their chests. Marty held firm to a spot in front of Dawson, as though protecting him.

Kari interrupted whatever conversation was taking place. "What the hell's going on in here? It looks like some macho standoff."

"And what's with all the media people?" I added.

Marty squared his shoulders and continued to stare at the detectives while he answered. "The detectives are here to take Dawson in for questioning. The media's here to watch it happen."

Marty had his lawyer face on. "On what grounds are you arresting him?"

"We've received the security footage from the night Metzger was killed. He had a pretty sophisticated system. It shows Dawson arriving at 9:10 p.m. and leaving at 9:35 p.m. No one came or went after that until Mrs. Metzger came home around 1:30 a.m. and found the body. Dawson's financial statements were laid out across the desk, covered with blood. It all fits."

"That's not conclusive evidence. Any hack can circumvent the security cameras. What about the wife? What about the maid?" Marty turned to Dawson. "You said they have a live-in, right?"

"Yes. Maria. Delightful young lady."

O'Mallory was stone-faced. "They both have alibis. Dawson had motive and opportunity. I've got to take him in."

Marty's face turned red. "That's ridiculous! There must be hundreds of more likely suspects—other clients of Metzger's who knew."

"No one else knew about the missing money until after the murder. They found out watching the morning news like everyone else. I gotta bring him in."

O'Mallory held firm, staring Marty down. "We can do it the easy way and walk out together and get in the car, or I can cuff him and drag him out there in front of all those cameras."

"Can we compromise?" I asked. "Can you have a car pull into our rear lot and bring Dawson out the back. We don't want any pictures of him being escorted by the two of you, with or without cuffs. We've got a reputation to maintain."

O'Mallory gave an affirmative nod to Howdy Doody, who took out his cell and made a call.

"Don't worry," Marty told Dawson. "There's plenty of time to have the bail hearing this afternoon and get you out this evening."

"That son of a bitch," Kari said. She was looking out the front window.

"Who?"

"It's Stuart Milligan. That good-for-nothing sleazebag is talking to the press again. And lots of people have gathered outside." Kari stomped her foot. "Oh no she's not! It's Chantel. That uppity bitch is handing out business cards and pointing people across the street to their office. I'm going back out there to shut them down." She marched toward the door.

"Kari, don't do anything," Marty said. "Stay put. We don't need any more attention."

Kari's nostrils flared like a charging bull. She stepped away from the window, arms crossed, taking deep breaths.

Howdy Doody was off the phone. "I've arranged to have another car come in through the alley. It'll be here any minute. Dawson, you ready to go?"

"Do I have time to iron my pants?"

The detectives laughed.

Dawson started unbuckling his belt and headed toward his office.

"He's not kidding," Kari said. "Can you give him time to iron his pants? It calms him down."

The detective shrugged. "Sure. You've got five minutes."

We followed Dawson into his office. His ironing board was at the ready. He laid his pants across the top and took a lint roller to the legs as he waited for the iron to heat up. He turned on his Bose system and the sound track to *Fiddler on the Roof* began to play.

"Dawson, you okay?" I asked.

"Sure. I'm okay. Marty will get me bailed out, and I'll be back here in the morning."

The iron beeped, signaling it was ready. Dawson began to press his pants. He was slow and methodical. "I didn't kill Harvey, you know."

"Of course we know that," I said.

"I know it looks bad. I was mad enough to kill him that night, but I'm no killer."

"O'Mallory has it in for you for some reason," Marty said. "Did you ever do anything to get on his bad side?"

"Not that I know of. He was working Vice until a few months ago. He put a lot of mid-level drug dealers behind bars." He flipped his pants over and worked the iron across them. "A handful got off by hiring savvy defense lawyers who managed to get the charges dismissed on technicalities—illegal searches, that kind of thing. But we never represented any of them. I figure he hates all lawyers."

"A lot of people do," said Kari.

We nodded in agreement.

Marty said, "Arresting a well-known local lawyer for killing the orchestrator of a Ponzi scheme jacks this into a high-profile case. That's what the police commissioner is trying to do."

"Trying to do what?" I asked.

Marty swiveled his head toward me and gave me an eye roll so severe it almost knocked me down. "He wants the publicity. Don't you get it?"

"So this is all for show? A way to send the message to the public that they are hard at work on this murder? Even if they have the wrong guy?"

"Yes. Even if they have the wrong guy."

Dawson looked up from his ironing. "Plus they need to distract the press from the drug money that went missing during O'Mallory's East Side drug bust a few months ago. The department's in the hot seat for that one. Over half a million in cash disappeared."

"I hadn't heard that part of the story," I said.

"It's back in the news because the top guy they nailed, Terrell Smith, he goes on trial this week," Marty said.

"I'm a pawn in their media manipulation. My arrest will take the media attention away from that bust and maybe even cover up corruption within the department."

Dawson started putting on his pants. "I found out about Harvey's scam because I wanted to take out a large sum. I wanted to diversify to prevent something like this from happening. A little too late, I guess. Harvey kept stalling and giving me excuses for days, so I finally went to see him. That's when he confessed."

"Car's here," Detective O'Mallory called from the outside room.

Dawson did a final check of his pants in the mirror behind his door, gave Bailiff a pat on the head, and joined the detectives with Marty at his side. Kari and I followed the four of them through the kitchen and stood at the back door. There was no press back there, but the helicopter was circling overhead. There would be no time for goodbyes. Before Dawson slid into the back seat, he yelled, "Hold down the fort, Jess."

They drove away. Marty followed in his car. Kari and I returned to the office and peeked out front. The press was still mulling about.

"Hard to believe none of them thought to peek around back," Kari said.

"They're not even making an effort. They've already convicted him. The headlines tomorrow will have Dawson pulling the trigger and kicking the corpse."

The phone rang incessantly, and the message light was blinking. Kari tended to the calls as I entered Dawson's office to turn on the news. He had a thirty-six-inch, high definition television and full cable package. I had to see if Dawson's arrest had been reported yet. It was mid-afternoon. All I could find were soap operas, but each station had a news scroll across the bottom of the screen that read: *Local lawyer arrested for murder. Dawson Garner, accused of shooting Ponzi scheme mastermind. Tune in at 5:00 for the full story.* Or some variation of that nonsense. I turned off the TV and joined Kari at her desk.

"We got a problem," Kari said and handed me several pink message slips. "Those are all client calls. Five of them so far. They all want to fire us. Every one of them said they didn't want to be represented by a murderer, and one of them specifically said he was going across the street to Stuart Milligan."

The news had spread like a wildfire. Dawson got arrested and we started to hemorrhage clients before he even reached the police station. Looking at the messages, I noticed four of the five were my files and one was Marty's. It was likely that Dawson never even spoke with these people. That meant Marty and I were guilty by association. Great. Where was the presumption of innocence?

The phone rang again. Kari answered it. "Dawson Garner & Associates, how can I help you? Yes, ma'am. Can you please hold?" She pressed the hold button and said, "It's Marjorie Howard. She's got her foul-mouthed self all worked up. Said she saw the news and doesn't want a murderer touching her case. She wants Stuart Milligan."

"Let me speak with her."

Kari put the call through to my desk. "Hello, Mrs. Howard."

"It's Miss Howard, and don't you 'hello' me. You people are a disgrace. Dawson Garner's nothing but a murderer pretending to be a lawyer. I don't feel safe with him. I want to take my case to Stuart Milligan. I hear he's a pervert, but at least he ain't no killer."

I didn't want to lose Marjorie's case. It could be a decent payout for us because she broke her wrist. Broken bones meant money. If I could get the adjuster to expedite on her file and give me a number, maybe I could salvage our fee. "Ms. Howard, I understand you're upset, but Dawson is no murderer. He's one of many suspects. He'll be cleared soon. Meanwhile, we're working hard on your claim and expect an offer before the end of the week." This last part wasn't true, but I intended to get right on top of it.

"Don't try to sweet-talk me, Miss Lady. Just get my file over to Milligan's office."

Since a rational approach wasn't working, I decided to stall. "No problem, Ms. Howard. I'm going to send you a form that I'll need you to sign and return. It will state that this firm is no longer representing you and that you would like your file transferred to Stuart Milligan's office. I'll send that out today."

"You do that." She hung up.

I went out to tell Kari about my conversation, but she was taking another message, and there was another call on hold.

The front door opened and a woman walked in. It was Helen Holman, a reporter I recognized from WTTZ news. I wondered how she got past the two uniformed officers, then realized that they must have left as soon as Dawson was carted away. Helen was an industry veteran in her mid-fifties. She was dressed in a simple, navy-blue V-neck top tucked into crisp white jeans with a crease down the middle that even Dawson would envy. An air of confidence preceded her as she bounded into the office.

"I'm Helen Holman." She reached her hand out to shake mine. Kari spotted Helen and rushed around her desk to shake Helen's hand, too.

"I'm a big fan, Ms. Holman. I've seen you on WTTZ Channel 7. But not lately, now that I'm thinking about it. You're even prettier in person. You want some coffee or a bottle of water? We've got some cookies in the kitchen. How about a cookie?"

I was irritated at Kari for her overt girl crush on this woman. Helen Holman was the press. She was the enemy.

"No, thanks. And I'm no longer with WTTZ. I'm an independent reporter now. The networks get all caught up with the ratings and political correctness. It stifles my search for the truth. Hey, can I use your bathroom?"

I directed her down the hall toward the restroom. When she was out of earshot, I turned to Kari. "Do not say anything to that woman. She's on a witch hunt for dirt on Dawson. She can bring us down with one catchy headline, so don't say a word."

"I know how to handle the press," Kari said.

Helen returned from the restroom. "It's so damn humid. Look at my hair. I tried to run a comb through it, but it's no use."

"Jess has that same problem. It's because you white women don't use enough product. I told Jess she should—"

"Ms. Holman isn't here to discuss common Caucasian hair ailments." I turned to Helen. "How did you find out that Dawson was arrested? How did any of the media know?"

"It was that lawyer across the street, Stuart Milligan. He sent emails and called the tip lines at all the local stations. I found out from an old friend at WTTZ." She dug into her purse and pulled out a copy of an email chain that originated from Milligan's office. It was time stamped at ten this morning.

I saw red. My pulse quickened. My hatred for Stuart Milligan took an ugly turn. I would somehow make him pay for this. But for now, I needed to focus on helping Dawson. "Everyone else is gone. Why are you still here?"

"I'm here to find out who murdered Harvey Metzger."

"Then you're in the wrong place. Dawson didn't murder Harvey," Kari said.

"I'm not here to talk to Dawson. I know he left out the back with the detectives. I wanted to talk with you two. Listen, those other reporters out there, they're convinced of his guilt because that's the easy story. They're young. They're lazy. I like to assume the old adage is true." She looked at me. "You know. The one they teach you in law school—'innocent until proven guilty.' It's a real gem."

I was beginning to like Helen Holman.

"Who's the lead detective on the case?" she asked.

"O'Mallory. He focused on Dawson right away, which doesn't make sense considering there are so many other people with motive." I studied her. "What's your angle?"

"I'm looking at the wife."

"Olivia?"

"Yup. What do you ladies know about Olivia?"

Kari's left eye started to twitch. She knew something but didn't want to blurt it out. Such restraint was uncommon for her.

"Helen, would you excuse us for a moment?" I motioned for Kari to follow me into my office and closed the door.

"So, what do you know?"

"How do you know I know something?"

"Because some juicy nugget of gossip has you practically jumping out of your skin."

"It's Olivia. She was having an affair with her Pilates instructor, Juan Carlos."

"Juan Carlos?" I'd recently added Pilates to my exercise routine with minor success. I wasn't good with group fitness. Juan Carlos was my instructor, too. "What makes you think Olivia and Juan Carlos were having an affair?"

"My stylist, Paulette."

"At The House of Hair?"

Kari nodded. "That place has the pulse on this city."

"Then it's a rumor. Helen Holman won't act on a rumor."

"So I can tell her then?"

"Sure, why not?"

We rejoined Helen in the reception area.

Kari wasted no time. "Olivia Metzger was having an affair with her Pilates instructor, Juan Carlos."

"Did you witness this affair?" Helen asked.

"No, but it was all the talk at the House of Hair last week."

Helen's face brightened. "The House of Hair. That's a great resource. Those ladies were the reason I got a front-page story last month on the now-disgraced Reverend Tappalo."

"That was you?" Kari said. "That was some good investigative reporting."

"Thanks. I owe it all to the relentless gossip ring at the House of Hair. One of the ladies there grew up with Tappalo and knew him to be a scheming degenerate since he was thirteen years old. The story practically wrote itself."

"What's this world coming to when you can't trust a reverend?"

It was five o'clock. Time to watch the news.

Kari locked the front door, and she and Helen followed me into Dawson's office. I turned on local Channel 6. The requisite male-female pairing sat at the news desk. The guy wore a crisp, dark-blue suit with white starched collar and a bold striped tie, like the kind worn by prep-school students. He was fit and tan with chicklet-white teeth. The woman, whose teeth were even a shade whiter, had impossibly blonde, shoulder-length hair. She wore a red dress that clung to her body and revealed her size D cup cleavage.

Kari said, "Turn it up. Let's hear what Ken and Barbie have to say."

Helen laughed. "That's why I never made the news desk." She gestured across her own chest. "Not enough in the booby department."

We pulled the chairs from around Dawson's conference table and huddled up close to the television. Traffic and weather updates dominated the news at this hour. Then finally:

"In local news," Ken began, "The death of Harvey Mezzer is being—"

"Metzger," Barbie said.

"What?"

"Harvey Metzger. His name is Metzger. I mean was Metzger. Harvey Metzger."

"That's what I said."

"No, you didn't. You said Mezzer."

"Did not."

Barbie rolled her eyes at the camera. Ken continued.

"In local news, the death of Harvey METZGER, has turned into a murder investigation. Dawson Garner, a Baltimore attorney known for his ubiquitous advertising on billboards, buses, and benches across the city, has been arrested. The motive for the murder has not been revealed, but there is speculation that Garner and Metzger were involved in a love triangle that turned deadly..."

"What! A love triangle?" Kari said. "They're making shit up."

"Wouldn't surprise me," said Helen.

I couldn't listen to it. I turned the volume down on the television.

"We need to save Dawson from these lies."

"The only way to do that is to shift the media focus onto something else," Helen said. They're like kindergartners. They have short attention spans. They'll forget about Dawson if they have something juicier to talk about."

"How about a UFO sighting?" Kari asked. "I can call one into 911. We can Photoshop a few pictures together to make it look like it was flying over Camden Yards. That would catch a lot of attention. No one would be interested in hunting down a murderer when there are aliens watching baseball."

"We can't lie," I said.

"They are," said Kari, gesturing toward the television.

"True, but I'm a lawyer, I'm supposed to represent the truth."

There was silence for a few beats before we burst into laughter.

#

Mrs. Bianco was sitting on her porch with the twins. Kaitlyn and Kristin were around my age and lived in the row house on the other side of mine. We had become fast friends when I moved in. Having lived there for four years, they were my social connection to the happenings in Canton and Fells point, and they were big sports fans. When the Ravens or Orioles played, they had an open house for viewing on their sixty-inch wide screen with surround sound. On nice evenings, they moved it onto their front porch for outdoor viewing.

"Hey, Jess. You coming over to watch the O's game on Friday?" Kaitlyn asked.

"Sure, I'll be there."

They stood to leave. "We'd love to stay and catch up, but we're meeting a client." The twins were real estate agents. I was glad they couldn't stay. I wanted to talk to Mrs. Bianco about Franco Giovanni. While I loved hanging out with the twins, I didn't trust them to keep our conversations confidential. Their gossip circle was almost as big as the one at the House of Hair.

After they left, Mrs. Bianco said, "I saw the five o'clock news. What a story they tell about your boss."

"Dawson didn't do it. He was just the last one to see Harvey alive, according to the security cameras. His financial statements were tossed around Metzger's desk when they found him. The rush to justice has Dawson tried and convicted. Marty's hoping to get him out on bail so he won't have to spend the night."

She poured me a glass of port and freshened hers.

"Do you know a guy named Franco Giovanni?" I asked.

"Franco Giovanni?"

"Yeah, big guy, nice hair, intimidating security detail. Do you know him?"

"I play bingo every week with his mother, Cecilia. And I knew his dad, Franco Sr. He had nice hair, too. Franco Sr. did some business with Mr. Bianco. But I can't talk about that. How do you know Franco?"

"I'm representing a guy who fell and was injured at Brenner's Market. He's a male dancer. Franco owns Brenner's. He offered to settle. I told him it was too soon to negotiate a settlement. He didn't take my refusal well."

"He does not like to be refused." She took a pull on her Tiparillo. "Franco Giovanni is more barker than biter. You earn his respect, and he'll be fair."

"How do I do that? I'm a rookie here."

"You be confident. Fake it if you have to." She shrugged." Don't let him know he intimidates you. Respect him, but demand his respect, too. If you cross him..."

"What?" I asked. "If I cross him, what?"

I saw in her roaming eyes that she was searching for the right words. Then her eyes settled on mine. "Things could get unpleasant."

"I don't intend to cross him."

"You do, you end up like Harvey Metzger."

She took a long sip of port, eyes still on me. "You know, the Giovanni family invested some money with Harvey Metzger, too." She watched my face as the implications of this information sunk in.

Did Harvey get whacked by a Giovanni hit man? I thought that only happened in the movies.

"Mrs. B, does the mob still whack people?" I asked.

"I don't know for sure, but if it was a Giovanni who ordered the hit, who could blame them? I wanted to kill Metzger myself."

We sat in silence for a moment, watching the foot traffic. There was a young couple about my age strolling by, holding hands and talking intently to each other. It made me think of Mark. I had a quick school-girlish daydream about me and Mark walking hand in hand along the docks by the harbor, soaking in the warm sun and falling in love. My expression must have changed because Mrs. Bianco said, "What are you smiling about?"

"A funny thing happened at work yesterday. I accidentally set a dumpster on fire with one of Dawson's cigars. The fire department came and had to put it out."

"There are some good-looking firefighters in this city," Mrs. Bianco said.

"I know. A couple of them showed up. I talked to one of them."

"Did you introduce yourself?"

"Not exactly, but I did confess to starting the fire."

"That is good. Confessions are adorable," she said and chuckled to herself.

"His name was Mark. He had warm blue eyes and a nice smile."

"How's he going to ask you out if you didn't introduce yourself?"

"Well, he knows where I work."

Mrs. B shrugged. We enjoyed another quiet moment as we sipped our port.

It had been a long day, filled with unexpected and troubling events. I was worried that I hadn't heard from Marty or Dawson. Was he still locked up? It was hard to imagine him tossed into a cold holding tank filled with drunks, drug dealers, and pimps. I didn't want to think about it. We needed to figure out a way to get him back in the office and clear his name before we lost any more clients. If Olivia was having an affair, then Detectives O'Mallory and Johnson need to be made aware of that. I decided to check things out at the House of Hair tomorrow. There was also the possibility that the mob was somehow tied in Harvey's murder. If Franco had money with Harvey and lost it, ordering a hit would be another day at the office for him.

My phone rang and I was oddly relieved so see that it was Marty.

"He's out. We posted bail."

"That's such a relief. I wasn't going to be able to sleep if I knew he was locked up with a bunch of dirty, derelict, lowlifes."

"You watch too much television. There were only two other guys locked up with him. One was 22-year-old law student who blew over the legal limit after two beers. The other was a 60-year-old pervert they hauled in for exposing himself to a group of ladies having a picnic lunch in front of the Science Center. They both recognized Dawson from the commercials. They want us to handle their criminal cases."

"They're okay being represented by someone charged with murder?"

"Neither of them had seen the news about Dawson's arrest and didn't seem to care why he was in there."

"So, not a bad day then?" I asked.

"Guess not."

"I've got a lead on who may have killed Harvey. Did you know that his wife, Olivia, was having an affair?"

"How'd you find out?"

"At this point, it's a rumor, but I plan to check it out tomorrow. We need to establish Dawson's innocence before we lose more business. The press has him convicted and clients have been calling wanting to fire us. Stuart Milligan is circling, waiting to feed on our scraps."

CHAPTER EIGHT

The next morning, I drove past the front of our building before parking in the rear. A small contingency of the press had returned. There were two vans, two cameramen, and two reporters. I passed without being noticed. When I pulled into the lot, Marty was right behind me.

"Did you see the press out front?" I asked. "Looks like most have lost interest."

"Don't be naïve. They're not done with us yet."

Dawson pulled in as I was opening the back door to our office. Marty and I waited for him by the door.

"Do you think prison changed him?" I whispered to Marty. He inched away from me.

"He was locked up for five hours. It wasn't a big deal." He rocked his head back and forth in a way that confirmed he thought I was an idiot.

Still, I was happy to see Dawson, and not just because he was carrying a box of doughnuts.

Dawson joined us and handed the doughnut box to me. "Let's get inside and have a meeting over breakfast. Kari's got bagels, too."

We could smell the coffee. Kari was sitting at the kitchen table and flipping through *People* magazine. When she saw Dawson, she said, "You don't look like an ex-con. Where's your prison tattoo?"

"Prison wasn't nearly as bad as I thought. Although when I got home, I threw my clothes in the trash and took a twenty-minute shower." He handed Kari some paperwork. "I picked up two clients while I was in there. Criminal cases. They should both be in today with the retainer money. Then you can set up the files."

Kari listened while she pulled a foiled tray of bagels out of the oven. "Compliments of Dr. Cohen," she said. I was standing next to the refrigerator. "Jess, can you grab the cream cheese?"

I laid out some knives along with the cream cheese. Between the bagels and the doughnuts, it was a carb feast. We dug in shamelessly. It looked to be an amicable breakfast among co-workers until Marty and I grabbed the same sesame bagel. I dug my nails in for a better purchase.

"Jess, let go of the bagel."

"You let go."

It was a bagel standoff. We positioned our elbows on the table for added strength and held firm. Moments passed. Dawson and Kari watched on in silence. Maintaining my grip, I leaned forward, whipped out my tongue, and licked the top of the bagel.

Marty let go. "That's disgusting."

Kari passed me the cream cheese. "Well played, Jess."

Dawson gave me a quick wink and brought our attention back to business. "We've got a PR nightmare. Did you see the news yesterday? The press has me convicted."

"So do some of our clients," I said. "A couple have asked to transfer their files."

"Not to Stuart Milligan, I hope," said Dawson.

"Marjorie Howard asked for him."

"So did Walter Reese and Taylor Lawson," Kari said. Marty and I looked at her. This was news to us, too. "They both left angry voicemail messages. They didn't mention Stuart by name, but said they wanted their files sent across the street to the TV lawyer."

"I'll talk with all of them. Bring me their files after breakfast. These people just want their money. They don't care which attorney gets it for them. If I can convince them that changing attorneys at this point will delay their settlement, they're likely to stick with us. At least for a little while longer."

"We won't have to worry about losing more clients once the press turns its focus on Olivia," Kari said.

"That's ridiculous. What makes you think Olivia killed Harvey?" Dawson asked.

I jumped in ahead of Kari. "We heard it from a reliable source."

"Who's the source?"

"The ladies at the House of Hair."

"A gossip ring?" Incredulity filled Marty's eyes and he let out a puff of exasperated air. "You're not serious?"

I ignored him. "I'm going over there today to check it out for myself. If it proves to be a solid lead, we'll alert Detective O'Mallory."

"You're wasting your time. O'Mallory already talked to Olivia," Marty said. "They always interview the wife."

"Yeah, but at the time he had Dawson pegged as the perp."

"Perp?" No one says 'perp' anymore."

"They do on *Law & Order*," I said, raising my eyebrows and wiggling my head at him.

#

I had to set the murder investigation aside to lock in my first exploding-toilet case. Delroy had convinced his cousin to meet with me to discuss representation. Delroy and Kari came with me.

Parking was easy this time of day in Marshall's Druid Hill neighborhood. I found a spot across the street. We proceeded up Marshall's front porch. Marshall opened the door immediately.

"I saw you pull up. Come on in. Wipe your feet." Marshall was a large man. Defensive-tackle kind of large. Not fat, but very big, very strong. He could have played for the Ravens. He was dressed in a short-sleeved collared shirt and sweatpants. His feet were bare.

The houses in Druid Hill were built in the 1950s, but this one was updated We stood in the taupe painted hallway on top of the matching carpet. The home had a comforting monochrome palette. I admired a couple of bright botanical prints framed in black. On the opposite wall, a pewter-framed mirror hung over a narrow sideboard. Marshall motioned for us to follow him into the family room. He moved with caution toward the biggest recliner I'd ever laid eyes on and lowered himself gingerly, grimacing as he came to rest. The three of us spaced ourselves evenly across the matching leather sectional sofa.

"Why don't you tell me what happened," I said.

For a monster-sized man, he was surprisingly soft spoken. He stared at his fingers in his lap and said, "It exploded. The toilet. It exploded. I had just flushed and was…" He paused, looked up at Kari and me. "I'm sorry for being indelicate here, but ... I hadn't ... I hadn't even pulled up my pants yet when *bam*! I felt this sharp pain in my side and heard the explosion at the same time. Next thing I know, I'm on the floor. My head is pounding. My side"—he gestured toward his left midsection—"was bleeding like I had been cut in two. I felt sick to my stomach. It hurt so bad." He stopped and shook his head from side to side.

"I see you got started without me." We all turned our heads toward the woman in the doorway. I assumed it was his wife, Lucinda. She was wearing a floral blouse, white capris pants, and a scowl on her face that made me feel I got caught with my hand in her wallet. She had her hair pulled back off her face and her makeup was severe. Marshall sat mute. "Marshall told me Delroy was bringing over a lawyer. Where is he?"

He? This ought to be fun.

I stood and stepped around the coffee table with my right hand stretched out. "Hello, Mrs. Ball. I'm Jessica Snow with Dawson Garner & Associates." She took my hand and released it like it repulsed her. I turned toward Kari. "And this is my assistant, Kari Cruz."

Kari also stood to shake Lucinda's hand. "Nice to meet you. Can I call you Lucinda?"

"No. I prefer to be addressed as Mrs. Ball." She turned back at me and studied my face. "I've seen you on that billboard over on North Avenue, near the Market." She looked me up and down from head to toe. "They must have airbrushed you. Amazing what they can do with a little airbrushing." Her voice and her eyes dared me to a verbal sparring.

Her personal assault fired up my anger, but I held it in check. I replied in my most saccharine voice, "Aren't you sweet to notice."

A vein in Kari's neck pulsed purple anger. She was ready to jump to my defense. I motioned for her to stay calm.

We resumed our seats and Mrs. Ball stepped over to stand by Marshall's chair. There was a coldness about the woman that put me on edge. Marshall reached for a prescription bottle on the table next to him and shook out two white pills. He tossed them down his throat and chased them with whatever was in his coffee mug.

"What can you do for us, Ms. Snow?" Lucinda asked.

"Should Marshall choose to hire me, I intend to get him a substantial amount of money to compensate for his pain and suffering, his permanent scarring, and any other permanent injury he may have, as well as compensation for his time missed from work. Also, we would seek compensation for the damage to your bathroom."

Lucinda tapped her fingers are the back of Marshall's chair. "What about loss of constitution?"

Marshall stiffened and lowered his eyes again.

I had no idea what Lucinda was talking about, so I turned to Kari. "Consortium. I think she means consortium."

Lucinda rolled her eyes. "That's what I said."

Oh, boy, this should be fun. Under Maryland law, both spouses can make a claim for the loss of consortium. That is, loss of marital intimacy due to injuries caused by the negligence of a third party. In other words, they can get paid for not being able to have sex while Marshall is recovering. It's a statute that is rarely called upon because the questions that need to be answered to prove its value are intrusive and embarrassing. If Marshall was embarrassed about being injured with his pants down, wait until he tried to justify a loss-of-consortium claim.

I sat forward in my seat and made direct eye contact with Mrs. Ball. "Certainly, we *could* make a claim for loss of consortium, but I don't recommend it. Those claims, even if proven, carry so little value that it's not worth the embarrassment that is inevitable when certain questions about your intimacy need to be answered. I'm talking very personal questions requiring very specific answers."

I could tell Mrs. Ball was not happy with my answer when she stepped forward, hands on hips, and said, "What do you know? Have you even graduated from high school?"

Kari started to rise to my defense when Delroy put a gentle hand on her shoulder and addressed his sister. "Lucinda, that's enough. Ms. Snow is a smart attorney. I know she looks young, but she's an ace. I wouldn't have brought her here if she weren't. Come on, let's you and me go to the kitchen and get a cup of coffee while these folks work things out." He took her by the elbow and led her through the door.

Marshall looked up. "I'm sorry about that. She means well. She gets a little carried away is all. What else do you need to know?"

"Tell me more about your injuries," I said.

"The doctor said I have a concussion from hitting the floor. And this." He angled his hips so that his left side was facing us and lifted his shirt to reveal at least a dozen staples pulling his flesh together. They formed an angry line from the top of his hip down below the waistline of his sweatpants. "Doc did a good job patching me up, but it hurts like hell. I can't work for at least two weeks."

I made a note. "What kind of work do you do?"

"I drive a delivery truck for Big City Distributors. No way I can haul pallets of beer until this thing heals. Doc says it could rip right open."

"Had you been having any trouble with the toilet? Was it making any noise, or not operating properly? Any reason to believe there was something wrong with it?"

"No. Not a thing. It was fine up until this happened. I hate to think that this might've happened to one of my kids. Could've killed them.

Someone needs to get the word out about these toilets."

"Can I see where it happened?"

The bathroom was on the first floor between the family room and the kitchen. The porcelain tank was split into two large pieces, each with thick, jagged edges. One side had a dark stain that I assumed was blood. There was also dried blood on the floor. Marshall wasn't exaggerating when he said this could have killed someone. I stepped around the debris and moved closer to the toilet bowl. It was still intact. The name of the manufacturer was K.L. Meglan. "Where did you get this toilet?"

"I bought it at Deckles Home Outlet a few months ago. Me and a buddy redid the bathroom. I had a licensed plumber install the toilet and all the plumbing."

I reached into my purse and pulled out my phone. "I'd like to take a few pictures." He backed out to give me room to maneuver around the bathroom. I shot several photos, then joined him in the family room. "I hate to ask this, but we should get a photo of your wound."

He walked over the front window for light, lifted up his shirt, and inched down his sweatpants. I snapped a few pictures and we returned to our previous seats in the family room. It was time to talk business.

"Marshall, you've got a good case here. I'd like to represent you." I nodded to Kari. She was better at this part than I was.

Kari picked up a folder and went to sit closer to Marshall. "You're hiring the best there is in this business, Mr. Marshall." She opened the folder and went through the standard documents. "This here is our retainer agreement. It's standard for this type of case. Our fee is one-third of any settlement, plus expenses. If it goes to trial, our fee is forty percent, plus expenses. But we don't see this one going to trial." She moved on to the other documents. Marshall gave a blank stare and said nothing. Was he even listening?

"These four papers are all the same. They are medical releases so we can get your records from the hospital and your doctors." Kari reached into her bag and pulled out a pen. "We're gonna need you to sign these, and we'll hit the ground running." She handed the pen to

Marshall. He didn't take it.

"I should talk to Lucinda about this before signing anything. I'm sorry."

Damn it. I had a feeling we'd need to win over Lucinda before this was said and done. "That's fine. We'll leave the paperwork here. You and Mrs. Ball talk it over and let me know."

Kari stood first and headed toward the hallway. "I'll go get Delroy."

"Marshall," I said extending my hand, "it was a pleasure to meet you. Please call me with any questions you or Lucinda have." I gave him my business card. "Take care of that wound."

The others filed out of the kitchen. Mrs. Ball had a sour look on her face. I made one last attempt to be cordial. "You have a lovely house, Mrs. Ball. I can tell you've had some work done. It's beautiful."

Her face brightened. "Thank you. The bathroom was also beautiful until the accident."

"I can tell that it was. I promise that if you and Marshall decide to let me handle his case, I will get you money to fix that bathroom."

"We'll talk about it," she said as she opened the front door.

Once Kari, Delroy, and I were in the car, I said, "I know Marshall would have signed up if Lucinda wasn't there. Don't you think? Don't you think he'd hire me?" That sounded way more desperate than I intended.

Delroy hesitated a moment. "Yeah, Marshall liked you. I could tell. The problem is Lucinda tends to intimidate the big man. She'll make the final call. You may have to do something else to win her over. The television was on when we were in the kitchen and she saw Stuart Milligan's commercial. She wrote his number down."

There was no way I was going to lose this one to Stuart Milligan.

CHAPTER NINE

The idea of calling Chip Woodward thrilled and terrified me at the same time. My schoolgirl crush still lingered. I was worried that I would say something stupid. He had two years at the State's Attorney's office and I was a newbie ambulance chaser.

I had given a lot of thought to what I was going to say. It was straightforward and professional with a touch of carefree humor. But when I got his voicemail, all my preparation failed. My open mouth hovered over the phone like I was taking a tentative bite from it. Kari entered my office as I hung up in disgust.

"What's wrong?"

I gave her a brief explanation. "I froze when I heard his voice on his voicemail. I'm paralyzed with fear of embarrassing myself."

"It's becoming a habit with you. You did the same thing when we saw Mark the other day. You gotta learn to relax."

"I know. Maybe it's because he's out of my league. Maybe I should lower my expectations. Find a short, fleshy guy with no teeth who lives with his mother."

"There's always Dr. Shon. He's been asking you out for drinks for weeks now."

Kari lowered herself into the chair in front my desk and pulled my desk phone toward her. "God knows you need some help in the dating department. Here's what we'll do. I'm your assistant. I'll make the call. At least it will appear that you're important."

Great, I'm an idiot with an assistant. "No, but thanks. I need to jump right in and do this."

I redialed his number. This time he answered. The familiarity of his voice picked up my pulse.

"Hi, Chip," I said finding a measured, professional tone. "This is Jessica Snow. We met in law school. Domestic Law, Professor Portione?"

"Sure, I'm reminded of you every time I head up the JFX and see your billboard." His voice was breezy but had a sharp edge. "Nice photo." Was that sarcasm?

I laid on the breezy with a sharp edge, too. "Yeah, well, I gotta pay the rent." I could hear him try to interject something, but I forged on with my business. "I'm calling because I represent Sharlyn Monroe in a civil matter. She got a message that you wanted to speak with her about Darnell Black."

"Right. I've got him on a simple possession charge, but he's more than a user. My intel suggests he's got a direct link to a heroin distribution center out of Houston. He's the lead guy and has runners in Baltimore and Prince George's County. Heroin's become a statewide problem. There's been a renewed movement to track down the dealers."

We agreed to meet at my office tomorrow at noon. With our business concluded, he shifted to a casual tone. "So, how've you been?"

We chatted in general terms about our work until I was interrupted by Kari, who had wandered back in and stood in my doorway, demanding my attention. She indicated that I had an important phone call on the other line.

"I've got to go, Chip. There's a call I have to take. See you tomorrow." We disconnected and I asked Kari who was on the line.

"No one. I'm hungry and want you to go get lunch with me. Hal's got a special on crab cakes today."

"I could go for some crab cakes."

#

After lunch, we headed to the House of Hair. It was on Eutaw Street near the Bromo Seltzer Arts Tower. I was glad to have Kari with me. She was a regular there and would be able to get the gossip girls chatting about Olivia.

We found meter parking a few blocks north of The House of Hair. We stepped into the salon and were greeted with the scent of mingling hair products. A beautiful dark-skinned woman with pinkish hair, a nose ring, and a black T-shirt with sequins in the shape of a gray tabby cat looked up from the head she was working on. "Whatcha doing here, Miss Kari? You're not on the schedule."

"Whatz up, Paulette?" Kari said with her best inner-city girl attitude.

Paulette looked like she was in her early thirties, but it was hard to tell with all the makeup. Her hands worked with unimaginable speed, tugging and pulling on the hair of a twenty-something woman. I could see her pained face reflected in the mirror.

"We're here to gather some information. This here's my boss, Jessica. Jess, this is Paulette. She owns this place."

I smiled. "It's nice to meet you."

"What's wrong with your hair?" Paulette asked me.

"It's the humidity." My smile faded.

"Don't she look like a white Diana Ross with hair like that?" Kari asked. All eyes turned to me and laughter filled the room.

I changed the subject. "You've got a nice place here." It was a small salon with eight styling chairs, four against each wall. A seating area consisting of a circle of four love seats facing a center coffee table was located in the center of the shop. Two manicure and two pedicure stations had been set up along the right wall.

Kari's eyes followed mine. "When did you get the mani-pedi set up?"

Paulette beamed. "Last week. I had to take a loan to do it, but it'll pay off soon. Our regular hair clients are staying here for their mani-pedis rather than going across the street to Sung Yee's Nail Palace. We cater to male clients, too. See." she pointed across the room. "I hung a flat screen and run ESPN on it all day."

Overall, the salon was the perfect configuration for a gossip ring. That day, the gossip circle included two seated customers in the midst of their transformations, one with Paulette and one with another stylist who wore a leopard-print unitard and four-inch heels. There were also two customers seated in the pedicure lounge chairs being attended to by two young nail technicians.

"What kind of information are you after?" Paulette continued to work on the head of her customer while she spoke. I noticed her efforts were transforming an unruly head of long black hair into gorgeous braids.

"The indiscretions of Olivia Metzger," Kari said.

Paulette's fingers stopped working. The other stylists, nail technicians, and patrons all stopped what they were doing and swiveled their heads in our direction.

"Is it true she was having an affair with her Pilates instructor?" I asked.

"If you mean Juan Carlos, that's old news," said Leopard Print. "She hasn't been especially discreet."

Leopard Print was fitting a dark-skinned woman with a blonde wig of shoulder length, wavy hair. Blonde Wig tried to turn her head toward us, but Leopard Print held her in place, so she had to speak to us through the reflection in her mirror.

"I saw them last week going at it like schoolkids in the back of her Mercedes in the middle of the day."

The woman in the waiting area added, "I saw them getting all frisky in the office at the Pilates studio. I was standing outside having a smoke. It was getting dark, but they had the lights on and the shades weren't drawn. It was like watching bad porn." She made the sign of the cross with lightning speed across her chest.

"When was that?" I asked.

"Sometime last week."

"Olivia's husband was murdered two days ago." Kari threw out this fact like fuel on a fire.

"I heard about that," said Leopard Print.

"You mean Juan Carlos murdered Olivia's husband?" asked Blonde Wig.

"The two of them hired a hit man I bet," said Leopard Print.

"I bet she's pregnant," said the woman in the waiting area.

"And her husband threatened to kill her," Paulette added.

"So it was self-defense then," Blonde Wig said.

Speculation was being kicked around like a hacky sack on a college campus. I had to get them back on track.

"Have any of you seen them together since the husband's death?" I asked.

They stopped their chatter, some in mid-sentence. The stylists stopped working and turned toward me, and the customers all swiveled their chairs in my direction. There was obvious annoyance at my tedious follow-up question. I had interrupted their flourish of conjecture, which they had turned into an art form.

Paulette answered. "All's I heard was that folks saw them together last week."

"Yeah," Leopard Print said. "Not since last week." The rest muttered agreement and went back to the business of hair.

Our visit had proved that what Kari and Helen Holman had told me was true—the House of Hair gossip ring was a great resource for local information.

Kari and I thanked them and turned toward the door.

The women being fitted for the wig was moving on to the next topic. "Anyone hear about Ms. Trudy's unfortunate accident yesterday?"

Being a trained professional, the word "accident" did not escape me. Kari heard it, too. We turned around.

All eyes turned to Blonde Wig. "What happened?" Paulette asked.

"You have to promise not to spread this around. It doesn't leave here, okay?" There was false agreement all around. Even I agreed, but I had my fingers crossed.

"She was cleaning her toilet. She gave it a flush and the bowl exploded. It flew right off the wall. She had turned toward the door when a piece of flying porcelain ricocheted off her rear end."

There were gasps all around. Each gasp evolved into a snicker.

"Was she hurt?" Leopard Print asked.

"Yeah, she was hurt," Blonde Wig said. "The force of the porcelain projectile knocked her down and she broke her wrist. She's also got a large cut and a wicked bruise on her left butt cheek."

The mental image of a bruised butt had everyone trying to stifle a giggle. Kari didn't miss a beat. She strolled over to Blonde Wig and handed her my business card. "You have Ms. Trudy call us. We've handled these exploding toilet cases before. We can get her some money for her pain, suffering, and indignity."

Blonde Wig took the card. "You mean this has happened before? Ms. Trudy was so embarrassed. She thought she did something wrong when she was cleaning. She tends to be overly aggressive with the abrasive cleanser."

"You tell Ms. Trudy this was not her fault. We've discovered a line of defective toilets that are exploding across the country. Have her give us a call. The sooner the better."

Kari and I were making a second attempt at our exit when we heard a panicked voice from the back of the salon. "El fuego, el fuego!"

Paulette translated. "Fire! Fire! Inez?" With each word, she turned up the volume. She ran toward the back as a hysterical Hispanic woman ran to the front. They collided.

"El Fuego, el Fuego!" Inez repeated, and by now the smell of smoke was unmistakable.

"Call 911," I told Kari. "Paulette, where's your fire extinguisher?"

She reached behind the reception counter and handed me a small red canister that was covered with dust and old hair trimmings. The hardware was rusty. I grabbed it and ran to the back. The smoke was coming from the back of the clothes dryer. Flames were climbing to the ceiling and spreading across the window curtains. They would soon reach a stack of linens and gallons of hair chemicals. Kari had moved in behind me. "Oh shit, it's gonna blow. Let's get out of here."

"Wait, let me try." I held up the antique fire extinguisher, removed the rusty pin, and pulled on the trigger. It sputtered and let out a short burst of spray that backfired. I felt cold droplets on my face. Then it sputtered again, and a white froth oozed from the spout and onto my shoes.

"Okay, you tried," Kari said between coughs. "Let's go." She grabbed my wrist, and we ran for the door.

When we hit the streets, we heard the sirens approaching. Kari smiled up at me and pumped her eyebrows. "Guess who's on the way?" I realized with equal amounts of dread and excitement that Mark the firefighter was on his way to the second fire in less than a week that erupted in my presence.

We joined Paulette, Leopard Print, Blonde Wig, Inez, and the others outside the building. Paulette was holding her cash box and laptop while she watched her business burn. She was wide-eyed, shaking, and muttering, "No, no, no."

Over the sound of the sirens, there was the unmistakable screech of a transit bus as it braked to a stop across the street. There was Delroy, once again waving to me. I forced a smile and returned the wave.

As the fire truck got closer, we moved to the other side of the street to stay out of the way. I caught a glimpse of the first firefighter out of the truck right before he put on his protective hard hat and shield. It was Mark. He and six other firefighters moved with choreographed precision to get the hoses ready. One of them broke the front window before he entered through the door. I heard Paulette gasp at the sound. Dark-gray smoke escaped through the opening.

There was an Italian deli on one side of the House of Hair and a thrift shop on the other. Two firefighters entered each building. I assumed they wanted to make sure that everyone had been evacuated. Minutes later, they returned to the street and set up a perimeter with yellow caution tape. The smoke abated quickly, which gave me hope that the fire had been contained and the damage was minimal. After about twenty minutes, the firefighters began to trickle out onto the street. The smoke was gone. Their job was done. I turned to Paulette, who still had a death grip on her laptop and cash box.

"You should go speak to them," I said. "Let them know it's your building. They'll want to know what happened."

"But I don't know what happened. Inez said she was running the laundry like always and then saw the flames."

"Well, you have to at least tell them that," Kari said. "Come on. Jess and I will go with you." She winked at me, grabbed Paulette's elbow, and nudged her across the street.

"Excuse me," Kari said to the closest firefighter. He turned toward us and I realized it was the same firefighter who put out the dumpster fire. Not Mark, but the other one. Kari continued. "This is the owner of the building, Paulette Wells."

"Sorry about your building, ma'am. The fire was contained to the back room, but there's a lot of damage. You need to call your insurance company. We've got the fire inspector on the way."

"Can she go inside to get the rest of her belongings?" I asked.

He turned to look at me. "Are you all right? You have something on your face." His gaze lingered. "I remember you." Then he saw Kari. "You're the ones who started the dumpster fire a couple of days ago."

Kari spoke for me. "This is attorney Jessica Snow. She tried to stop the fire before it spread too far. She's very brave."

Mark approached. "It's clear she didn't have the proper equipment." He looked at me with that same smile he gave me last week. He came closer, real close, and took the extinguisher from my hand. He winced. "This thing dates back to the Truman administration."

"It's all I could find."

He laughed. Then with a more serious demeanor, looked into my eyes. "Are you okay?"

"Yes, I'm fine."

"You know you've got some white stuff on your face." He waved

93

his gloved hand across his own face as a visual aid. I reached up and touched my cheek. The stuff had dried and formed a speckled crust all over my face.

"Not a good look for you," Kari said. Turning to Mark, she said, "It's the humidity that does that to her hair. It doesn't normally look like that."

I started to back away. "I better go get cleaned up."

Mark stepped toward me with a smirk. "You've been at the scene of two fires in the last three days. Is this a lucky coincidence or do you have pyromaniac tendencies?"

"It's a lucky coincidence, all right," Kari said. "We were planning another toaster fire, and now we don't have to." Mark tilted his head, looked at Kari, then back at me like he was trying to figure out what to make of that comment.

His fellow firefighters called to him.

"I better get back to work, and you should go clean up. That stuff's toxic." He hustled off to join his crew.

We wished Paulette luck with the insurance company. I gave her my card and told her she could list us as witnesses.

As we walked back to the car, Kari said, "That was a productive outing. We got the scoop on Olivia, and you got to see Mark again."

"Look at me. I'm a disaster. I didn't want to see him like this."

"You're getting hung up on the details. You made another connection. That's the important thing."

CHAPTER TEN

Back at the office, I scrubbed the white crust off my face and changed into my workout gear. Kari and I drove to the Pilates studio in her car. I was the only one in the class who did not refresh her makeup, coif her hair, or don a cute, sporty, matching exercise outfit to pant and sweat in front of Juan Carlo. Some of these women were shamelessly flirty with him. The remodeled studio had a soft color palette, large windows, and beautiful plush carpeting. We were not allowed to sweat on the carpet, so we brought our own mats and towels.

The studio was a huge room with Pilates reformer machines on the perimeter. On the first day of class, my classmates and I were admonished not to use the reformers, not to go near them, not to touch them. In fact, we weren't allowed to even look at them. The penalty for breaking this rule was to have your ID photo blown up to an 8 x10 and posted on the community board under the heading Rule Breaker. It would remain there for a full week. If you broke the rule a second time, you were escorted out of the building and banished for life, or until you signed up and paid in advance for the next series of classes.

It was a system of humiliation designed to encourage Pilates 101 students to quickly progress to the intermediate level, where using of the Reformers was required. We 101 people were not yet worthy.

"Okay ladies, are you ready to get started?" Juan Carlo asked with his sexy Latin accent. He entered the room wearing biker shorts and a tight spandex T-shirt with the slogan Do The 100. The ladies all jumped to attention while adjusting their clothing and painting on smiles. "Yes, Juan."

"Now let's take three big cleansing breaths." He planted his feet shoulder-width apart, crisscrossed his arms in front of his privates, then lifted them out to the side and up over his head. "Breathing in, and now out." He released his arms back to their starting position. This was a familiar warm-up during which I rarely lost my balance. I could hear the women in the front exaggerating their breathing.

As I followed along with Juan, I scanned the room and found Olivia. She was front and center, following Juan's every move with precision in her black-on-black mourning spandex, not a hair out of place. I could see her and Juan Carlos exchanging glances. There was a sudden change in her movement. She slowed her momentum and walked off without a word. She entered a room marked Office and closed the door behind her. Juan's worried eyes followed, but he continued to guide us through our workout.

I kept an eye on the office door. Olivia was still in there when the class came to an end. Several women approached Juan, but he tore himself away from his bevy of admirers and rushed off to join Olivia. I left to find Kari.

It was a beautiful Baltimore evening. The sun hovered low in the sky, leaving a soft glow about the city streets. Kari's car was parked in front of the studio, but she wasn't in it. Scanning the streets, I found her standing near the metro bus stop among several people. I could see her chatting with them and handing out business cards. She looked at me and said something to the small crowd. They all waved.

Kari joined me at the car. "Those were some nice folks. I thought it wouldn't hurt to give them your card. You know, spread the word. Get your name out. Hey, what happened in there?" she pointed to the Pilates studio. "Was Olivia there?"

"She was there, but she was upset. A few minutes into the workout, she left the floor, went into his office, and stayed there."

"So now what?" I asked Kari. "Do we wait and follow her?"

"You bet we do. While you were in class, I went over to Brenner's and got us a couple of chef salads and a bag of crab chips. Olivia's Mercedes is parked right over there." She pointed across the street. "We can sit in the car and eat dinner while we wait for her to come out."

I found myself enjoying being an unofficial private detective with Kari. We had no idea what we were doing, but I think we were faking it pretty well. Kari had enough confidence for both of us.

About midway through our salads, we saw Olivia emerge from the studio. She looked up and down the street before heading to her car, passing the front of Kari's Camry on the way. She didn't notice us. Her eyes were puffy and red like she'd been crying. We closed up our salads. Kari put the Camry in gear and followed her.

"They say you're supposed to leave a couple of car lengths between you and the car you're tailing," Kari said as she maneuvered behind a gray sedan which was behind a black minivan which was behind Olivia's Mercedes. Then Olivia's car changed lanes. Kari had to move directly behind her. "This is harder than it looks on TV."

"Don't worry. Fall back a little, but stay close enough so we can see which way she turns."

Olivia headed up Charles Street and merged onto Route 83 North out of the City. It was the tail end of rush hour, so it was easy for Kari to stay a few cars back and still have Olivia within our sight. The Mercedes signaled to get into the right lane and headed up the exit ramp onto Northern Parkway. Olivia's route brought us into Mount Washington—my parents' neighborhood. Mount Washington has two faces. The block I grew up on was aggressively average with mid-sized homes, postage stamp lawns, and sidewalks sprinkled with kids on bikes and dogs on leashes. The street we followed Olivia to was distinctly different. At first glance, I counted six gabled roof lines on her three-story, tutor-style home, plus a single-story addition off to one side. The house sat amongst Volkswagen-sized azalea bushes with bright pink flowers. Two monstrous magnolia trees brandishing blooms the size of dinner plates stood on either side of the front entrance. All of it rested under an umbrella of oak trees.

It was almost impossible to believe a murder had been committed here, yet the eclectic fleet of media vehicles, television cameras, and satellite dishes that crowded the street were a stark reminder that something newsworthy had happened behind those walls.

Olivia turned into the circular driveway and stopped in front of the walkway and porch leading up to her front door. The media crowd sprang into action, cameras flashing. To her credit, Olivia emerged from her Mercedes with her head held high. She kept her mouth shut, waved a disinterested hand at them, entered her home, and shut the door.

"She's a cool cucumber," Kari said. "Why didn't we see this coming? The TV people being here, I mean?"

"Because we're amateurs."

"We may be amateurs, but we're smart. Come on, let's go talk to these vultures. Maybe we'll learn something."

Kari and I approached the first reporter we saw. At least we assumed he was a reporter. He was wearing eyeliner, an excessive amount of bronzer, and an air of self-importance.

Kari got right to business. "What do you know about the Metzger murder?"

He took a step back and looked at us like he feared we'd steal his lunch money. "Just like that? Just like that, you think I'm going to give my work product over to two strangers." He snapped his notepad closed and stuck it in his jacket pocket. "This is journalism, ladies. It's cut-throat, okay?" He gestured toward the other media crews. "Look at the competition. We're all looking for that newsworthy nugget that will get us on the front page, and you think you can simply put your hand out and I'll give it to you?" This guy was strung a little tight.

"We're not reporters. We're curious, that's all," I said.

An exasperated exhale fluttered past his lips. His camera-ready bravado deflated. "I've got nothing. The police aren't talking. The securities regulators aren't talking. And, as you may have noticed, the wife isn't talking either. My only other lead is a local attorney named Dawson Garner who was questioned. You must know him from his advertising. He's an ambulance chaser. Sleazy by nature, you know the type. We're going to follow up on him now."

This guy didn't recognize me. I needed to keep it that way and get him off the Dawson trail. Avoiding direct eye contact and keeping my advertising-smile at bay, I said, "That's a dead end. He was cleared about an hour ago." The lie rolled off my tongue with disturbing ease. "His alibi panned out."

This guy was a day late on the Dawson angle but got in early on the Olivia investigation. He'd follow any lead that was dangled in front of him. I decided to have a little fun.

"Surely you've heard about Harvey Metzger's mistress?"

"No! He had a mistress? Who is she?"

This was too easy. I smiled at Kari, who gave me an encouraging wink. "Her name's Chantel Devista. She works for Stuart Milligan."

"The lawyer? The other accident guy?"

"That's the one. Metzger was paying for her condo, bought her a cute little Prius convertible, promised to always take care of her, then pulled the rug out from under her. Her condo's being foreclosed and they repo'd her car."

The reporter was taking notes without asking for details or verification. He grabbed the cameraman. They jumped into the conspicuous van bearing the name and logo of their network and sped off, burning rubber.

Kari buckled over with laughter. "I thought you weren't supposed to make shit up."

CHAPTER ELEVEN

I got to the office early to work on a couple of things before the filming of the commercial began. My first call was to Tony. He'd been discharged from the hospital soon after my initial visit. His diagnosis was a bruised coccyx and mild concussion, both of which required no further medical intervention. Time would heal all. And once it did, I could negotiate a settlement with Franco Giovanni. I got Tony's voicemail and asked him to call or stop by to let me know how he was feeling.

Yesterday had been so busy I hadn't checked my email. I sat down to run through it. There was the usual spam: loan offers, discount solar panels, secrets to maintaining a youthful appearance, and offers for penis-enlargement apparatus. I scanned through and found one from mjenkins@wagnerbeamlegalteam. The subject line said, "We'd like to Schedule an Interview." My pulse quickened. I glanced at my door to make sure no one was coming into my office. This was a private matter. I did not recall applying for a position at the Wagner & Beam. The truth was, I'd never heard of them. I scrolled down for an address. They were in Towson, north of the city.

The content of the email said that they had an entry-level position and would like to interview me for the job. I closed that window, opened another one, and googled them. According to their homepage, they were an intellectual property firm. That meant they worked with cases involving patents, copyrights, and trademarks. All very interesting stuff. I sent them an email stating that I would be interested in an interview and asked them to give me a few dates and times to choose from. I hit send and sat back in my chair.

Wow. A real law firm was interested in me. I didn't want to get ahead of myself, but I visualized a world where my face would be absent from buses and billboards. A world where I never had to hear the word *ambulance chaser* directed at me. A world where my mother could proudly say her daughter was an intellectual property lawyer and people would be impressed, even though they wouldn't know what the hell it meant. It just sounded smart and cool.

"What's that dumb look on your face?" It was Kari. I hadn't seen her in my doorway.

I rolled my eyes. "I was concentrating. What's up?"

"You ready for this commercial thing?" She studied me. "Stand up. Let me see what you're wearing."

I stood and spun around. I had on a simple blue suit with a snug, but not slutty, fit, a short skirt, but not too short, and, of course, sensible shoes.

"You pull off that boring blue suit pretty well. Let's hope the camera stays high and doesn't catch those grandma shoes you're wearing."

There was some commotion as Sal arrived with the camera crew, lighting people, and everything else needed for a low-budget commercial. I stepped out to witness the action. They were setting up in the conference room. Our extensive collection of law books would serve as the backdrop. Kari hustled in and started dusting and polishing the table. Sal was conversing with the camera crew. Marty and Dawson were standing together looking over what I assumed was the script. It impressed me that business proceeded as planned despite the pending charges against Dawson.

They didn't look like themselves. Dawson had shed his khakis and bowling shirt and donned a dark-gray suit, collared shirt, and a bow tie. His graying hair was trimmed and styled into place. It surprised me to see he was wearing makeup. So was Marty. It was subtle, but I could see a matte foundation covering their faces and a single swipe of eyeliner under each eye. Marty's usually disheveled hair also appeared to have received extra attention this morning. It was parted to the side and combed back without a strand out of place.

"Good morning," I said. "You two are looking sharp. What's your secret?"

"She's in my office waiting for you," Dawson said.

"Who's in your office?"

"Paulette. My hair stylist." Dawson waved his hand about his head.

"Paulette from House of Hair?"

"That's the one. Go see her. We'll get started as soon as you're done."

I grabbed Kari. "Did you know Paulette was going to be here?"

"Yeah. Dawson asked me to call her last week. I didn't tell you because I wanted it to be a surprise." She paused and read my face. "Surprise!"

We entered Dawson's office and found Paulette. Her hair was still a pinkish hue, but she had added orange tips. Today, her black t-shirt had an orange sequined Orioles mascot. She looked up from her magazine, smiled, and gave me the once over with her eyes.

"Come sit. Dawson said to give your hair some sex appeal."

"What the hell does that mean?" I asked, touching my head.

"It means we leave it long, soften the ends with some gentle waves, and puff up the top a bit."

"I don't want sexy hair. I'm a lawyer. I'm not supposed to look sexy. I'm supposed to look smart. I want Sarah Palin hair. She looks smart. Give me Sarah Palin hair."

Kari winced. "You want to look like a hockey mom?"

"No. I want to look like a strong, educated woman."

Paulette motioned me to the chair. "I'll give you a young, sexy Sarah Palin. Sit."

Her skilled hands moved about my head. She pulled and twisted and shoved bobby pins into my skull.

"How's the shop looking after the fire?" I asked.

"It's coming along. It could have been a whole lot worse. On the upside, I'll be able to make some improvements with the insurance money. The front of the shop was spared, so I can see clients while the work is getting done. Hey, you two still interested in Olivia Metzger? I may have some information for you."

Kari closed in. "Yeah, we're still interested. What'd ya hear?"

Paulette continued her tugging and turning and bobby pinning as she spoke. "She came in so I could touch up her roots. I was running behind so she was waiting in the waiting area talking on her phone. She was talking in Spanish. What she doesn't know is that my stepfather is from Ecuador and I picked up the language from him. It sounded to me like she was talking about travel plans. From what I could piece together, she had purchased two one-way tickets to Barcelona."

When all the hair was off my shoulders, she shielded my eyes and dispensed a thick fog of hairspray onto her creation. She and Kari looked at me and nodded their approval. Paulette handed me a mirror.

I didn't hate what I saw. Paulette had managed to soften my hair and give it some gentle waves. I looked polished, mature, and almost sexy.

"Nice work," I said, admiring my hair in the handheld mirror.

Paulette took the mirror out of my hand. "Now let's do your makeup."

"Not too much. Make it look natural. And no eye shadow."

While Paulette covered my face with a series of cosmetic products, I tried to piece together what Olivia was up to. We knew her husband was dead and he had lost a lot of people's money. She planned to leave the country. She and her lover should be suspects in the murder. All signs pointed to her and Juan Carlos, but Detective O'Mallory didn't seem anxious to explore that angle. He'd arrested Dawson on very little evidence. Why?

I needed to have a talk with the detective.

Paulette swept mascara onto my lashes, swiped lipstick across my lips, and handed me the mirror again. For a woman who had pink hair, a nose ring, and three colors of eye shadow, I marveled at her restraint with me. The makeup, while way more than I ever use, wasn't too over the top.

Marty appeared in the doorway. "Are you all finished in here? We're ready to go." He looked closer at me. "You look a little creepy."

"She doesn't look creepy," Kari said. "She looks like an educated woman with style and dignity."

"Just what our clients are looking for." Marty rolled his eyes.

I thanked Paulette and followed Marty into the conference room.

"Jess, you look perfect," Sal said. "Smart and dignified. Let's get this started. Dawson, you stand here." He pointed to a spot in the middle of our bookcases. "Marty and Jess, you stand on either side of him. You two can rest your hands on the top of the chairs or fold them in front. Whatever feels natural. Dawson, you hold this." He handed Dawson an iPad. "We want to project the image that we are using state-of-the-art technology."

"Whose iPad is this?" Dawson asked.

"My daughter's." Sal's daughter was in middle school. "Okay, let's run through the lines before we roll the cameras."

"I'm attorney Dawson Garner, and these are my associates. We may be a small law firm, but we get big bucks for our clients. Have you been injured? We can help. Over the last thirty years, we have recovered millions of dollars for people like you who have been wronged through the negligence of others. We'll take care of everything. All you need to do is call us. Or," Dawson motioned with the iPad—"you can email us any hour of the day."

Now it was Marty's turn. "That's right, I'm Marty Ferguson. We want to help. Call us at 1-555-WANNASU, or email us at GetMeMoney@DGA.com. You'll get a response from one of us"—he made a sweeping gesture with his hand—"within the hour." Now it was my turn.

"I'm Jessica Snow, and I promise that we will successfully resolve your claim and put money in your pocket. No matter how big or small, your issue is important to us. With our combined experience, we will fight the insurance company and move your claim along quickly and efficiently. All you need to do is get better and figure out what you're going to do with all that money. Right, Dawson?" Marty and I turned toward Dawson.

"That's right, Jessica. We are the real deal. We care about you. While you heal from your injury, let us work on getting you the money you deserve."

In unison, we say, "Has an accident messed up your day? Call DGA!"

"Not bad," Sal said. "Let's try it with the camera rolling."

After a few takes, we were done. It was easier than I expected. While the dialogue was trite and robotic, it was far less embarrassing than I had imagined. At least there was no close-up. Maybe I'd go unrecognized, blend into the bookshelves.

#

I dialed Detective O'Mallory, who answered on the first ring.

"O'Mallory here."

"Detective. It's Jessica Snow. I work for Dawson Garner."

"I remember you. I've seen your face three times this morning. You should know that the billboard on Charles Street North is looking a bit tattered. It ages you a few years."

"Thanks. I'll tell my agent. Look. I'm calling because I think I know who killed Harvey Metzger."

"Sure you know him. You work for him."

"No. Not Dawson. Dawson didn't do it. It was his wife."

"Dawson's not married."

"Metzger's wife. Olivia Metzger. She was having an affair with her Pilates instructor, Juan Carlos."

"How do you know this?"

"I saw them myself. Apparently, they've been seeing each other for a while. Long before the murder."

"I don't act on rumors."

I fought to control my frustration. "It's more than a rumor. It's a fact. I also know that she's booked two one-way tickets to Barcelona. They're planning to leave the country."

He was silent for a beat. I imagined trying to contemplate a reason for dismissing this piece of information, dismissing me, but he couldn't ignore it. "Text me the info on the guy. I'll look into it."

"Thank you. I will. Do you have any other leads, besides Dawson and Olivia, I mean?"

"Yeah. I got a tip from a reporter. Metzger had a mistress. A paralegal. As a matter of fact, she works across the street from you for another ambulance chaser."

I fell silent. This was insane. O'Mallory was following up on the bogus story I gave that reporter last night. Should I tell him the truth? Should I tell him I messed with a reporter to get him off Dawson's trail? This guy was a cop after all. Was I withholding relevant information? Could I be charged with interfering with an investigation? I didn't know the answer to any of these questions, so I said nothing.

"You still there?"

"I'm here. Sorry, I've got another call coming in. Gotta go." I hung up and went to find Dawson.

He was practicing his putting when I entered his office. "I have a question for you."

He kept his eye on the ball. "Sure, what's up?"

"Let me put it to you as a hypothetical. Let's say my friend learned that a cop who's investigating a murder is following a bogus lead. And let's say that friend knows this because she planted the bogus lead on a meddling reporter to distract him, not knowing the reporter would tell the investigator. Should my friend admit to the investigator that she started the rumor with the reporter?"

"It depends."

"On what?"

"Is this cop a detective named O'Mallory?"

"Yes."

"Will this distraction keep him from finding the real killer?"

I was starting to feel stupid now. Obviously, we want O'Mallory to focus on actual leads. I lowered my head and said, "Yes."

Dawson could have drawn this exchange out, asking questions with obvious answers, deepening my humiliation, but he didn't. He said, "So, tell your *friend* to set O'Mallory straight."

"I'll do that. Thank you."

"By the way, what is the bogus lead O'Mallory is following?"

"That Harvey Metzger was having an affair with Chantel Devista."

"Stuart Milligan's Chantel Devista?"

"Could there be more than one?"

"I change my mind. Don't call off O'Mallory. Let's let Stuart get a little taste of what it's like to have his business disrupted by a wayward police investigation."

We exchanged conspiratorial smiles and Dawson sunk another put.

My cell phone rang. "Jessica Snow."

"Hi, Ms. Snow. This is Marshall. Marshall Ball. We met yesterday."

"Yes, Marshall. How are you? How's your injury healing?"

"I'm doing fine. Thanks. I wanted to let you know that my wife, Lucinda, she wants me to hire a different lawyer. It's nothing personal. You seem real smart, and all, but she wants to use someone else—"

I interrupted, "Is it Stuart Milligan? Is that who she wants to represent you?"

"Well, yeah, how'd you know?"

"Is Mrs. Ball at home with you now?"

"Sure. You want me to put her on the phone?"

"No. I'm coming over to speak to her. I'll be there in twenty minutes." I disconnected the call. "Damn it!"

Dawson lined up another put. "What's up?"

"The guy I spoke with yesterday. He's like 350 pounds and is getting pushed around by his pencil-sized wife." My tone grew with anger. "She wants to hire Stuart Milligan instead of me!" I stormed off toward the door. "I'm going to talk her out of it. I want this case."

"Do you want me or Marty to go with you?"

I hated to admit it, but I was sure that if I took either of these two mature, male attorneys, she would sign right up. I wanted to nail this newbie by myself. I had done the research. I was prepared. This baby was mine.

"No thanks. I got it."

CHAPTER TWELVE

I grabbed the file from my office and fled out the back door. My pulse raced. I knew this woman was discriminating against me because I was young and female.

I hopped on the JFX. Traffic should have been light heading North this time of the morning, but the left lane was closed for construction. I moved into the middle lane. A Cadillac SUV passed me on the left and cut in front of me without signaling. I hit my brake to avoid rear-ending him. I could see he was talking on his cell phone. It's illegal in this state, but that doesn't stop its habitual practice. People do it all the time. Distracted driving has been quite good for business. I hated to think that way, but it was true.

I parked at the curb across the street from the Ball's house, grabbed the file, marched up their front steps, and rang the doorbell. Mrs. Ball answered.

"Didn't Marshall tell you that we're hiring Stuart Milligan? What are you doing here?"

"Listen. I hate to let you make that mistake. Give me five minutes. If I can't convince you to hire me instead, I'll leave you alone. Five minutes. That's all."

"Oh, all right." She stepped aside and cleared the threshold. I felt a small victory. We sat down in the family room. There was no sign of Marshall.

"Where's Marshall?"

"He's resting. He took a pain pill. What did you want to tell me?"

"Mrs. Ball, I've done my research. I know the name of the company that made the defective part. I also know where the toilet was manufactured, who the wholesaler is, and who the distributor is. So far, I've got four defendants to go after. I think we could punitive damages on top of what we discussed yesterday."

She was sitting forward in her seat now, eyes focused on mine, taking it all in. "What's punitive damages mean?"

"That means the court could add on additional money in any amount to punish the companies for failing to warn of the dangerous toilets. Looks like they issued a recall, but it was not widely publicized." I sat forward on my seat. "So you see, Mrs. Ball, I'm prepared. I could get this started, stir the pot, and have the other side losing sleep tonight over what we are going to do on Marshall's behalf. Do you think Stuart Milligan is ready to do that?"

"He could be. Maybe he's done the research, too."

"Maybe he has. When did you talk to him?"

She shifted in her seat. "Well, I didn't talk to him. I talked to his assistant, Chantel."

"What did she say?"

"She said Mr. Milligan would like to handle Marshall's claim and she'll mail me the paperwork."

"When do you and Marshall get to meet with Stuart Milligan?"

Maybe I was being too abrasive because Lucinda tightened her jaw and narrowed her eyes. "I'll call her right now and schedule a meeting."

She pulled out her cell phone, punched a few buttons, and waited with the phone to her ear. "Hello, this is Mrs. Ball. We spoke yesterday about my husband's case." She paused and nodded her head. "Yes, he's fine. Thank you. I was hoping Marshall and I could schedule a meeting with Mr. Milligan before we sign the paperwork." Another pause. "For how long?" She stared at the floor. "Okay. I see ... No, that's not necessary. Goodbye."

She disconnected and handed me the phone. "He's leaving for Hilton Head tonight. He'll be gone for two weeks." After a moment of quiet contemplation, she looked at me. "You win."

The file I left yesterday was sitting on the coffee table. She tapped it. "I'll have Marshall sign these when he wakes up."

"No need. I'll sign them now." Marshall's frame filled the doorway. He gave me a wink and a smile.

With signed retainers in hand, I headed back to the office victorious. I called Delroy from my car on the way back to thank him again for setting up the introduction.

"That oughta bring in a nice fee for DGA. How about throwing a little something my way. You know, like a referral fee?"

This was a touchy subject for me. I was fresh out of law school and hadn't forgotten what I learned in ethics class. Lawyers are restricted from giving referral fees to anyone other than other lawyers. The reality, however, is that it's done all the time. Some lawyers have runners who are aggressive, streetwise people who know where to drum up business. For each new client they bring in, they receive a monetary reward, discretely distributed and always in cash. I wasn't sure about Dawson's policy on this, but I assumed it was rather relaxed. Delroy had proved to be an asset and could be valuable in the future. Not to mention, I thought he deserved a reward.

"Right. Let me talk to Dawson and I'll see what we can do."

I glided into the office with my new file in hand.

Kari looked up. "From that smile on your face, I assume you signed him up?"

"Sure did. Lucinda was ready to sign with Milligan, but it turns out he's in Hilton Head for the next two weeks." I leaned over her desk and lowered my voice. "Delroy connected me with this case and came out with us yesterday for the meeting. How do you think Dawson would feel about giving him a little something... you know, for the referral?"

"He does it all the time." She pushed the button on her intercom. "Dawson, Jess needs a withdrawal out of petty cash for Delroy."

"Tell her to come in here."

Gliding through Dawson's door, I waved the new file in my hand and sunk into my spot on his sofa. He handed me a small stack of twenty dollar bills and sat down across from me. "That's for Delroy. Tell me about this new case."

I relayed the important details about Marshall's incident and added what I found from my research about similar occurrences. Dawson's eyes lit up. He leaned forward and steepled his fingers. The corners of his mouth turned up, almost at right angles, like the Grinch on Christmas Eve. "Do you know what this means, Jess?"

I gave him my best Grinch grin in return. "Yes. It's got class action potential." Knowing that this could translate into big fees, it was hard to contain our greedy smiles.

Energy radiated off of Dawson. He jumped up. "Wait. Marty's got to hear this." He bounded to the door to speak to Kari. "Tell Marty to come into my office, and I want you in here, too."

Dawson had me explain my new case to Marty. When I said the words "other incidences" and "defective valve," Marty turned to Dawson with a sly grin and nodded. He knew the potential, too.

Kari was the only one who wasn't smiling. "We don't know the first thing about how to handle a class action suit. We're small fry. We don't have the manpower for massive litigation. And I'm not working overtime. I got a life."

Dawson spoke. "That's not going to be a problem. If we get enough clients who were injured by these toilets, we farm the whole lot out to "Jenkins, Doyle, and Robb." I know John Doyle. He's a class action king."

Marty nodded. "That's the way to go. They do the work. We get a nice chunk of change for funneling our clients to them."

The men high-fived.

Dawson turned to me. "Well done, Jess. This could be big."

Marty looked at me without his usual contempt. "Yeah, Jess. I have to admit you've tapped into a potential windfall here. Good job."

It's ironic that my moment of validation from Marty arose from a toilet.

Dawson slapped the top of his desk. "We've got to get this ball rolling, get our name out as the experts on toilet explosion litigation before anyone else thinks of it. Here's what we do, I'll call Sal and get him over here so we can tweak the new commercial lineup. We need to include a 30-second spot about toilet explosions. We'll blast it out over the next two weeks. Kari, call our web designer. We need a site dedicated to exploding toilet injuries that links to our website..."

I heard about half of what he said after that. My mind was thinking about the 30-second commercial. I was hoping it didn't involve me. Somehow it seemed undignified to talk about exploding toilets on television. My mother wouldn't like that.

We concluded our meeting to the sound of tires screeching in front of our building. Marty was the first to the window. "What's with all the commotion over at Milligan's office?"

We hustled over to the front windows. "This is great," Dawson said. "Look at all the TV cameras. This is payback. This is karma."

"I don't see O'Mallory's car. The press must have beat him here," I said.

"This town sure does take its gossip seriously," Kari said.

"What's going on?" Marty asked.

"I ran into a reporter in front of Olivia's house last night. He was giving up on the Olivia angle and turning his focus back to Dawson. I didn't want him showing up here, so I diverted his attention by telling him that Harvey Metzger was having an affair with Stuart Milligan's secretary. I guess word travels fast. O'Mallory was even talking about it."

A smile started to form on Marty's face. "You mean you lied? You made shit up to protect Dawson?"

That's exactly what I had done, but I hadn't planned it, and I certainly couldn't have foreseen that my spontaneous lie to a single reporter would turn into a media circus. I was helping Dawson at Stuart's expense. That was fine with me.

"Yeah. I guess I did."

"Well played," he said and gave me a pat on the shoulder. This little chum fest was mildly disturbing. Was Marty starting to like me because I was becoming more like him?

O'Mallory had shown up with his partner, Howdy Doody. They double-parked in front of Stuart's office, blocking two of the four television news vans that were parked against the curb. The two detectives were mauled by reporters as they worked their way to the front door of Milligan's office.

We opened the window and strained to listen.

"Is it true that Harvey Metzger was having an affair?"

"Are you here to question Metzger's mistress?"

"What's the connection between Stuart Milligan and Dawson Garner?"

O'Mallory's partner responded with "no comment" to all questions as he shoved his way through the swarm of reporters, O'Mallory right on his tail. They entered the building, and the reporters retreated to their former positions on the sidewalk. We moved away from the windows and regrouped on the sofas in the reception area.

"I'm enjoying this," Dawson said. "The negative attention is on Stuart, at least for the time being. Have we had any more clients calling to fire us?"

We each replied in the negative. "Then I think we're in pretty good shape. I spoke with the others who wanted to leave and convinced them all to stay. Everyone except Marjorie Howard. That woman has a trashy mouth for an elementary-school teacher. You'd think she could expand her assault vocabulary beyond the words *asshole* and *douche*."

"It's time we let her go anyway," I said. "I got an email this morning. The insurance company is denying her claim. In short, they can't accept liability because they have two witnesses who say Marjorie was the one who ran the red light."

"Don't we have a witness that says otherwise?" Marty asked.

"Yeah, but what Marjorie didn't tell us is that he's her half-cousin from her mother's side, so he's biased. Also, there's a bit of history with him that won't play favorably in court. He's been convicted twice of drug possession and has a pending indecent exposure charge."

"Let's dump her fast," Dawson said. "Send the file across the street as soon as the dust settles over there."

"I'd' like to personally deliver it so that I could tell Stuart what a sleazebag he is," I said.

"You better take Kari with you."

"Yeah, I'll tell him where he can put that file."

#

By the time the street was clear of the news vans and reporters, it was approaching four o'clock. Kari and I wanted to deliver Marjorie's file before the end of the day.

I went through the paperwork and pulled out all correspondence and documents pertaining to our own efforts to resolve Marjorie's claim. I gave Kari what remained, which was all Marjorie's medical records and the denial letter from the insurance company. In short, Marjorie's claim wouldn't settle out of court. It was no longer easy money. I had Kari hide the denial letter within the stack of medical documents so Stuart wouldn't see it right away. She put the half-inch pile of paper inside a giant envelope and we headed out across the street to make our delivery.

Stuart's office building was another converted row home. I was disturbed to find the setting quite different from our own. Even though our practice areas were similar, Stuart's offices were worthy of the cover of *Architectural Digest.* I hated to admit it, but the place was gorgeous. A tribute to the legal profession. The back wall of the reception area was covered from floor to ceiling with integrated wood panels. In large, gold-colored letters were the words Law Offices of Stuart Milligan, Esq. Chantel was seated behind a custom workstation made of the same wood adorning the walls. It had a granite transaction ledge on which sat a vase of fresh flowers. Kari and I walked through the small waiting area, past the matching leather chairs that surrounded a coffee table. The table was made out of the same wood as the walls and the reception desk and had a granite top.

Kari leaned in and whispered, "It all matches."

Chantel looked up from her computer screen with a toothy smile and welcoming eyes. A practiced look that faded when she recognized us.

"What do you two want?"

Kari responded. "That's no way to greet us, but I'll let it pass this time. I bet you're a little shaken up by the cops and the press getting in your face and all."

"How do you know about that?"

"Jess and I are helping the detectives investigate the Metzger murder. We're on the inside and have access to that kind of information. Plus, we could see it from across the street. They decided not to take you in for questioning, huh?"

"There's nothing to question me about. I never even met Harvey Metzger."

I decided to stir the pot. "Didn't Stuart have his money with Metzger, too?"

"Maybe. I don't know." She was trying to file some paperwork as she spoke, but her hands were shaking so much, her bracelets rattled.

Her nerves were shot. I almost felt bad about steering O'Mallory's investigation toward her. She always appeared tough skinned, but apparently, O'Mallory had gotten to her.

"If you two came here to interrogate me, you need to turn around and leave now. I didn't know Harvey Metzger, and I wasn't having an affair with him."

"Calm down. We're here to give Stuart the file he requested," I said, holding up the envelope.

"Which file?"

"It's Marjorie Howard. The others are staying with us."

"How long does it take you people to copy a file?" She reached her hand out to take the envelope.

"No, I need to deliver this to Stuart myself. Is he in?"

"Yeah, he's in, but he's busy. You can't walk in here and demand to see him."

"Fine," Kari said. She grabbed the wrist of my right arm which was holding the envelope. "Tell your busy boss that as soon as his schedule frees up, we would like to deliver this file to him ourselves. We'll be across the street."

"You can't take that file. She's our client now."

I was sure, like me, Chantel didn't know at what point in time a client becomes a former client to one attorney and a new client to another. Like most of the law, there's a lot of gray area to play around with. Even though normal business etiquette would suggest I comply with the client's request and leave the file there, I didn't want to make it that easy. I needed to say my peace with Milligan. "There is a matter of our expenses that needs to be discussed before you get the file," I said. It was a lie, and it didn't bother me a bit.

"What expenses?" Stuart appeared in his office doorway wearing an expensive looking suit. "I've got a few minutes. Come in."

When he turned his back to reenter his office, I gave Chantel my most professional sneer. Kari smacked her hand on the reception desk and put her finger in Chantel's face. "Don't mess with us."

Stuart's personal office space was as impressive as the reception area. His dark wood desk had polished-brass details. There was a conference table with six upholstered chairs to the right of the doorway. The difference between here and the reception area was the clutter. There was clutter everywhere. Files and random papers were strewn across his desk, accented by a few Styrofoam carryout boxes. There were bags and boxes on the floor. One end of the conference table was covered with clothing and a pair of running shoes. He made no apologies for the mess.

"Have a seat," he said, indicating the two leather chairs across from his desk. "What's this you said about expenses on the Marjorie Howard file?"

"There are no expenses worth discussing. I wanted to sit face to face with you and tell you what a conniving disgrace to our profession you are."

"And you're a slob," Kari added.

He sat poised in his chair with his arms resting on the desk, hands folded. The elbows of his silk suit came close to what appeared to be the gooey remains of an egg-and-cheese sandwich.

"I'll make no apologies for the way I conduct business. I've done nothing illegal."

"You sabotaged Dawson by calling the press."

"You have no evidence that I called the press."

I turned to Kari and nodded. She reached into her purse and pulled out one of Helen Holman's old business cards and handed it to Stuart, "She's with WTTG. She took the call and had it traced here, back to you." Of course, none of this was true, but he didn't know that.

Stuart took the card, gave it a quick glance, and then flicked it back at Kari.

"I'm tired of you two amateurs. Give me Marjorie's file and take your wild accusations elsewhere. I've got a plane to catch."

I handed him the file. "We've notified Penn Casualty that we've withdrawn representation, so she's all yours."

"What about the others? I've got four more of your clients wanting to jump ship."

"No, you don't. They've decided to stay with us."

Stuart's face reddened, and he raised his voice, pointing to the door. "Get the hell out of here."

As we passed Chantel's desk, we saw her picking at a hangnail and mumbling to herself.

CHAPTER THIRTEEN

Mrs. Bianco and I swung in her glider, sipping port in comfortable silence. The same young couple that we saw the other night strolled by again. She had her arm linked around him and leaned on his shoulder. A thoughtless display of love and romance, given my chronic singledom. Mrs. Bianco saw them, too.

"What a lovely young couple," she said. "That reminds me. Did you run into that handsome fireman again?"

"Yeah, but it was not under very social circumstances."

"What do you mean?"

"There was a fire at the House of Hair. I tried to put it out with an old fire extinguisher and ended up with white crusty stuff all over me. I was speckled with white splotches, and my hair was frizzed out from the humidity when Mark and his crew showed up. I was a mess."

She winced. "I'm sure it wasn't as bad as you think. Don't give up."

"I'm taking it as a sign that maybe it's not meant to be."

"No. I don't think so. I think the third time will be ... what is it they say? The third time will be charming."

"You mean the third time's the charm."

"Right. Third time will be the charmer."

I changed the subject. "Do you know a Ms. Trudy?"

"Sure, I play canasta with her mother, Theresa."

"So you heard about her accident?"

"Yes, poor dear. Theresa says she uses too much elbow grease." She moved her arm in a back and forth motion.

"The thing is, I don't think the accident was her fault, and I'd like to get word to her. I have another client who had a similar injury." I told Mrs. B about Marshall, the defective toilet valve, and the many reports of exploding toilets. "So you see, she may have a claim against the manufacturer."

"I will call Theresa in morning and give her your number."

"Thank you." I said good night to Mrs. B and walked down her porch stairs and up mine. I planned to binge watch *Law & Order* and was anxious to get to it. As I reached for the door, Mrs. B said in a hushed voice, "Jessica." I turned to look at her and she nodded her head toward the sidewalk. That disgustingly affectionate couple walked by again. "Remember the third time with be charming."

#

I don't believe in pajamas per se. It seems contrary to me that at a time when we are most vulnerable, while we are sleeping, we should wear silly cotton sleepwear that does not function well in an emergency. What if there's a burglar? I imagined myself wielding my baseball bat and threatening to bash in a burglar's skull while wearing pajamas with cute bunnies eating ice cream under a rainbow. It didn't fill me with confidence. This is why I sleep in a pair of gray running shorts and an oversized T-shirt and have a baseball bat resting on my nightstand.

I was grateful for my practical sleepwear when I heard sirens at two-thirty in the morning. I hear sirens all the time, but these were close. So close the flashing lights beamed right below my window. The fire truck had stopped in front of my house. I didn't smell smoke. Since I'm in a row home, it could be the house on either side of me. Mrs. Bianco? I ran downstairs in my bare feet and out the front door and jumped over the railing onto her porch. I was reaching for the doorknob when I heard my name.

"Jessica, I'm here."

I turned toward the street and there was Mrs. Bianco standing next to Mark. Mark looked as surprised to see me as I was to see him. His eyes met mine and they got wider. He whispered something to Mrs. Bianco and she nodded her head. Two firefighters casually walked past me on their way into her house. From their slow gait, I gathered this was not a certifiable emergency. My own eyes jumped back and forth between Mark and Mrs. Bianco. I was inclined to jump back over the rail and into my house. Instead, I held my head high and walked down Mrs. Bianco's porch steps to join her and Mark on the sidewalk.

"You scared me." I turned to Mark. "What happened?"

"We got a call about an odor. Mrs. Bianco said it smelled like an electrical fire, but there was no smoke. We came to check it out."

"Mrs. B, you should have called me."

"I not want to wake you. I know you are busy attorney. You need your sleep." What a crock of meatballs. This feisty Italian widow was so desperate to get me a date that she faked an emergency. I wondered if Kari was in on this. A small crowd of our neighbors gathered to see what was going on. "Oh, there's Mrs. Delrico, I need to go see if she'll give me a ride to bingo tomorrow." And off she went.

"Not that I'm keeping score, but you've been at the scene of three fire calls in as many days."

"It's four days, but I'm not keeping score, either. This had nothing to do with me. I live next door." As I turned to point to my house, I took a small step sideways and felt a slimy, gooey grossness under my foot. It was a slug. I jumped away from it and into Mark.

"Gross. It's stuck to my foot. Gross, gross, gross." I held on to him while I balanced on one foot and scrapped the other against the sidewalk to get the icky slug off my foot. "Get it off!" I was dizzy with disgust.

Mark supported me by putting a muscled arm around my back and wrapping warm, rugged hands around my waist. "It's okay. It's a slug. It can't hurt you."

"It can gross-me-out to death. That's a real thing you know. Ew, I can still feel it."

"It's gone. Look, I think you killed it." He pointed toward the ground.

"I don't want to look. I'm already sick to my stomach."

In an effort to minimize my contact with the pavement, I continued to balance on one foot and hold on to Mark.

"I know this seems crazy," I said. "But I've had this phobia since I was a kid. Slugs. It's irrational, I know. I'm sorry."

"It's alright." He took off his long firefighter gloves and laid them at my feet. "Here, stand on these."

"Thank you." I had no excuse now. I had to let go of his arm.

The two guys who entered Mrs. Bianco's house had now returned. They hadn't found anything unusual. The house was safe. Their job here was done and they were getting ready to leave. Mark would need his gloves back, and I would have to negotiate the twenty feet of sidewalk to my porch and hope there were no more slugs. I was staring at the ground when Mark said, "Here's what we'll do. Don't move. I'll get a flashlight and we'll find a slug-free path to your door."

He went into the cab of the truck and returned with a flashlight. "Ready?"

He shined the flashlight at my feet. "Orange nail polish?"

I shrugged. "I'm an O's fan."

There were no slugs in sight, so I stepped off the gloves, bent down to retrieve them, and handed them to Mark.

"Thank you." He walked with me, shining the light on the pavement. "This is nice of you. I feel kinda foolish."

"I've got a cousin with a weird phobia, too. She's afraid of kiwis. Can't even look at a picture of them. It's fine if it's a whole kiwi, but sliced up—it freaks her out."

"It is one of the scarier fruits. I can see that."

At my front door, he turned off the flashlight and reached for the door knob, but didn't pull it open. He studied my face. "You sure you're okay?"

I held his eyes and smiled. "I'm fine. Thank you for not making me feel like a complete idiot."

He paused, looked away, and then back to me again.

"Would you like to have dinner with me sometime?"

Finally. Celebratory trumpets sounded in my head. There was confetti, too. I fought to keep my smile at a level beneath desperate-single's-dreams-come-true. "Sure. No escargot though."

He started to pull my front door open. "Good. I'll call you and we can figure out the details."

"Do you have my number?"

"I see it several times a day on billboards and buses. I have it memorized, counselor."

CHAPTER FOURTEEN

Given the craziness at work, I was grateful for a quiet weekend. I watched a couple of chick flicks, slept late, got some reading done, and washed my car. It's a good thing I was well rested for Monday morning because it set the tone for another stressful week. It started with a phone call on my way to work.

"Jess, there's a problem." It was Art Miller calling about Sharlyn's claim.

"What kind of problem?"

"My guy changed his story. I'm denying liability."

My stomach knotted up and I stopped breathing for a moment. This couldn't be happening. I had this all but wrapped up last week.

"What do you mean he changed his story? You already offered me $28,000."

"It's off the table. Darnell Black says your client, Ms. Monroe, was beating him about the head and shoulders while he was driving, which caused him to cross over the center line and hit the other car."

"That's a load of crap."

I knew what Darnell was doing. He was getting revenge on Sharlyn for moving on and moving out. If he couldn't get his hands on the insurance money, neither would she. Or was there more to it? Maybe he had learned of Sharlyn's intent to testify against him. Maybe he wanted to trade his cooperation with the accident case for her silence on the drug charges. I needed time to think about that. For now, I kept my response simple.

"He's a dirty, vindictive, jilted boyfriend. He's only saying that because she broke up with him and moved out. You don't believe him do you?"

I knew it didn't matter what he believed or what I believed. If it remained in dispute, it would come down to the question of what a jury would believe. I didn't have the time for a jury trial and neither did Sharlyn. She needed to move on with her life and leave Darnell behind.

"You know I have to take his word for it until I see evidence otherwise."

"Keep the file open. I'll call you tomorrow."

I went out to tell Kari what had happened. "That man is a menace. Why can't he go to jail peacefully and leave Sharlyn alone?"

"He wants to bargain."

"In other words"—Kari said—"he'll do the right thing if she does the wrong thing."

"Exactly."

We held silent over this troubling turn of events until Kari changed the subject. "So how was your weekend?"

My face lit up. "Mark asked me out."

"The firefighter?"

"Yup." I gave her the details about Mrs. Bianco's imagined electrical fire.

"Electrical fire, huh? She's a clever one, that Mrs. B."

Moments later, Sharlyn showed up for our meeting with Chip Woodward. She wore a conservative pale blue dress and carried an umbrella.

"Is it raining yet?" Kari asked. "I heard we were supposed to get another thunderstorm. Channel 23 even posted tornado warnings."

"Not yet, but the sky is getting black and the wind's picking up," Sharlyn said.

"How're you feeling?" I asked.

"I'm nervous about this interview, Should I be nervous?"

"No. You have to answer his questions truthfully, that's all. You've done nothing wrong. Hooking up with the wrong guy is not a crime."

Kari looked up from her desk. "I sure hope not, or lock me up and throw away the key."

There was a loud clap of thunder. We turned toward the front windows as if it would break through the glass.

"Sharlyn, I'm afraid I have some bad news. It's temporary though. I'm sure things will turn around."

"What is it?"

"Darnell's changed his story about the accident."

I explained what Art had told me and that it meant the insurance company has to deny his claim unless there is evidence contradicting Darnell's version, or unless he changes his story back to the truth.

"But how can they believe anything he says? He's trying to screw me over for breaking up with him. It's obvious he's lying."

"You and I both know that. But if he holds his position, we will have to file suit and let a jury decide."

"I don't have that kind of time. I need that money to get my own apartment."

"Don't worry. I'm not giving up on this," I assured her.

Chip Woodward came through the door. He stood tall and slender in a slim cut Daniel-Craig-as-James-Bond suit. The memory of my earlier crush tapped me on the shoulder and said, *I'm still here.*

"It's coming down hard." He closed his dripping umbrella and settled his warm brown eyes on mine. "Hi, Jess," he said, moving toward me. I wondered, was this a huggable moment? We'd spent some time pouring over notes in our study group, but it was more like parallel playing, and we hadn't seen each other in a while. What was appropriate? A long embrace, a quick hug, a meaningful handshake? I didn't know the answer, but I was alert to the clue when he presented it. He put his umbrella down and reached out his right hand. "So good to see you." Okay, so no hug. I'd get over it.

I took his hand. It was damp from the rain. He had soft skin, but a strong grip. I held it a few seconds longer than I would a complete stranger as a homage to our past and said, "Good to see you, too."

I introduced Kari and Sharlyn before directing him toward the conference room. Kari asked if she could get us anything to drink. Everyone declined, and Kari returned to her desk.

Chip had a tall, muscular build from which his tailored suit hung perfectly. A platinum Tissot watch peeked out from under his cuff as he hoisted a black leather briefcase onto the conference table. I knew his salary as a public servant couldn't pay for these niceties. Chip came from money. His father had local political influence and was one of the developers who benefited from the renaissance of the city's Inner Harbor.

Sharlyn and I sat down while Chip remained standing, going through his briefcase. "How long have you been working for Dawson Garner?" he asked.

"About six months now."

"How's it going? Do you like this kind of work?"

Once again, I couldn't decipher his tone. Was he putting me down? I wasn't sure. I decided not to get defensive.

"It's been kind of a whirlwind. I've learned a lot while flying by the seat of my pants. In six months, I've closed about three-dozen files and was top earner here for the last two months. So, yeah. I do like it here." The easy truth of this statement shocked and confused me. It was true. I was falling into step as a personal injury lawyer. The more my confidence rose, the more I liked the job. So why, I wondered, was I excited about my interview with Wagner & Beam?

"How about you?" How's the State's Attorney's office treating you?"

"Not bad. I've put a lot of reprobates away and made several important connections. I plan to run for office someday. I figured this is a good place to start."

His tone hinted at arrogance. He thought this job was beneath him, a necessary step up the ladder.

"Sounds like a good plan," I said.

As we spoke, he pulled out a tape recorder, a manila file, a yellow legal pad, and a fountain pen. He closed the clasps on the briefcase, used both hands to relay it from the table to the floor, then seated himself in the chair.

"So how does this work?" I asked.

"It's simple. I'm going to turn on the recorder and ask Ms. Monroe for her permission to record this session. Then I'll ask questions to determine whether or not Sharlyn knows anything that might help put Darnell Black away."

Chip managed to put Sharlyn at ease with his relaxed manner, but my brain was telling me not to let my guard down with this guy. Warning sensors sounded at the mention of recording the meeting. I couldn't let personal feelings cloud my judgment.

"I'm not comfortable with having this meeting recorded," I said. "Sharlyn's here voluntarily as a courtesy to your office. She'll answer your questions, but until we know what she has that might help you, we're off the record."

"I understand." He gave me a I-didn't-think-I'd-get-away-with-it-but-had-to-try smile and returned the tape recorder to his briefcase.

Nice try.

Chip began by asking Sharlyn for her full name, address, age, and occupation. He jotted all this down like it was new information. Then he got into what Sharlyn knew about Darnell.

"How long have you known Darnell Black?"

"About eight months. I moved in about four months ago because my lease ran up and it was a free place to stay." Her head was down and her hands were taking the top of a pen on and off. I knew she was not proud of her association with him. "We come from a neighborhood where Darnell has power and respect. He always had money. Lots of money. He was good to me most of the time, took care of me when I needed taking care of. But now I see that his lifestyle is not what I want." She looked at me. "I know I can do better. Jess helped me get a job, so things are looking up for me." I received an approving nod from

Chip. His gaze lingered like he was trying to figure me out.

The interview went on to reveal that Sharlyn had seen Darnell take possession of shoe-sized boxes that contained small zipper-lock baggies. She watched as money changed hands in exchange for those little baggies. "But I never helped him. I never approved. I stayed in the kitchen if it happened at home, or stayed in the car if it happened somewhere else." Her tone became a bit defensive. Chip noticed it, too.

"Don't worry. I'm not after you. I need to know if we can count on you to testify against him."

She stiffened and gave me a scared look, but I saw determination on her face. "I'll help you. I moved out a couple of days ago. I don't want nothing more to do with him."

"Okay then," Chip said. "I'll have a subpoena issued for you this afternoon."

Chip must have noticed the concern on her face.

"Don't worry. It's a formality to secure your testimony and let the other side know you'll be testifying for the State."

"So, Darnell will know?" Sharlyn asked.

"His attorney will get a copy of the subpoena and will contact Darnell."

Sharlyn squared her shoulders. "That oughta piss him off."

I knew it wasn't relevant to the criminal case pending against Darnell, but I had to tell Chip about the civil claim Sharlyn had against her ex-boyfriend, and the bunk he was pulling.

"Darnell's messing with Sharlyn's civil claim against him. We almost had it settled when Darnell changed his story about how the accident happened. Now the insurance company is denying her claim. She was counting on that money to get started building her new life."

Chip was packing his briefcase. "The man's a piece of work. It will be my pleasure to put him behind bars. But I'm not sure how I can help with the civil end."

"If he pleas out, can't it be part of the plea deal that he also admits to the accident?"

"I don't see how." His tone was arrogant and dismissive. Here he was asking for Sharlyn's help and not even pretending to be interested in helping her. My law-school crush was dimming.

As we filed out of the conference room, the front door slammed open. Delroy and his friend, Ronald, walked in holding up a young man who was dragging his leg behind him, at an impossible angle.

"I got another one for you, Jess," Delroy said, as though I was collecting the wounded from the streets of Baltimore. I needed to help this guy, but my first, shameless concern was to let Chip know that we don't make a habit of hauling in clients this way.

Kari sprang into action first. "Delroy, get him to the couch. I'll call an ambulance."

Once the man was seated, I addressed Delroy. "Why did you bring him here? Why didn't you call an ambulance?"

"It happened two blocks from here. I figured you'd know what to do. Besides, Stuart Milligan's runner works that corner. I didn't want him getting this case when I could give it to you."

I was mortified to have Chip hear those words. This was textbook ambulance chasing. It walked the fine line between being an ethical attorney and being a scumbag. I felt like a scumbag.

I admonished Delroy, channeling my mother's strident tone. "Next time call an ambulance. His medical needs come first." I raised my voice. "They always come first."

Delroy shrunk from my verbal assault. "I'm sorry. I thought I was doing the best thing by him. You always help people, so I figured..." He let his words trail off and I felt like a heel.

"It's okay. I'm sorry. I know you were trying to help."

The injured man had not uttered a word or a moan since he arrived. He sat motionless, yet he seemed to be following the conversation with his eyes. He was studying Kari while she spoke to the 911 operator.

I turned to Chip. "Sorry. Our business is done, right?"

"Yes. Go do what you have to do. I'll touch base with you later." He looked down at the injured man. "Hope it's not too bad, buddy."

While we waited for the ambulance, I learned that the injured man was named Maurice Townsend. He was crossing St. Paul Street in the crosswalk with the crossing light when a woman driving an Audi SUV turned right on red and knocked him to the asphalt. Delroy saw it happen and got the driver's name and tag number before scooping Maurice up and dragging him and his dangling leg to my office. Now wasn't the time, but Delroy and I were going to need to talk about personal injury protocol. Maurice mustered the strength to pull his cell phone from his cargo shorts and asked us to call his girlfriend.

She arrived at the same time the paramedics walked in. She looked at Maurice, then at me and said, "You're that lawyer lady, right?"

I nodded.

"How much you think we gonna get out of this?"

CHAPTER FIFTEEN

Sal brought over lunch from Sabatino's. He must be flush with all the commercial production work we'd been giving him. Over pasta and salad, we hammered out the details of the thirty-second toilet-explosion spot. Sal took the lead. "We need to keep it short and factual. Because the issue involves a toilet, the image can make people uncomfortable. It will conjure up pictures of people flying through their bathrooms with their pants down. To some that's a comical image." He paused while we chuckled. "But to those who have been injured, it's embarrassing. So we set out the facts about the faulty toilets and we detail our contact information. Also, we squeeze in a word about the recall and suggest that people check their toilet's manufacturer before their own toilets explode."

"Sound's kind of boring," Dawson said.

"It is, but it will be effective. Trust me. You may even get a tax break because we can claim it as a public-service announcement. I suggest we put Jess's name up there, as well as one of you two. That way we have both genders covered. A woman with a lacerated backside is not going to want to talk to either of you," Sal said, pointing at Dawson and Marty. "And a young man with a punctured penis is not going to want to talk to you," he said, pointing to me.

"So no live shots of me?" I asked.

"No. We can use the stock photos we have on hand and add some new graphics. Do you have any photos of the exploded toilets?"

"I've got photos from my one client, and I'm hoping to sign up a second. Either way, I would have to get their permission."

"Get me whatever you can as soon as possible. We want this in production by the end of today and on the air tomorrow."

I had to hustle. There was a lot to do before my interview with Wagner & Beam later this afternoon.

First, I called Marshall and asked if we could use the images of his bathroom in the commercial. He consulted Lucy, then gave me the verbal okay. I needed it in writing to protect us from the remote possibility that Marshall would deny his consent and come back to sue us later, but time was of the essence. I emailed Sal the photos so he could get them in production, then I worked on drafting the consent form. The short and practical version would be, "I, Marshall Ball, give Dawson Garner & Associates permission to use images of my bathroom, post-explosion, in their future commercials and all visual media." Period. But the law doesn't make things so simple. You have to throw in some fancy words such as *irrevocable, inclusive, fiduciary*, and *in perpetuity*, to construct a tangled and verbose document that no one understands, yet attorneys pretend they do.

I did my best to use the proper language to protect DGA within the constructs of two long, torturous paragraphs. I titled it "Consent to Utilize Specific Photographs in all Visual Media." Even the title was a snooze fest. I printed out two blank consent forms and stuck them in my bag to have at the ready next time I saw Marshall.

#

As I drove north on York Road to Towson for the interview with Amanda Chamberlain, the sun fell behind a bank of dark clouds that moved in from the west. It was four thirty in the afternoon, prime time for a typical Baltimore summer thunderstorm. It wouldn't last long but would dump a heap of water and bring crazy winds, upsetting the balance of things before it moved off. This storm had an attitude. It skipped the telltale warning sprinkles and went straight to large buckets of water slapping my windshield.

Several things happened at the same time. I flipped my windshield wiper control to maximum, saw brake lights ahead, slammed on mine, heard the screeching of tires, and then silence. A couple of seconds went by before the impact to my rear bumper propelled my car forward, missing the sedan in front of me by an inch. It was impossible to see. The irritating cadence of the windshield wipers combined with the pounding of the rain made me anxious. Since traffic had stopped, I turned the windshield wipers off and took a deep breath. What now?

I knew that information needed to be exchanged. However, I decided it would be dangerous to exit the car at this point. Not to mention the water hazard to my hair, my tailor-fitted power suit, and opened toed, three-inch strappy heels. I couldn't show up for my interview like I had just climbed out of a pool. It seemed reasonable to wait until Mother Nature decided to stop dumping vats of water on our cars. These things don't last long. It would be a matter of minutes before I could get the necessary information from the driver who rear-ended me.

In the midst of my rational justification for staying put, the car behind me started to reverse. I could feel his bumper disconnect from mine. The bastard was trying to pull a hit-and-run. Oh no, not on me. I was a professional!

With complete disregard for the rain or my dignity, I leaped from the car and started banging on his driver's side window. He didn't bother turning his head in my direction, but I could see his devilish smile. He raised the middle finger of his left hand and kept backing up. After clearing my car, he shifted to forward and started pulling away. He wouldn't get anywhere fast. The other northbound lane of traffic was stopped for a red light. I ran back to my car and grabbed my cell phone, grateful it had a waterproof case. I caught up to him and started taking pictures of his car, being sure to capture the license plate number. He was still stuck at the light, so I stepped up to his driver's side again and snapped a few shots of his wretched face laughing at me.

Then the light turned green and he pulled off. I was left standing wet and foolish in the middle of York Road. Traffic maneuvered around me, but not in a nice way. There was some horn blowing and verbal abuse as I returned to my car. My rear bumper had tolerated the impact. The accident had left a small dent not worthy of the indignity I had suffered.

Mother Nature had downsized the pummeling to a moderate rain. I found a metered spot one block up and sat in the car to contemplate my options. My clothes were soaked, my hair was matted to my head, and I had an interview in thirty minutes. I could cancel the interview, but I didn't want to risk losing this opportunity. I could present myself as is and share my witty story about the hit-and-run driver who escaped my grasp. I decided to use the bathroom in the lobby of The Towers to assess my appearance and then make a decision. The Towers is an upscale office building with ample indoor parking. Before entering, I noticed that the rain had given way to the sun, making a mockery of my recent ordeal.

With twenty minutes to spare, I entered the lobby and located the elevators. Wagner & Beam was on the third floor. I took the elevator to the second, hoping to find a ladies' room. The bathroom was styled with granite counter tops and three infinity sinks. To my delight, there was an air hand dryer located on the far wall. I dug a brush out from my purse, pushed the metal button on the dryer, and stuck my head under it. In two minutes, my hair was dry, but it was a jumbled mess. Ignoring that for now, I took off my jacket and held that under the dryer, then I did the same with my skirt. I used paper towels to dry my legs and shoes. After dressing, I stepped back to examine myself in the mirror. The clothes were presentable, but my hair was scary.

The door to the ladies' room opened. A woman about my mom's age came in. She must have noticed my distress. "You alright?"

"I got caught in the rain. I have an interview in ten minutes, and look at my hair."

"Stay here. I'll be right back." She went back out through the door and returned moments later with a giant handbag. She pulled out a wide-tooth comb, a giant spider clip, and a can of Aqua Net. "Hold still," she said. She had magical hands because I hardly felt her tugging on my unruly locks.

I noticed her watching my reflection in the mirror. "I know you. You're that bus lawyer."

"Guilty," I said.

"I don't get it. You've got a good job, but you're here to interview for another?"

It was not lost on me that she referred to my current job as good.

"To be honest, I didn't take my current job thinking it would be my lifelong career."

"Seems to me you got a real job. Your firm represented my sister's husband's first cousin when he was injured at the Dunston Plant a couple of years ago. Dawson Garner did well by him." She grabbed the hair clip in one hand, did some tricky little loopy thing with the bulk of my hair, and jammed the clip onto it. When she was done, the spider clip held most of my hair behind my head. A few gentle curls were allowed to escape, giving it a soft look.

"Close your eyes and hold your breath," she said. I complied and heard the can of Aqua Net dispense a sticky fog of aerosol lacquer over my head. After the air cleared, I turned to the mirror and examined her handiwork.

"How'd you do that? It looks better than before I got caught in the rain. Very professional." I turned my head from side to side, looking at my reflection and nodding my approval.

"I have four daughters. We call this 'interview hair.' So who's this interview with anyway?"

"Wagner & Beam. They do intellectual property law."

"I know who they are. You don't want to work for them."

"Why not?"

"You'll find out soon enough. I work down this hall at the engineering firm. My name's Janice. Come see me when you're done."

Wagner & Beam shared the third floor with an accounting firm, a fertility clinic, and a canine therapist. The entrance had large glass double doors with heavy hardware pulls. I pulled one side open and slid into their reception area. It was sparsely decorated in an intentional way. The round reception desk had wood-inlaid panels and a granite top. It was free of any paperwork. No files, no mail. Just a computer. The seating area had a large leather sofa with two matching wingback chairs on either side of a circular glass coffee table. The whole place was cold and impersonal.

A young woman with severely pulled-back black hair, dark red lipstick, and fake eyelashes was poised behind the desk. She looked up from her computer monitor. "May I help you?"

"I'm Jessica Snow. I have an appointment with Amanda Chamberlain."

"Oh right. You're here for the interview." She stood and looked at me a little harder. "I should have recognized you from the ads." She stood higher on her tiptoes and leaned across the reception desk to give me the once-over with her eyes. I felt self-conscious about my appearance. At the same time, I was insulted by her condescending scrutiny and wanted to punch her in the face.

"Is there a problem?" I asked with a saccharine smile.

"No. Follow me to the conference room." She led the way down a short hall and gestured toward the doorway of a glass-walled conference room. "Can I get you some coffee, or water, or tea?"

I declined the offer of refreshments, and she retreated, promising to let Ms. Chamberlain know I was here.

Surveying the surroundings, I concluded that if there was an HGTV makeover show for law offices, Dawson Garner & Associates would be the "before" and Wagner & Beam would be the "after." The second-hand, almost-matching chairs Kari found for our conference room at a consignment store in Cockeysville seemed sullen and dull compared to the crisp, tight leather swivel chairs adorning this room. I selected a chair by the window so I could look through the glass wall into the hall. I sat my handbag on the chair next to me and pretended to look at my cell phone. Through my peripheral vision, I noticed two people standing in the hallway on the other side of the glass. Looking up, I noticed it was a man and a woman about my age, wearing business suits and arrogant demeanors. Both associate attorneys, I assumed.

When they saw me looking, they transformed their smirks into serious faces and hastened down the hall. I was getting used to being recognized once in a while—a natural consequence of DGA's advertising—but I didn't like this. Had they been laughing at me? Indignation burned in my chest. Before I could contemplate their behavior further, a figure appeared in the doorway.

"You must be Jessica. I'm Amanda Chamberlain." She glided toward me and presented a well-manicured hand. I stood, took her hand, and practiced my firm, one-pump handshake.

She had about fifteen years on me. Her tailored suit made mine look like I'd pulled it off the rack at a thrift shop. Hers was a subtle, houndstooth print in a gray tone. She brightened it with yellow, bobbled earrings and a matching bracelet. Highlighted hair swung an inch above her shoulders. She motioned for me to resume my seat and lowered herself with the grace of a dancer at the head of the table. While we were about the same height, she sat taller than me. I checked my posture, threw back my shoulders, and elongated my neck. Still, I felt like a kid at the adults' table. I looked at the two chairs adjacent to me and noticed their seats were the same height as mine. Her chair was set higher. The room was designed for intimidation, and it was working.

The receptionist came in and placed a crystal glass filled with ice water and a lemon slice in front of Amanda Chamberlain. "Are you sure you don't want anything?" she asked me. I politely declined again and she retreated through the glass door, leaving it open.

Amanda Chamberlain took a sip of the ice water, opened a folder in front of her, and looked down at my resume.

"I see you work for Dawson Garner."

It was not a question, but I replied in the affirmative anyway.

"Why would you want to leave such"—she paused for effect and painted a smirk on her face—"stellar employment." I was confused by her characterization. While I retrieved my rehearsed answer from my brain, I noticed yet another man in a suit peering at me from the hallway. He pretended to consult a file folder. When I met his eyes, he moved along down the hall with a not-so-subtle nod at Amanda. I redirected my attention to my answer.

"I'm looking for more of a challenge," I replied.

"And why are you interested in intellectual property law? Isn't chasing ambulances challenging enough for you?

Her condescending tone bit hard at my core. She was trying to humiliate me. They all were. It almost worked. A small cluster of people pretended to have a meeting in the hallway. They were busy stealing glances at me. I recognized three of them from earlier. The air tensed with their arrogance. I knew then that this interview was not about hiring me. They wanted to see the ambulance chaser who didn't want to chase ambulances anymore. They wanted to see if the real Jessica Snow resembled the one they'd seen on billboards and buses. To them, I was a circus sideshow—their afternoon entertainment. Amanda Chamberlain acknowledged their presence with a wink and turned back to me.

Avoiding her question, I rose, gathered my purse, and went to stand over her before she had a chance to stand on her own. "I've made a mistake. I'm sorry to have wasted your time." It felt good to reject her before she rejected me, but something was missing. It was a muted victory. I needed to even the score.

The gawkers in the hallway were no longer pretending to discuss work. They were lined up against the glass staring in. Perfect. In one seamless motion, I reached for Amanda's water glass, poured it over her head, and watched as the lemon struck her nose. I dropped the glass in her lap. Squaring my shoulders, I skated through the door past the dumbfounded, pompous brigade of onlookers and let myself out. Damn, that felt good.

Once in the elevator, I hit the button for the second floor. I wanted to share my victory with Janice. The office of Vector Tech, Inc. was more low-key than Wagner & Beam. Its furnishing resembled that of Dawson Garner & Associates. I asked the receptionist if Janice was available and she buzzed Janice on the intercom, then directed me down the hall to the first door on the right.

Janice was sitting at a drafting table. She removed a pair of reading glasses, let them fall on a chain around her neck, and gestured toward a drafting stool right next to her.

"So, how'd it go?"

"You were right. I don't want to work there. They were awful to me."

"I should have warned you, but I figured that's something you needed to judge for yourself." She reached for a bag a Twizzlers, grabbed one, and passed the bag in my direction. I pulled out a piece. "Some folks enjoy the arrogant atmosphere and the posturing of pompous pricks. I had a feeling you weren't one of them."

"They were making fun of me. It was like they called me in for the interview to see the real thing—like I'm a freak show." I took a bite of the licorice then pointed it toward the ceiling. "But I got the better of Amanda Chamberlain."

"What did you do?"

I told her what I had done. She laughed so hard she nearly fell off her stool.

"So what now? Do you have any other interviews set up?"

"No. My resume is still out there. I check job postings a couple of times a week. Something will come up." I stood to look around. "So, you're an engineer?"

"Nice deduction, counselor." She smiled. "Yup, I've been with Vector for almost twenty years now. I was hired not long after it was founded. We do government contract work for the most part. Nothing fancy or groundbreaking, but it's steady work, and I like the people I work with." She looked up at me. "Do you like the people you work with?"

My eyes narrowed. "I know what you're doing. You're trying to make me realize that I have a great job."

"Another savvy deduction, counselor."

I suspected she might be onto something, but I wasn't in the mood for a deep discussion about my motivation for seeking employment elsewhere. For now, I wanted to wallow in my victory.

"I shouldn't keep you from your work any longer. How about I call you next time I come to Towson? I have business at the courthouse once in a while. Maybe we can meet for lunch?"

We agreed to stay in touch, and I resolved to make an effort to keep that promise.

On the drive back to DGA, I considered two opposing views. Janice was from my mother's generation and she saw the value in the job I was doing. My mother, on the other hand, didn't approve of my work. Could she be the reason I felt the pull to find something else?

CHAPTER SIXTEEN

Sharlyn was sitting in the reception area when I returned from my clandestine interview.

"What's up?" I asked.

"Kari said you wouldn't be long. I've got to get back to work, but I wanted to show you this." She handed me her cell phone and I looked at the displayed text message. *Keep your mouth shut or I'll cut out your tongue.*

"Who's this from?"

"I don't recognize the number. It could be from Mad Dog. He's Darnell's boy. Does whatever Darnell says."

The office phone rang, and Kari went to answer it. She listened for a few moments and held the phone out to me. "I think it's for you."

"This is Jessica Snow."

"You need to tell Sharlyn to shut the fuck up about Snake. If she rats him out, she's dead, and so are you."

"Who is this?"

"I'm your worst fucking nightmare, bitch." He hung up. The phone shook in my hand as I returned it to Kari.

"You're paler than your normal pale," Kari said. "What'd he say?"

I relayed our brief and heartwarming conversation, then went to rap on Dawson's door. "Hey, we've got a problem out here."

He called from inside his office. "Give me a second to put my pants on."

"Kari, check the phone and get the number from that call. Let's see if it's the same as the number on Sharlyn's phone." We compared the numbers. They were the same.

Dawson emerged from his office with crisp seams on his pressed khakis. "What's up, Jess? You look a little pale."

"Sharlyn's been subpoenaed to testify against her rat bastard ex-boyfriend. He's being tried for heroin distribution." My voice was shaking. I took a deep breath. "We got threatening messages saying that if she talks, we're dead."

He shot me a questioning look. "And, what? You're not worried about that are you?"

"You bet I'm worried! I'm not ready to die. I've almost got a date lined up."

Marty joined us. "What'd I miss?"

"These two"—Dawson said, pointing at Sharlyn and me—"received a threat suggesting that if Sharlyn testifies against her ex-boyfriend in his drug trial, then they're both toast."

Marty looked at us. "And, what? You're not worried about that, are you?"

I felt like I'd been transported to another dimension where people had nine lives, like a cat. So why worry about one routine death threat?

Dawson tried to reassure me. "These kinds of threats happen all the time. Right, Marty?"

"All the time," Marty said. "In fact, I've had clients threaten witnesses."

I narrowed my eyes at him.

"I didn't know about it at the time, Jess. I may bend the rules, but I would never condone that. It happens in drug cases all the time." Dawson pulled me to my feet. "You need to get your mind off this. Everyone, we're closing early and going to happy hour."

"Come to Hal's," Sharlyn said. "We've got a special on steamed shrimp, and it's half-price burger night."

We filed into Hal's and got a booth overlooking the street. Marty and Dawson on one side, Kari and I on the other. Hal brought us a mountain of steamed shrimp coated in heaps of Old Bay seasoning and a pitcher of Natty Boh. We each ordered a burger and fries.

After filling our mugs, Dawson raised his glass. "Here's to persevering in the face of adversity."

Clink, clink, clink. Our four mugs met in the middle.

Dawson continued. "A lot has happened in the last week, beginning with Harvey's murder and then my arrest. Now Jess has been threatened by some lowlife drug dealer. But I'm feeling very positive."

"How's that?" I asked.

"For starters, I shot a 74 at the Baltimore Country Club yesterday."

I raised my eyebrows. "That's why you're positive?"

"No, I was bragging. I'm feeling positive because we've got a killer team here." He gestured around our booth. "Despite the troubles of last week, we've kept our clients, gained new ones, even increased our criminal practice. Plus, Jess is on to a new line of personal injury claims with the exploding toilets. The future is bright." He raised his glass again.

Clink, clink, clink.

Dawson's team building speech made me happy to be recognized as part of this burgeoning legal squad. At the same time, guilt gnawed at my stomach. Here was Dawson, praising our four-person team when a couple of hours ago, I sat for a job interview. I felt like a traitor. Why was I looking for other work? Sure, our area of practice lacked the prestige and honor of other fields, but we helped a lot of people. We did good, honest work. I was getting the hang of this business, and I had become a true asset to the firm. Who cares if a drug-dealing lowlife had threatened to kill me? At that moment, I loved my job.

I raised my glass. "Here's to DGA."

We finished our meal. Marty and Dawson stayed behind to shoot some pool with Hal. Kari and I walked back to the office to get our cars and head home.

#

Kari jumped right into her car and drove off. I backed out and turned left down the one-way alley. My headlights illuminated the path in front of me. I glanced in the rearview mirror. The other end of the alley was partially lit by a floodlight over a single-car garage. Standing in that wash of light was a man. He straightened his arm in front of him, raised one hand, and leveled it at me. I saw a flash of metal. In a small fraction of a millisecond, as adrenaline coursed through me, a few simple things went through my head—this asshole was going to shoot me. I would die alone and never get that date with Mark.

I sank into my car seat and floored it down the alley. The horrifying sound of gunfire exploded. The car lurched to the left. Gripping the wheel tighter, I guided the car toward Biddle Street. It was well lit, which provided me with some comfort. I turned left onto Biddle, the car hobbling along on three tires, when Delroy crossed the street in front of me. I slammed on my brakes and blew my horn at the same time. Delroy jumped like an NBA superstar and stumbled forward, but caught himself. He clutched his chest. I feared he was having a heart attack.

I didn't want to stop or get out of the car because I didn't know if the shooter was following me. But I couldn't leave Delroy.

I lowered the passenger window. "Get in the car. Delroy. Get in the damn car!"

"Jess. Is that you?" He was trying to steady himself after his near-death experience, still clutching his chest.

"Yes, don't ask any questions. Get in the goddamn car!"

We drove in silence for three blocks then pulled over at a busy intersection.

Delroy reached again for his chest, this time going inside his jacket. He brought out a flask, took a long pull, and handed it to me. I took my shaking hands off the wheel, grabbed the flask, and choked on its contents. I needed both hands to control it. Then I took another swig. It had an instant calming effect.

"What happened back there?" he asked.

"Someone shot at me as I was leaving the alley."

"Damn. Who'd you piss off?"

I explained that it was most likely a drug dealer.

He gave me a disparaging look. "You shouldn't be doing drugs, Jess."

"I don't do drugs. I'll explain later. You alright?"

"Sure. I'm fine. You got a spare tire in this tin can?"

"Yes, but I don't know how to change a tire." I looked at him. "And you shouldn't be changing a tire, either. I thought I gave you a heart attack."

He suggested I limp the car a couple more blocks over to his pawn shop. He lived above it, and his son lived half a block away. He called his son and told him to bring a tire iron and a jack.

While we waited, I told Delroy about the threat I had received from Mad Dog. He reiterated what Dawson and Marty had said about those threats being harmless.

"But the guy shot at me. That's not harmless."

"It was a warning shot. If he wanted to kill you, he would have."

I didn't find that at all comforting. "What's your son's name?"

"Marcus. That's him." Delroy pointed toward a figure on the sidewalk and got out of the car. Marcus was carrying a jack and a toolbox. He appeared to be in his early twenties, clean shaven, cropped hair. He wore his shorts low on his hips, but not so low as to reveal the color of his underwear. His T-shirt bore the logo of the family business, Delroy's Pawn Palace.

There was a good amount of activity on the street. I scanned the near vicinity for anyone pointing a gun at me. Seeing no immediate threat, I joined Delroy and Marcus on the sidewalk.

Delroy made the introductions. Marcus grabbed my right hand with both of his and pumped it. "My dad says you're the shit when it comes to attorneys."

"High praise, thank you. And thanks for coming out to help with my tire."

He shrugged. "It's no big deal. Dad said someone shot at you. That happen often?"

"First time."

"You get used to it."

He asked me to pop my trunk, pulled the spare out, and got to work. "You're lucky. I think the rim's in good shape."

I sat on the curb close to Marcus and watched the activity on Holliday Street. Delroy was chatting it up with a cross-dresser at the corner. There were bouncers stationed outside of three different establishments along the street. Each had bright neon signs screaming to be noticed while Marcus was quietly humming a tune.

After thanking Marcus and Delroy for their help, I headed home. I was still a bundle of nerves. Someone shot at me and he might try again. I was tired, sweaty, and dirty from sitting on the street. I needed a shower, but all I could think about was getting stabbed in my bathroom. I couldn't go home alone. I decided to call on Mrs. B. At least she had a gun. It was tough to find a parking space at this hour, but I managed to find one half a block away. I fast-walked toward my house with my phone in my hand pretending to talk to someone, staying vigilant. The only people I saw were that disgraceful young couple practically groping each other while their dog pooped. Then I noticed Mrs. B sitting on her front porch. I was so happy to see her.

"Jessica, I worry for you. You usually home by now on work night." As I got closer, concern registered on her face. "What happened? Have you seen your hair? You don't look too good."

Mrs. B poured some port into a teacup and handed it to me.

"Thank you. It's been a bad night. Someone shot at me. Blew my tire out." I took a long drink and held my cup out so she could top it off.

"Who would do this?"

"I got a threat from someone earlier. One of my clients is supposed to testify against a drug dealer, and he's threatening to kill my client and me if she talks."

"I see. You know, witness intimidation is common."

"But he shot at me!"

She shrugged. "He missed."

What was wrong with people? Dawson, Marty, Delroy, Marcus, and now Mrs. Bianco were all taking this death threat in stride. Had they become so hardened by city life that a death threat was no bigger deal than Sabatino's running out of chicken parmesan on a Friday night? Or was I overreacting to a common occurrence? I was too tired to contemplate the cosmic meaning of it all. I wanted to shower and go to bed.

"Will you come over while I shower?" I didn't care that I sounded childish. I was out of false bravado.

"Sure. I'll turn on the news."

"You got your gun?"

She nodded, patted the pocket of her housecoat, grabbed the bottle of port, and followed me.

"That stunt you pulled yesterday with the fire department worked," I said as I unlocked my front door.

She beamed up at me. "You mean you have a date with Mark?"

"Yup."

"See. I told you. The third time is charming."

CHAPTER SEVENTEEN

Mrs. Bianco's port proved to be the perfect sleeping aid. I slept like the dead. No sooner had she left than I fell fast asleep and didn't wake until my alarm went off. The sun was out. I could feel the heat penetrating my blinds even at this early hour. I didn't need to see a forecast to know it was going to be another sweltering, sticky, frizzy-hair day. Of course, I had more to worry about than my hair. The events of last night replayed in my head. It scared me, but any follow through on these threats seemed unlikely according to common street logic.

My cell phone rang, and I saw Sharlyn's name on the display. It was 6:45 a.m. I knew it couldn't be good.

"Hi, Sharlyn."

"That punk-ass Mad Dog was here at my cousin's house last night. He stopped his car in front and shot out her porch lights. Both of them."

"Did anyone get hurt?"

"No. Just the lights. Two bullets, two lights. He's an excellent shot. Darnell always said that."

I supposed that if Mad Dog always hits his mark, then there was truth to what everyone was telling me. If he had wanted to kill Sharlyn or me, he would have.

"He shot at me last night, too. Took out my tire as I was leaving work."

"I'm sorry to have gotten you involved in this."

"I'm going to call the DA and let him know that we're being threatened. I'm not sure what good it will do, but he should know." I hung up with Sharlyn and gave Mrs. Bianco a quick call to thank her for taking care of me last night and apologize for being such a baby. She reiterated her offer to teach me to shoot and help me pick out a gun. "You are a young woman living in the city with a job where you meet not so nice people. You need a gun."

"Right now, I need a new tire. You know anyone I could call?"

She said her husband used to use a guy who owned a car shop on Read Street. She had his number and remembered him as Flat Face. I took the information, thanked her again, disconnected, and called the shop. The guy identified himself as Bucky. He remembered Mr. Bianco and said I could bring the car in this morning and he'd have it ready in a couple of hours.

I drove up Calvert and Monument Streets on the temporary tire with an abundance of caution, receiving angry honks and offensive middle fingers along the way. Kari pulled into the DGA parking lot at the same time. "What happened to your tire?"

"Someone shot at me last night."

"Girrrrl. You kidding, right?"

"I'm not kidding." I pointed to the alley. "Right out there, right after you drove off." I gave Kari in an objective play-by-play of events affecting an outward calm.

"That's some heavy shit, Jess. What're you going to do about your tire?"

"I was hoping you'd drive me down to Bucky's Auto on Read Street so I can drop it off."

"Sure. Let's step inside first. I need to check the messages."

Kari went to the front office. I stayed in the kitchen to make coffee. While it was brewing, I looked out into our parking lot. No bad guys looming outside. I watched Marty, Dawson, and Sal pull into the lot at the same time. Marty parked next to me and stopped to examine my rear tire. He pointed it out to Dawson, who shrugged.

"You get a flat yesterday?" Marty asked, holding the door open for Dawson.

"No. Someone shot at me." I was pouring myself a cup of coffee, trying to look casual. "Anyone want coffee?"

"What do you mean someone shot you?" Dawson said.

I gave them the details. "Now do you think those are empty threats?"

"How many shots did he take at your car?" Dawson asked.

"One."

"How many shots did he take at Sharlyn's two lights?"

"Two."

Dawson and Marty exchanged knowing looks. "The guy's an ace marksman. He's trying to scare you, is all."

"Well, it worked."

#

After Kari helped me drop off my car, we returned to the office. My first order of business was to call Chip. I dispensed with the usual pleasantries and got right to my point. "Sharlyn and I are getting death threats. She thinks it's Darnell's flunky, a guy they call Mad Dog. They're trying to intimidate us to keep Sharlyn from testifying."

"What kind of threats?"

"First we received a text and a phone call. Then last night, he shot out my tire as I was leaving work. He also shot out two of Sharlyn's porch lights."

"Who?"

"What'd you mean, who?"

"Which one did the shooting, Darnell or Mad Dog?"

"Sharlyn says Mad Dog's the marksman, so we assume it's him."

"How many bullets?"

"One for my tire—"

"And one for each light?"

"How did you know?"

"It's typical witness intimidation. You should file a police report.

151

I'll call Darnell's defense attorney and tell him about these intimidation tactics. He'll deny that Darnell's involved, but at least he'll know I'm aware of it. Let me know if anything else happens."

"Any chance he'll plea out so Sharlyn doesn't have to testify?"

"Doubtful."

"Well if talks do open up, remember, I still need a truthful statement from him about the accident. It would mean a lot to Sharlyn."

"At this point, I doubt there will be a deal. He wants his day in court."

#

Sharlyn came in carrying a tray of freshly baked something. "I brought you some of my pocket pastries. Hal wants your opinion before he puts them on the menu." She put the tray on Kari's desk. Kari and I reached for the biggest one at the same time. She gave me a look, and I chose another. They looked like puffed pastry stuffed with some kind of filling. They had icing and sprinkles on top. Like Pop-Tarts, but softer and prettier. I sunk my teeth into one and felt the gooey chocolate filling run down my wrist and my chin at the same time. I moved my head forward and stepped back to avoid getting any on my clothes. Kari had the same oozing problem, but neither of us could put the things down. There was no way I wasn't taking another bite. It might be messy, but damn if it wasn't the best pastry I'd ever had. As I opened my mouth to go in again, Sharlyn ran into the kitchens for napkins. My second bite was more problematic than the first. The rest of the filling squirted and landed on my shoe. Kari was smarter than me and shoved the whole thing in her mouth, where it exploded in a good way.

Sharlyn shoved napkins at us. "I'm sorry. I should have told you they're messy. Hal's going to put a warning on the menu and serve them with a paper bib."

I sat down on the sofa to get the chocolate off my shoe. "Don't apologize. It was so worth it."

"Umhh," Kari was still chewing. "Best thing I ever had." Her eyes rolled back in her head.

"Messiest one, too," I added, licking the rest of the chocolate off my wrist.

"Hazelnut," Sharlyn said. "The chocolate has hazelnut in it."

I was still licking my fingers when Tony walked in. "Musta been good."

"Damn best thing you'll ever eat." Kari pointed to the tray on her desk. "Try one. Sharlyn here made them. Sharlyn, this is Tony."

Rather than eyeing the pastries, Tony was eyeing Sharlyn. He stood up a bit taller, reached out his hand, and said, "Nice to meet you. I think I've seen you around. You work at Hal's, right?"

Sharlyn's eyes turned soft. She blushed.

Kari picked up the tray of pastries. "Here. You gotta try one of these, but hold up a few napkins. The insides will fly out."

Tony examined the tray, grabbed the smallest one, and used three fingers to shove the whole thing in his mouth. He smiled with his mouth closed and gave a thumbs up while he chewed. We all watched in silence.

"Oh, man. You're a magician with the pastries. That was the best thing I've ever tasted. Maybe if you make them smaller, they'd be more manageable and won't make such a mess."

"You're right!" Sharlyn said. "I can't believe I didn't think of it. I could make them bite-size and have four to a serving." She stepped toward him sheepishly and gave him a chuck on the arm. "I'll talk to my boss about it. Thanks, Tony."

I had to interrupt this awkward display. "Tony, can I see you for a moment?"

Tony came into my office. I resumed my place behind the desk while he took a chair on the other side.

"How're you feeling? What'd the doctor say?"

"I feel great, Jess. Good as new. The doctor said everything healed well. I can start work again tomorrow."

"Then I'm going to settle this thing for you."

This was unchartered territory for me. I had to make a deal with the mob. I couldn't have anything in writing. I'd have to tear up the retainer agreement. There'd be no record of this settlement. It would be a cash deal. Unmarked, small bills, delivered in a gym bag, at night, near the Penn-North Metro stop. Okay, maybe not that dramatic, but certainly unorthodox.

"To be clear, Tony, we're doing this outside of normal procedures. There will be no record of this. In fact, I will shred your file. It will be a cash deal. Not that there is anything wrong with this type of transaction. There is nothing illegal about two people coming to an agreement over an issue like this. It's a little unconventional, that's all."

"Got it. I don't care about the formalities. When do I get the money? Will he still offer fifteen grand?"

"Let's hope so. We'll remind him of the pain you suffered, the concussion, the fear you had that perhaps there was some permanent injury, things like that. I know how to sell it. I'll set up a meeting with him and keep you posted."

"Should I be at the meeting?"

"No, I go alone." That sounded more melodramatic than I intended, but it seemed kind of cool. Jessica Snow takes on the mob.

We returned to the reception area where Marty and Dawson were sampling Sharlyn's pastries. Chocolate was splattered everywhere. Dawson looked like a toddler at his third birthday party. Chocolate on his face, in his hair, down his shirt. Marty was a mess, too. Kari had a roll of paper towels and spray cleaner in her hands and was busy wiping away the mess.

Tony walked over to Sharlyn. He said something. She giggled. He said something else. She giggled some more and on it went.

I joined Marty and Dawson, who had moved into the kitchen for coffee.

"Tony's fully recovered from his accident at Brenner's, so I'm ready to make a deal with Franco Giovanni. I'm going to try to meet him within the next couple of days. Any advice?"

"Wear a vest," Marty said.

"And a garlic necklace," Dawson added.

"That's for vampires," Marty said.

"Oh. Meet in a public place?"

"Yeah, that's a good one. And wear comfortable shoes in case he drives you out to the desert and leaves you there."

"In that case, you might want to bring a bottle of water, too."

"Thanks, you guys. I'm so lucky to have such savvy mentors."

When I returned to the reception area, Tony and Sharlyn were still hanging out. They had their cell phones out and were exchanging contact information.

Moments later, she entered my office with a silly schoolgirl grin. "Tony seems kinda nice."

"Yes, I think so, too."

Her smiled faded and she stood still, staring at me. "Wait, you and Tony aren't a thing are you? I mean, I don't want to be stepping on anyone's toes. I'll back down. You can have him."

"Whoa, wait Sharlyn. No. No. No. Tony and I aren't a thing. I don't have any interest in him other than his being my client. He's all yours. But thank you for offering."

She giggled and tossed her hair. "Okay, good." Standing up tall, she straightened the spaghetti straps on her dress and bounced out the door where Tony was waiting for her.

The office phone rang. Kari went to grab it while I headed toward my desk.

"Dawson Garner & Associates, how can I help you?" There was a pause then I heard fingers snapping. Kari was trying to get my attention. I turned toward her to see a giant grin on her face. "... right, I remember you. How's the fire business going?" She listened to his response, her eyes locked on mine. "Don't I know it," she said. "Well, you be careful. You want to talk to Jess? Hold on." Kari pressed the hold button and put the phone down. "It's Mark." She started chanting, "Jess gets a firefighter, Jess gets a firefighter." She added some impressive dance moves behind her desk.

"Kari, you're making me nervous. Please stop singing, sit down, and put the call through to my desk."

"Don't you be acting like you're all calm and collected about this call. This is a big deal. We've been working on this."

I turned again toward my desk and did a little two-step with a twirl.

"Oh, girl, we gotta work on your dance moves."

I took a deep calming breath and picked up the phone. "Hi, Mark." Be cool. Keep it short and simple. Don't seem too anxious, but don't seem uninterested.

"Hey. Did you get the slug slime off your foot?"

"I was kind of hoping we could forget about that little scene. I like to think of myself as a pretty tough lady."

"Too late. I've seen the real you. Are you free Saturday night?

"I am. What did you have in mind?"

"I thought we could either have dinner downtown or go see the Orioles' game. They're playing the Yankees."

"Is this my first test?"

"Test?"

"Yeah. You want to know if I'm the kind of girl who wants to dress up and be wined and dined or a girl who would prefer to throw on a T-shirt and shorts and eat peanuts and ballpark dogs at Camden yards in the sweltering August heat."

"Great, I'll make the reservation. Should we go for seafood or Italian?"

"No way. I want to go to the game."

"Really?"

"As long as I can bring my giant, orange foam finger."

"It's a date then. Let's get there early and have dinner at Dempsey's. How about I pick you up at five?"

"You remember where I live?"

"Next to that crazy Italian lady who faked a fire so I could rescue you from slugs."

CHAPTER EIGHTEEN

I called Franco and told him I was ready to discuss the settlement of Tony's claim. He told me to meet him at Aldo's Italian Bistro at two o'clock.

Aldo's was located in the heart of Baltimore's Little Italy, a cozy community and cultural icon of Baltimore located east of Baltimore Harbor. Many of the tiny row houses were still owned by the families of immigrants who settled there a century ago. Aldo's offered vintage Italian mob style dining as depicted in the movie classics. Checkered table cloths, dim lighting, and booths with tall walls for private conversations. A handful of patrons occupied the front booths while a few more sat at the bar. They were all men, most of them staring up at a flat screen tuned to ESPN. I tore the bartender's attention away from the screen and told him I was there to meet Franco Giovanni. He directed me to a rear booth.

Franco sat alone in a booth reading the *New York Times*. I recognized Elvis and Paulie, his bodyguards. They were playing cards in an adjacent booth. All three wore dark suits, collared shirts, and ties. Franco's had a tailored fit and the sheen of quality silk. Diamond-studded cuff links peaked out at the sleeves. Elvis and Paulie dropped their cards as I approached and reached into their waistbands. Their eyes darted from me to Franco and back to me. Franco waved a hand at them, indicating I was not a threat. They relaxed and resumed their card play, clearly unaware of the mace and rape whistle in my messenger bag.

When I reached the table, Franco stood and gestured for me to take the seat opposite him.

"Thank you for meeting me."

With slow and deliberate movements, he folded his newspaper and pushed it up against the wall of the booth then raised his stern eyes to meet mine. Leaning across the table with a tight -set jaw, he said, "Don't thank me yet."

Ignoring his menacing tone, I held his gaze until I realized I wasn't breathing. I looked away, pretending to be interested in what Elvis and Paulie were doing.

Franco drained whatever was in the glass in front of him and signaled to a waitress. "You want anything?" He asked me.

Since I'd lost about a pint of bodily fluids through my sweat glands on the walk from the parking lot to the door, I asked for a glass of water. He ordered more iced tea for himself and his men.

I pulled a notepad and pen from my messenger bag. "We need to talk business."

"I tried to talk business at the hospital, but you were not so agreeable. I made you a good offer, you refused." He shrugged.

"I didn't refuse. I asked for more time to see how extensive my client's injuries were, a. And you agreed to that. You said to contact you when I knew where things stood. So, here I am."

The waitress returned with a pitcher of iced tea for the men and a tall glass of ice water with a slice of lemon on the rim for me. I took a few greedy gulps and sat the glass in front of me. I removed the lemon wedge from the rim, held it over the glass, and squeezed it. Lemon juice squirted into my right eyeball.

"Oh shit." I shut my eyes tight and dug the palm of my hand into my eye socket. The lemon juice burned like fire on my cornea. There was no maintaining composure. I rocked back and forth in the booth, waiting for the sting to go away. When I opened my good eye, I noticed Franco passing me a dry napkin.

"Here, take this," he said. "Paulie, go get another glass of water—no lemon, no ice."

Paulie returned with a glass of water. I dipped the napkin in it and dabbed my eye, squeezing extra water in it to dilute the citrus. I was all too aware of how pathetic I looked. Soon the acid burning reduced to a mere discomfort. The napkin I used was covered with a black smudge. My mascara. It must be all over my face. Franco noticed it, too. He passed me another napkin.

I took the napkin and held my head high, refusing to let my optical distress make me appear weak.

He sat back in the booth, smug and confident. "I realized after our last chat that I made matters far too easy for you by throwing money on the table without much consideration. My offer was too generous. I wasn't thinking straight that day. I blame nicotine withdrawal. I've been cigarette-free for seven days now."

"Good for you," I said. "I know it's not easy. My dad's trying to quit."

"He should get hypnotized. I know a guy."

"You got hypnotized?"

"Why does that surprise you?"

"Because hypnosis leaves you vulnerable and susceptible to suggestion."

"Right. That's why it works."

"So how do you know the hypnotist didn't say something like 'you will no longer desire to smoke, and by the way give me your offshore account numbers and passwords?'"

His eyes registered concern. "I never thought of that." He looked over at Elvis.

"Give me a piece."

My adrenaline shot up. A gun? Why was he asking for a gun?

Elvis reached into his jacket pocket and pulled out a silver sheet of plastic that looked like a pack of Chiclets. He popped one out and handed it across the aisle to Franco.

"Nicotine gum." He commenced aggressive chewing. "This hypnotist thing has me worried."

"I was using an extreme example. That guy wouldn't mess with your money. You're Franco Giovanni for Christ's sake."

His cell phone rang. He looked at the display and stiffened. "I gotta take this." He scooted out of the booth. "Hi, Mama," I heard him whisper as he stepped toward the back of the room, cupping his free hand over the phone.

Elvis and Paulie shared a subtle, knowing snicker. Franco paused near the restrooms as he spoke to his mother. She seemed to be doing most of the talking. His head hung low, shoulders slumping. I could hear him repeat, "I know," "Okay," and, finally, "Love you, too."

As he returned to the table, he resumed his authoritative posture and tone. "Now back to our business. Like I was saying, I was too easy on you. I want you to prove your case. Prove to me that your client didn't fall because his jeans were too tight and he took too big a step."

The security detail chuckled.

I realized Franco was amused by me. Business must be slow for him, so he was messing with the rookie ambulance chaser. Well, fine then. If he wants me to prove my case, I'll prove my case. No problem. I'm a lawyer. That's what lawyers do.

"Fine. You want me to document the obvious? You got it."

"And you must get me this proof in three days, or I pretend we never met."

As he looked at me, his focus lingered on my right eye, the eye that had suffered the citrus assault moments earlier. "You may want to give that a good flush with water when you get back to your office. And when you see Dawson, thank him for me."

"Thank Dawson? For what?"

"For killing Harvey Metzger. He saved me the trouble." He gave me a crooked smile. He was baiting me, but I wasn't having it.

"So it's true. You had invested with Harvey, too? How do I know you didn't whack him?"

"You don't."

I winced. He smiled at my discomfort.

I said goodbye to Franco, then to Elvis and Paulie who looked up into my right eye and cringed. Maintaining outward calm, I glided out the door. As soon as I hit the sun, my right eye burned in protest. I closed it tight and tore a path to my car guided by my one good eye. My Accord was a furnace inside. I started the engine to get the air conditioning going, then took a look in the rearview mirror. I gasped. Mascara had dried in streaky black strands down my right cheek. My eyeball was pink and the skin around my eye was splotchy red. That was one potent lemon.

I dug out my sunglasses to shield my bad eye from the sun and mask my hideous appearance while I drove the few blocks back to the office. I had been so distracted by the lemon incident that the fact that Tony's claim was in jeopardy was slow to take hold. If I hadn't been so stubborn, Tony would have taken the fifteen grand last week and this would all be money in the bank. In hindsight, I realized I'd rejected it without even discussing it with him. How the hell was I going to find evidence to prove that the water was on the floor and that management knew about it? And I only had three days.

I parked behind our building and took another look in the mirror. Staring back at my good eye, I said to myself, "You will find that evidence. You will get Tony his fifteen thousand dollars."

Kari sat behind her desk. She looked at me with alarm when she saw my eye. "Did Franco do that to you? I knew I should have gone with you. That son of a bitch!"

"No, he didn't do it. I did. It was an accident. I squirted lemon juice into my eye."

"Lemon juice. It looks like you got maced."

I excused myself and spent some time in the bathroom flushing my eye, reapplying my makeup, and mustering up my self-confidence and dignity. I returned to Kari's desk. "I need your help."

"Sure. What's up?" Kari asked.

After detailing my conversation with Franco, Kari hopped on board ready to help me hunt down a witness. "No problem. We need to head to Brenner's and snoop around a bit. There's got to be a worker there who knew the tank was leaking. Let's go talk to the guy at the fish counter."

We walked out the front door right into a wall of heat and humidity that melted the foundation on my face. Sweat beads formed in their usual spot on my hairline. By the time we reached the corner, I could feel a trickle of sweat drizzle down my cleavage. Well, where my cleavage would be if I had one. I looked at Kari, whose skin was dry as a bone.

"How come you never sweat?"

"I come from a long line of no-sweaters. It's in the genes. Doesn't mean I'm not hot, though. I'm hotter than a hot dog."

We reached Brenner's and welcomed the cool air inside. I noticed that there were now warning signs posted and orange caution cones placed at the ends of each aisle, even though there was no specific reason to be cautious. Franco had a ready-made defense for the next lawyer who tried to sue him.

"Let's see if they replaced the lobster tank," I said.

We cut through the middle aisle and headed back to the fish department. I was pleased to see that a new lobster tank had been installed. This one was about the same size but was housed in a deep cherry wood base. The tank was not glass, but some kind of transparent material that was an inch thick. It sat in shallow housing that would catch any drainage or condensation that might otherwise puddle on the floor. In the clear, fresh water, the lobsters looked happy—for now anyway. A wooden sign at the top of the tank had gold, engraved lettering: Please Ask for Assistance. Do Not Touch the Tank.

"Looks like you made this place a lot safer for the customers, Jess."

I hadn't thought of it that way. I supposed she was right. I just hoped I hadn't pissed off a mob guy in the process.

A tall, skinny guy wearing a white smock stood behind the fish counter. His left side faced us as he worked on something in the sink. I pulled Kari by the arm and we ducked into aisle number ten.

"We haven't rehearsed what we're going to say."

"Whatta'ya mean rehearse? You're a lawyer. Ask lawyerly questions."

I sighed. I wasn't one to wing it, but how hard could it be, right? I mustered my resolve and strolled up to the counter. The fish guy turned to me. He was younger than I expected, probably a freshman in college freshman. He had pale skin, narrow eyes, and thin, pursed lips. He looked like a fish. His name tag read "Ben."

"Hi, Ben. I'm Jessica Snow, and this is my associate Kari Cruz. We want to ask you about the lobster tank. I see you've installed a new one."

His hands stopped working but remained in the sink as he eyed both of us. "I know who you are. Your face is on the bus I take to get to work every morning. You're that lawyer. I bet you represent that guy who fell here. I can't talk to you about it."

I couldn't let him off the hook so easily. "We want to know if the old lobster tank was leaking that day, or if it had a history of leaking."

He looked down into the sink. "I said, I ain't talking to you."

"I'd like to try some fish," Kari said. "I'm a customer now. You have to talk to me."

"I have to talk to you about fish. Just fish. Now, what do you want?"

"I want to know if the old lobster tank had a leaking problem."

His pale face reddened and the veins in his neck pulsed. He glanced behind him, then over our heads, reached into the sink, and pulled out a slimy gray creature with a round top and long tentacles. He shoved it in Kari's face. "How about some octopus? It's on special."

The flailing tentacles slapped Kari's cheeks. She shrieked and tore down the paper products aisle. I followed close behind. She grabbed a roll of paper towels and ripped the package open.

"I got slimed." She rubbed the paper towels around her face and spat a few times. "He slimed me with a giant squid. I didn't sign up for this."

When Kari finished cleaning the goo off her face, I took what was left of the roll of paper towels to the register to pay for them. The cashier looked at the opened roll and said, "Guess you had a paper-towel emergency."

"You bet it was an emergency," Kari said. "Fish face back there shoved a giant squid in my face."

"You mean, Ben? Ben's strung a little tight. Takes his job very seriously."

I looked at her name tag. It read, "Karen."

"Karen, we noticed that there's a new lobster tank back in the fish department. What was wrong with the old one? Was it leaking?"

The smile faded and recognition registered in her eyes. She paused as if considering something and said, in a loud voice, "I know who you are. I can't talk to you." Then she lowered her chin and whispered, "You should talk to Roger. Roger brings the fresh lobsters every other day. How's Tony?"

So Karen knew Tony and wanted to help, but was being silenced. Franco must have called a staff meeting and threatened to throw them into the harbor if they talked to me.

"Tony's doing better. When do you expect another lobster delivery?"

"Tomorrow morning around six."

I whispered my appreciation, then Kari and I left with the paper towels and a new lead. "This is our chance. We'll get here early and stake out the back alley."

"Five forty-five? A.M.? I don't do mornings, not that early," Kari said.

"You have to come with me. I need your support."

She harrumphed. "You better bring doughnuts. And coffee."

CHAPTER NINETEEN

The streets of Baltimore were calm and quiet at five-thirty in the morning. Commuters were waking up to their alarms and getting ready to hit the roadways for their daily battle with traffic, and the local workers were still snug in bed. It was quiet and peaceful. I noticed a few lights on in places that serve breakfast and a handful of folks walking along the open sidewalks, perhaps on their way home after a long night. As the next two hours rolled by, the streets would become increasingly congested, people would grow more irritated, and the sun would pop up to blanket it all with the burden of its heat.

Kari and I arranged to meet in the law firm parking lot and take my Accord to our stakeout. I was armed with doughnuts, bananas, coffee, and a wicked determination to nail down this witness.

Kari lowered herself into my car. "Don't look at me."

She pulled a small, zippered cloth bag from her purse, threw the purse in the back seat, lowered the sun visor to access the mirror, and commenced the art of vehicular makeup application. "You can go ahead and drive."

By the time we drove the two blocks to Brenner's and parked in their rear alley, Kari had applied a foundation, face powder, eyeliner, eyeshadow, and two coats of mascara. She was looking and acting more like herself.

"I figure I can have three doughnuts for every banana I eat. That way the good balances out the bad." She was on her second banana when a refrigerated truck with an image of a giant sea bass and the words "Manny's Seafood" in bold red letters rolled in.

"Here's our guy," I said. We closed the box of doughnuts, wiped the sugar from our hands and faces, and waited for the driver to get out of the truck. I assumed the driver was Roger, the guy the cashier had told us about. He was a man of large proportions. He wore dark khaki shorts and a tan company T-shirt with an image that resembled the side of the truck. As he stepped from the driver's seat, he paused, winced, readjusted his position, and then lowered his feet to the ground. His gait was slow and cautious as he moved toward the back of the truck and raised the rear door.

"Looks like he has back pain," Kari said.

So as not to startle him, I closed my car door hard. He turned to face us as we approached.

"Are you Roger?"

"Who wants to know?"

"I'm Jessica Snow. My associate and I are doing some research. I understand that you make deliveries here every other day?"

"That's right." He turned back toward the truck and lowered a ramp. After conferring with a clipboard, he proceeded up the ramp, taking slow, small steps.

"Do you recall when Brenner's old lobster tank started to leak?" I had worked hard formulating this question on the way over here.

"That's a leading question. It assumes the tank was leaking." It turned out Roger watched *Law & Order,* too. He began loading boxes onto a pull cart.

"Well, was it leaking?" Kari asked.

"Yeah, it was an old tank, and not a real quality one, either. I noticed a small leak months ago and told the guy who works behind the counter. Ben is his name."

Aha! Ben knew about the leak, and he knew that Roger knew about it, too. That's all I needed to prove to Franco that Brenner's was negligent. I could see the fifteen grand dancing before my eyes. I pulled my cell phone out and found the icon that records. "I'd like to get your statement recorded. It won't take long."

"Oh no," he said. "I already said too much. Do you know who owns this place?"

I didn't respond. Kari stayed quiet, too.

"The Giovanni family owns this place. I'm dead if Franco finds out that I told you. I'll deny it and won't lose any sleep over it. Now I got work to do."

"You can't ignore the fact that Brenner's was negligent. I represent a young man who was injured when he slipped on the water that leaked from the tank. You're my only witness. I need your help."

"You need to find another way, lady. I'm not getting on the wrong side of the Giovanni family."

I had to admit that I didn't blame him. My dilemma was not life or death. It was money or no money; fee or no fee. I couldn't ask this man to put himself in peril, perceived or otherwise.

He wheeled the loaded cart down the ramp, grimacing with each step.

"How long have you had the back problem?" Kari asked.

"That obvious, huh? Since last week when my handcart broke and I had to make deliveries without it all day. Musta pulled something."

Kari pulled a business card out of her bag. "You've got a workers' compensation claim. We can help. We can get you medical attention and paid time off work. You need to rest that back." She took his clipboard and clipped my card to it.

As we walked to the car, Kari said, "Tony's case may be in the crapper, but we got ourselves a potential new client."

I felt defeated. I started to play a game with Franco and he out-played me. "Do you think I should have taken the $15,000 offer he made at the hospital?"

"You can't be second-guessing yourself like that. Think about it. Why did you turn down the offer in the first place? What was your reasoning?"

"I was worried. Tony was in the hospital, the test results weren't back, and he was in a great deal of pain. If his injuries were serious, fifteen grand wouldn't cut it."

"You did the right the thing then, and you'll do the right thing now."

"What is that?"

"I thought you'd know. You're the lawyer."

We brought the extra doughnuts and bananas into the office kitchen. Marty and Dawson were sitting at the table drinking coffee. Marty was dressed in his standard suit and tie, ready to head to court, and Dawson was wearing khakis and a golf shirt, which meant he would squeeze in a few holes later today.

"Where have you two been?" Dawson asked.

"Failing," I said.

"Don't be so melodramatic," Kari said to me. She turned to the men. "We went looking for a witness, found one who told us what we wanted to hear, and then he clammed up because he's afraid the mob will turn him into fish food if he cooperates with us."

"Let me guess," Marty said. "You found a witness for the stripper's case, but he won't roll over on Franco Giovanni?"

"First of all, he's not a stripper. He's a male dancer." I said.

"Yeah," Kari said, "On account of he doesn't show his junk."

"And second, yeah, you're right. He won't talk. He told us he knew the lobster tank was leaking. He even said he told Ben, the guy who runs the fish counter. But he's afraid of upsetting Franco." I poured myself some coffee. "And frankly, I don't blame him."

"Why? Because Franco Giovanni is a tough businessman?" Dawson asked.

"A tough businessman? No! It's because he's a modern-day Godfather."

"Rumors of Franco's savagery are greatly exaggerated. I ran into him last week at the House of Hair. Now that Paulette's got someone doing mani-pedis, that's where I go for mine. Franco does, too. He's the one who loaned Paulette the money. He's a tough guy, no doubt.

Very intimidating. I wouldn't want to cross him, but he's a businessman. He can be reasoned with."

I held my coffee cup in both hands and bowed my head toward it in defeat. "I've tried. It doesn't work."

"So that's it? You're giving up?"

I took a seat next to him as I contemplated my answer. My reflex response was to say, "Well, yeah, I'm giving up, what else can I do?" But as I rehearsed these words in my head, I realized they were words of defeat. In that moment, I decided I wasn't giving up. I wasn't a quitter. Tony deserved compensation, and I planned to get it for him. Maybe it was the sugar rush from the doughnuts kicking in, but I was determined to shake down Franco. I couldn't let him win.

"No, I'm not giving up. I'm going to talk to Franco again."

Dawson gave me an 'attagirl' chuck on the shoulder and said, "Better take Kari with you this time."

#

My cell phone rang. It was my mother calling.

"What is this I hear about you and exploding toilets? I was watching the *Meredith Viera Show* and saw your commercial."

"Hi, Mom. It's like the commercial says. There are thousands of defective toilets out there. A recall has been issued, but it hasn't been well publicized. People are getting hurt when their toilets explode. I already have two clients."

"You're helping them fix their toilets?"

"No, mom. I'm a lawyer, not a plumber. I'm helping them get compensation for their pain and suffering and money to fix their bathrooms."

"Good, because we didn't send you to law school to end up doing plumbing. Now, how do I know if our toilets are defective?"

There were three toilets in my parents' house. My mother said she was in the powder room on the first floor. I told her to lift the lid off the tank and tell me what she saw.

"I'm going to need both hands, so I'm putting the phone down and putting you on speaker."

"Let me know what you see when you look inside the tank."

"There's a black box that says 'Friendly Flush II'. Is that good?"

"No, that's not good. Don't use that toilet, mom. Put a note on the door. Don't let anybody use that toilet."

"Oh my god. Our house could explode. It's a ticking time bomb!"

"It's fine. Nothing will happen unless you flush the toilet. Just don't use it. Now, let's check on the other two." It turned out that the toilet in my parents' master bath was also a Friendly Flush II, but the one in the other bathroom on the second floor was not. That was the bathroom that my siblings and I used growing up. It still had the old five-gallon, super-flush, no-clog system that environmentalists hated. It was a great toilet.

"I'm going to hang up now and call a plumber."

#

The phone call with my mother made me realize how important it was to get the word out and encourage people to check their toilets. My earlier research had focused on the companies involved and the liability issue. I had skimmed over the practical aspects of the recall. It had been mandated by the Consumer Product Safety Commission. In response, the manufacturer of The Friendly Flush II established a system whereby consumers could call the 1-800 number or register at their website. Once the serial number on the unit was verified, a replacement part would be mailed to the consumer. The removal of the defective unit and the installation of the new unit was said to take about twenty minutes and could be done by the consumer. No need to call a plumber. The company recommended turning off the water supply to the toilet. For households with only one toilet, they suggest dumping two gallons of water into the bowl to generate a "gravity-style flush."

This was quite useful information that had not been widely publicized, resulting in injuries that otherwise could have been prevented. I thought the public should be made aware of these specifics so they could check for themselves before their toilets exploded.

I called my mother, told her to turn off the water supply to each of the defective toilets, and gave her the 1-800-number and request the replacement kits. Then I went in to see Dawson.

"I think our exploding toilet commercial is too general and self-serving. We should put more emphasis on encouraging the audience to check their toilets before they explode. We could include the 1-800 number for the recall. There are a lot of safety tips online. People should be informed about this stuff."

Dawson paused. "Hmmm."

"Dawson?"

"I'm struggling with a moral dilemma."

"What's that?"

"By notifying the public about the danger and warning them before any more injuries occur, we are effectively eliminating potential new business."

These were the words of a focused businessman. Do the right thing and you may lose money. Politicians face a similar dilemma—do the right thing and you may lose votes.

"Damn it, Dawson, stop thinking with your wallet. You know it's the moral thing to do. We can help people. It's that simple."

He lowered his head. "I know."

"Look. If it makes you feel any better, here's how it will go down. DGA will be getting the word out about toilet explosions. There must be many more Marshalls and Trudys out there who were injured and are either too embarrassed to come forward. We'll nail down all those victims. Plus, we will be helping save others who may have been injured. You will be a hero. Your name will be golden. The next time any of them need a lawyer for anything, they'll call DGA because they know they can trust us. After all, we saved them from an exploding toilet."

"I hadn't thought about it that way."

"Think big picture, Dawson. This thing has legs."

"You're right!" He walked behind his desk and picked up the phone. "I'll call Sal right now and have him revamp that thirty-second spot again. Send him what you have on the specifics of inspecting and fixing the toilets."

#

I called Franco and asked if he could meet Kari and me at Aldo's to discuss resolving Tony's claim.

"You must have found a witness. What did that cost you?" He laughed.

"I don't bribe witnesses. That's not how I do business."

"Not yet," he said. "You'll learn."

It bothered me that he assumed I'd get sucked into debased and unethical tactics to hustle a fee. There's a lot that I would do for a client, but I would never fabricate a witness. Even Marty wouldn't fabricate a witness. Maybe Stuart Milligan would, but even he wouldn't try to pull that on the likes of Franco Giovanni.

We agreed to meet at three o'clock. Kari came with me this time.

When we arrived, I expected Franco would be occupying his usual spot with Elvis and Paulie seated in the booth across from him, like the last time we met. But he wasn't there. I told the bartender we were meeting with Franco and asked if it was okay if we sat in that same booth.

"I wouldn't if I were you. Franco don't like to come in to find someone in his booth."

We took a seat at the bar and ordered two ginger ales.

"Guess it's too early for margaritas," Kari said.

"Yes. Plus, we need to stay sharp to get what we want out of Franco." I said his name and Franco walked through the door, Elvis in front of him and Paulie trailing behind. Kari sat up a little straighter in her chair and patted her hair.

"Hello, counselor," Franco said. "And Kari." He gave her a nod.

"I'm a little surprised you remembered my name," Kari said.

"I make it a habit to learn the names of the people I do business with. Come back to my booth."

We grabbed our drinks and slid into the booth across from him. Elvis and Paulie took the booth adjacent to us.

"I had planned on getting here early to order you a large water with lemon." He laughed. Elvis and Paulie joined in. Kari laughed along with them. I kicked her under the table.

"What? That was funny." More laughter.

I knew I should let it go and laugh along with them, but I was too uptight about the business at hand.

"I'm glad you all could share a laugh together at my expense." A server came by and sat a mug of coffee in front of Franco and two Cokes in front of his associates. When she retreated to the front room, we began our meeting.

It turned out to be a short one. I explained to him, without naming names, that we had spoken to two employees and one vendor who both said with certainty that the lobster tank was leaking, that it had been brought to at least one of the managers' attention, and he took ineffective steps to remedy the problem. I further explained that none of these people would come forward to make a formal statement for fear of losing their jobs or facing other unsavory repercussions should they disappoint Mr. Giovanni.

As I concluded my statement, he was nodding and smiling. "Such loyalty from my people. It warms my heart." He pressed both hands together over his heart in mocked gratification, quite pleased with himself. "So you see why your dancer has no claim."

Anger pressed its heat against my cheeks. "Mr. Giovanni, I don't think you play fair."

"Of course I don't play fair. This isn't a game of Monopoly. This is business. Still a game, yes, but we're playing with real money."

He was right about one thing—this was a game involving real money. But he was wrong about not playing fair. I didn't think you had to cheat to win. This kind of game was won by strategizing and outmaneuvering your opponent. I had lost this round because I had been naive enough to think that he would want to do the right thing.

At the same time, it was clear that Franco was amused by me.

"Don't quit on me now, counselor. It's your move."

#

Mrs. Bianco was standing on a stepladder cleaning her front windows with a bottle of Windex and a wad of newspaper when I arrived home.

"Mrs. B, you should wait and have me help you with that. You shouldn't be standing on a ladder by yourself."

"I can handle a stepladder. Look," she said, climbing down. "I'm done." She stood back and admired her work. I looked from her windows to mine and realized they needed cleaning, too.

"Sit. Let's have a glass of port together, and you can tell me about your day. I'll be right back with glasses." She took the old newspapers and Windex inside and returned with two glasses and a bottle.

"Tell me about work. How is your stripper case going?"

"It's not going well."

"What do you mean?"

"Remember I told you that Franco made an offer of $15,000, but I had to turn it down?"

"Yes, I remember."

"Well, now he refuses to pay anything."

"How can he refuse?"

"He wants evidence even though he admits the tank was leaking."

"What kind of evidence?"

"That's my dilemma. I have witnesses, but they're afraid to come forward, and Franco knows it. I can tell he's having fun with this."

"That's not right. He's intimidating witnesses. He's acting like bully." She slammed her glass down on the table, stood up, and stamped her foot. "I'm telling his mama. When I see her tonight, I tell her what you told me. She'll set Franco straight."

Now I was amused. Was it possible that Franco's own mother could shame him into settling with me? I quickly assessed this plan. It had some potential, but something was bothering me. If Franco knew that I complained about him to Mrs. Bianco and got his mother involved, he'd be furious with me. I'd seem childish and unprofessional, and it would upset his mother. Even if he settled to appease Cecelia, he'd be pissed at me for involving her. I'd be a fool to piss him off.

"Here's the problem," I said to Mrs. Bianco. "You can't say anything to Cecelia. It will upset Franco. I'll lose any respect he may still have for me.

She sat for a moment staring into her empty glass of port. A sly smile played at the corners of her lips.

"This is what we do. You drive me to bingo tonight. Franco always drives Cecelia there. Once he drops her off, you confront him about the whole stripper thing and I happen to overhear the conversation. I be waiting around corner and sneak up from behind. Then I'll scold Franco and threaten to tell his mama unless he offers you good money to settle."

I let this plan settle in for a few moments, looking for flaws. I couldn't find one. I called Kari to run it by her. "That's an excellent plan. Let me tag along."

"Hold on." I said, taking the phone away from my ear. "What time is bingo?" I asked Mrs. Bianco.

"It starts at seven thirty, but we should get there around seven."

"Kari, I'm coming to pick you up. We'll stop to get some takeout for dinner and meet Mrs. B back here."

We stopped at Brenner's for takeout. I felt good about giving my business to them since I was going to strong-arm the owner into giving me money. It was the least I could do.

Staring down at the ready-made food options, we locked in on the fried chicken. "How about some Cajun rice to go with it and a veggie salad?" Kari asked.

I knew Mrs. B had a sensitivity to MSG, so I asked the guy working the counter if the Cajun rice or the fried chicken had any. He assured me that they did not. "We use all natural spices," he said.

With dinner in hand, we headed back to Fells Point.

Mrs. B was dressed for bingo when we arrived with dinner. It was a rare occasion that she wasn't wearing a housecoat. She had on a pair of black slacks and a floral blouse. She wore a hint of mascara, and her hair was pulled back into a neat bun.

I had been in her home many times before, but this was Kari's first venture inside. While our homes had been constructed at the same time and were identical in size and design, hers had some interesting modifications that her husband had made years prior to his death.

The front door was made of reinforced steel and had locks worthy of Fort Knox. Her front windows were made of three separate layers of bulletproof glass. They were sealed shut.

Kari noticed the windows and rapped on one. "This is one secure home you got here, Mrs. B."

"Mr. Bianco was a cautious man." She led us back into her kitchen. "Not that it did him good in the end. But I feel safe in this house." The back door leading from the kitchen to the backyard was the same size as the one in front, and the two kitchen windows over the sink were also bulletproof glass. There was a panel box near the back door that I knew controlled all the lighting in the backyard, as well as an electrical output that would zap anyone standing on her back porch either by the door or by the window. There was a similar panel in the front of the house.

I unpacked the bag of food while Mrs. B laid out some plates, utensils, and napkins. Kari poured us sweet tea from a pitcher Mrs. B pulled from the refrigerator.

Mrs. B eyed our mini buffet. "That Cajun rice looks good. Do you think it has MSG?"

"No. I asked the guy."

We helped ourselves to healthy portions and started eating.

"How far away is the bingo hall?" I asked.

"It's a few blocks west of here, outside of Little Italy. It's at the VA hall."

As we ate, Mrs. B explained Franco's recent routine for dropping off his mother. "Most folks enter through the side of the building because that's closest to the parking lot. But Franco will pull up in front. He always walks her through the front door, helps her to her seat, and then leaves."

"Does he drive the car, or are his bodyguards with him?" I asked, grabbing a second chicken leg.

"I don't know. I'm always inside the building when she arrives. I get there early, you know, so I can get a seat up front. That's where all the action is."

Kari helped herself to seconds on the salad. "So when do we strike? When he returns to the car?"

"If we do it then, we may also be facing his security guys. How about we snag him in the hallway after he sits her down and before he heads out the door?"

"That'll work," Mrs. B said. "There a closet right around the corner. I can hide in there until you need me to come knock some sense into that boy."

"We should get there before Franco does for a trial run," Kari said.

We hurried to finish our meal. I gathered all the trash and Kari wiped down the table while Mrs. B loaded the dishwasher.

Since it would be dark when we returned, Mrs. B punched a few buttons on the rear control panel. "I keep the backyard illuminated at night. They'll go on automatically once it gets dark." She punched a few more buttons on the front panel as we left. "That sets the alarm."

There were a few cars in the fire station lot when we arrived. We entered and found a handful of elderly, yet quite spry, men and women bustling about, setting up the tables where the bingo paraphernalia and refreshments would be sold.

"Hey there, you're early, Magda," a gray-haired woman said.

Magda? That was Mrs. B's first name? It never occurred to me that she even had a first name. It was strange hearing it for the first time.

"Hi, Emma. These are my friends, Jessica and Kari. They drove me here. I'm showing them around."

"See you at the table," Emma said.

We glided toward the front of the building. There was a set of double doors leading out into the front hallway. The hallway was empty except for a water fountain and a banquet-sized table that held an array of colorful brochures. Another set of double doors led out to the front steps.

"So, this is what will happen," I said. "Franco will pull up to these steps, then escort his mom through both sets of doors, deposit her in her seat, and return through the first set of doors. That's where we'll meet him. Kari, you'll stand by the doors leading outside while I talk to him. You need to be checking to make sure neither of his security guards tries to come inside."

"If they do, I'll go out and chat them up to stall them." Kari pulled her shoulders back and smoothed out her hair. "That Paulie one's kinda cute."

"Alright, that'll work. Mrs. B, you stand around the corner." I looked at Mrs. Bianco to make sure she understood. Her face was pale with a hint of green. She had a distressed, pleading look in her eyes and was holding her stomach with both hands.

"I need to get to the bathroom." She headed down the hall. Kari and I followed her.

"What's the matter?" Kari asked.

"I'm having an intestinal disturbance," Mrs. B said as she pushed her way through the ladies' room door. "Don't follow me."

Kari and I waited outside.

"I sure hope it wasn't the food," Kari said. "Because we'll be fighting each other for bathroom time."

"I feel fine. How about you?"

"I feel great. I was even thinking about getting me one of those snickerdoodles that lady was putting out."

The bathroom was around the corner from the entrance hall. We heard the front doors open and watched from a distance as Franco walked in holding his mother's arm. They proceeded straight through to the bingo hall.

"Damn," Kari said. "Our plan is in the toilet."

CHAPTER TWENTY

The Metzger murder investigation was stalled. There was no new information. The charges were still pending on Dawson. I feared the real killer was getting away and no one seemed to care.

I expressed my concerns to Kari. "Nobody seems interested in finding Harvey's murderer."

"That's because its last week's news. People have moved on."

"But Dawson's name hasn't been cleared yet."

"He doesn't seem to mind. The clients who threatened to fire us decided to stay. Plus we've got more criminal cases than ever. In fact, the suspicion of murder seems to attract a certain clientele. Dawson's setting records with new criminal defense cases. I guess they're more comfortable with one of their own."

"But Dawson's not one of them. He's not a criminal. He didn't murder Harvey."

"Well, now that's almost too bad. It sure is good for business."

Sheesh.

I went to see Dawson to refute such idiocy. His door was closed, so I gave it a knuckle knock and announced myself. He summoned me in where I found him seated next to the safe. He was counting out money and wrapping small stacks of it with rubber bands. He had a clipboard next to him with a list of clients and dollar amounts next to each.

"What's going on?" I asked.

"I'm doing the filing."

"You're filing money?"

"Just keeping track. I have to collect our retainers up front on all these new criminal cases, and I'm trying to devise a system. We've never had so much criminal work. Marty and I have court almost every day for the next two weeks." He stacked the money in rubber-banded bunches inside the safe.

"You don't seem too concerned that your name hasn't been cleared yet."

"It'll all be forgotten soon. Meanwhile, we need to take care of business."

He reached back in the safe, grabbed a wad of cash, and tossed it to me.

"That's a bonus. Use it to make a down payment on a new car."

"My car runs fine."

"Your car's a blue-collar car. You need a car that tells people you're a professional."

Good grief. I never did care much about cars, and I didn't feel like discussing it now. I clutched the money and held my hands behind my back. "You may not care about clearing your name, but it's important to me."

He waved a dismissive hand at me and returned to his filing.

#

I called Helen to see if she had any new information on the investigation. She didn't.

"I'm disappointed in O'Mallory. He seems to have dropped the ball on this," she said.

"He has. I called him last week to explain my concerns about Olivia's plan to leave town. He was unimpressed. Maybe you and I should go talk to him together. He doesn't think much of me, but he respects you."

Helen made arrangements to meet O'Mallory at a coffee shop in midtown. He was surprised to see me tagging along.

"How's your boss doing? He hasn't booked a flight and packed his bags has he?"

"Funny. Ha ha. He's got nothing to do with this, and you know it."

Helen placed a gentle hand on my shoulder and jumped in. "Kevin, we have a theory about the murder, and we can back it up." With her hand still on my shoulder, she guided me into the booth and slid in next to me.

I looked at Kevin O'Mallory. His eyes showed fatigue. He was wearing an ill-fitted blue blazer with a wrinkled collared shirt underneath. A bit of a contrast from when he first stepped into our office. I wondered what had him so out of sorts. It didn't seem to be worry over who killed Harvey.

"Let's hear what you got. I don't have a lot of time. I'm due in court at eleven."

"I'm heading there, too," Helen said. She turned to me to explain. "The trial for Terrell Smith starts today. He's the alleged head of the East Side drug ring that Detective O'Mallory took down a couple of months ago."

I looked at the detective. "You're testifying?"

"Yeah, so let's make this quick."

Helen took the lead. "We have reason to believe that Olivia Metzger killed her husband, and Juan Carlos may have helped."

"I've investigated Olivia. She didn't do it. Just because the woman is having an affair, doesn't mean she murdered him."

I inhaled and was starting to form my words when Helen kicked me under the table.

"There's more to it than that," Helen said. "She's fleeing. We know she's booked a one-way flight to Barcelona. Two tickets. She's on the run, and you're letting her slip through your fingers."

As she spoke, I realized how lame our theory was. Sure, Olivia was an adulterer. Sure, she's getting out of town with her boyfriend. That didn't make her a killer. Maybe O'Mallory had read her right. Maybe she was innocent. And if so, she may be as interested in finding her husband's real killer.

"Who else knew that Metzger was running a Ponzi scheme?" I asked.

"Dawson was the first to find out, on that night. The night he killed him."

This guy wouldn't let it go. He was plucking my nerves. Helen must have noticed my agitation. She spoke before I exploded. "Look, Kevin, you can't know that for sure. Have you checked the phone records, talked to the other investors? It's too easy to hang this on Dawson. You're a detective—you have to dig deeper."

O'Mallory's face reddened. His tired eyes narrowed, and he jabbed an angry index finger at Helen. "Don't you tell me how to do my job." He stood up, threw a couple of dollars on the table, and walked out.

"I've never seen him lose his cool," Helen said. "I guess I went too far."

Helen and I returned to the office and told Kari about our chat with O'Mallory.

"Looks like we're on our own," she said. "Any ideas?"

"Let's assume O'Mallory is right—that Olivia and Juan Carlos didn't do it. Maybe she knows something that can help us. She's a source of information that we've been avoiding because we thought she was a killer. I think it's time we pay her a visit," I said.

"I tried to talk to her," Helen said. "She slammed the door in my face."

"That's because you're a reporter, no offense," Kari said.

Helen shrugged.

"Kari and I will go talk to her. We'll say Harvey left some personal items with Dawson and we are returning them. Then we'll strike up a friendly conversation and see what we can get out of her."

Helen left for the courthouse to watch the Terrell Smith trial. Kari and I went to tell Dawson of our plan.

He was counting money again.

"Kari and I are going to talk to Olivia Metzger. We think she may be able to tell us something about Harvey and the Ponzi scheme or something that might help get you off the suspect list."

"You're still hung up on that?" He put some cash in the safe and closed it. "I guess it's worth a try. I know there are rumors about her infidelity, but Harvey understood. He truly did love her."

"Do you have anything that belonged to Harvey?"

"Yeah. I borrowed his putter last weekend." He walked over to this golf bag near the window and pulled out a club. "I also have his cigar cutter."

"She won't want the cigar cutter."

"She'll want this one. It's a rarity. Olivia gave it to him for their anniversary last year. Take a look."

He reached into a zippered compartment on the side of his bag, pulled out a small object, and handed it to me. "It's made from a Mammoth's tusk. Presumably ten-thousand years old. Thing's worth about $400."

I examined the cigar cutter. It had some markings on one side. "What do these mean?"

"That's to show its authenticity. They produced a limited quantity. Each one is numbered. It's kind of a status symbol among cigar smokers to own one."

We took the putter and the cigar cutter and left his office.

"Before we head out to see Olivia, I'd like to peak in at the Terrell Smith trial for a little while. Chip is second-chairing, and O'Mallory is testifying at eleven. I thought I'd catch a little of it, to get a feel for the criminal trial process."

"Sure," Kari said. "I've got some paperwork I need to do here. We'll see Olivia once you get back."

CHAPTER TWENTY-ONE

The Circuit Court for Baltimore City was housed in a mammoth stone building that occupied an entire block of downtown Baltimore. I was not a regular here because most of my cases were settled out of court. I joined the security line to be screened for weapons. It was similar to the security at the airport. I laid my handbag and briefcase on the belt and watched as it moved through to the screening box. I was glad I remembered to leave my can of mace in the car, or I might have been strip searched.

I walked along the marble-lined corridors and entered the courtroom through solid wood-paneled doors. All eyes were on the witness. It was Detective O'Mallory. There were about forty to fifty spectators. I recognized the back of Chip's head. He was sitting next to the State's Attorney. Helen had found a spot a few rows back and was at full attention. To my surprise, Franco Giovanni was sitting in front of her. He was flanked by his boxy duo. I slid into the bench next to the door, out of direct sight of anyone facing forward. There was no jury. Judge Binderhoff would decide the case.

O'Mallory must have just taken the stand. I recognized the standard questions setting forth his credentials. Through another series of questions, the State's Attorney established probable cause for the search of Terrell Smith's home. I could see Franco looking down into his lap as if checking his cell phone, or playing Candy Crush. Then came the details about what was found at the scene. A massive amount of heroin was recovered, as well as some firearms. Franco raised his head and watched the exchange between the prosecutor and O'Mallory.

"What about cash?" asked the prosecutor. "Did you find any cash in the house?"

"Yes, there were stacked bills in two shoe boxes we found under the bathroom sink."

"How much money was recovered?"

"The money was counted by one of the officers on the scene. It was just under $30,000."

I looked at Franco. He was working his jaw muscles, and his hands gripped the back of the seat in front of him. He turned to say something to Elvis and saw me. His eyes locked on me. He whispered something to Elvis, who nudged Paulie. They turned their expressionless eyes toward me. After a few uncomfortable seconds, they focused back on the front of the courtroom. I decided it was time to go and started sliding across the bench toward the door when my cell phone rang. I'd forgotten to silence it. It continued ringing while I fumbled around for it in my messenger bag.

Now everyone looked at me. O'Mallory rolled his eyes, Franco gave me a curious smile, and Helen laughed out loud. Chip gave me a blank stare.

"I'm so sorry, Your Honor. I'm leaving."

#

Kari and I hopped in my car for the short trip up the JFX to Olivia's house. I stared straight ahead as we passed the billboard bearing my face, pretending not to see it.

I was concerned about our conversation with Olivia. She didn't know me, and I didn't want to be too pushy. We had to earn her trust and ease into a conversation about her husband's dirty business, all within a short window of time. We also had to be sympathetic. After all, she did lose her husband.

"I've met Olivia before. I think I should do the talking," Kari said.

"Okay, but how do we segue into our real purpose? How do we ask her about the Ponzi scheme?"

"We don't. We talk about other things and wait for an opportunity to present itself. Don't worry. I got this."

Kari's confidence comforted me. It often did. I took a route that avoided my parents' house on South Road. If we saw them out in the yard, we would have to stop for a quick chat. I was not in the mood to have my job disparaged.

Olivia's Mercedes was parked in the circular driveway. I parked at the curb under a magnolia tree to keep the sun off my car. We walked up the stairs, enjoying the scent of the azalea bushes, and knocked on the front door using a brass knocker that was shaped like a dollar sign. The door was opened by a petite, young woman with brown skin and dark hair. She had a Spanish accent.

"Cain I help you?"

"We're here to see Mrs. Metzger. We have some items that belonged to her late husband," Kari said.

"I see if she can see you. What's your name?"

"I'm Kari Cruz, and this here is Jessica Snow."

The woman turned from Kari and looked at me for the first time. "Oh. The bus lady. I see you on the bus."

"Yes, I'm on a few buses." I nodded and gave her my bus smile.

"I tell Ms. Olivia you here. Come in." She swung the door wide, directing us into a small foyer that was adorned with maroon and gold striped wallpaper. We stood on a circular oriental rug. There was a small table on the side of the stairwell that supported a lamp and a gold-trimmed bowl that held Olivia's Mercedes key chain.

"Hello." We turned to see Olivia descending the stairs. It was the first time I'd seen her in anything but her workout clothes. She was wearing a pressed white-collared shirt tucked into capris-length jeans. The simple outfit was accented with a brown leather belt and cheetah print flats. More understated than I had expected.

"Hello, Mrs. Metzger. I'm Kari Cruz. We met a while back when you and your husband came to our offices—Dawson Garner & Associates?"

"Yes, I remember you. Dawson was a good friend of my late husband."

"This is Jessica Snow, one of Dawson's attorneys."

"Hello, Mrs. Metzger. We are deeply sorry for your loss."

"Thank you. It's been a difficult time. Maria said you have something of Harvey's. Come on in and have a seat. I'll ask her to get us some iced tea."

I was surprised to find Olivia so pleasant and well-spoken. Why had I suspected hostility? Perhaps because I had her fingered as a murderer. My research had discovered that she was forty-five years old. She had been born in Spain but moved here when she was in her teens. She had graduated from the University of Maryland with a degree in Political Science. She was no dummy.

The living room had grand ceilings and miles of fine fabric adorning the windows. Kari sat in a wingback chair on one side of the fireplace. Olivia and I shared the adjacent love seat. I set the cigar cutter on the coffee table and handed the putter to Olivia.

"Dawson borrowed the putter from Harvey a while ago and had his cigar cutter in his golf bag. He wanted to return them both to you."

She ignored the putter and picked up the cigar cutter. Rubbing the ivory tusk with her thumb, she whispered, "I gave this to Harvey for our anniversary last year."

We fell silent as Maria entered with a pitcher of ice tea and three frosted glasses. She set them out on the coffee table and exited the room.

Kari picked up a glass and poured herself some tea. "Who do you think killed Harvey?" she said like she was asking about the weather.

I stiffened and gave Kari a wide-eyed glare. She ignored me and looked over her cup at Olivia. Olivia was still fondling the cigar cutter. "I know people think I killed him, but I didn't. I loved Harvey."

"You were cheating on him."

"Yes. He knew it, too. He was consumed by his work. I was always second in line."

"Did you know about the Ponzi scheme?" I asked.

"No. I heard about it on the news like everyone else." She paused, sat the cigar cutter down, and said, "Not only have I lost my husband, but I've lost a fortune. They've put a freeze on our accounts. I'm broke. I'm so broke, I pawned several of my designer handbags."

"Didn't Harvey have life insurance?"

"Yes, but they won't pay out anything until the investigation into his death is done and my name is cleared."

"Since you didn't know about the Ponzi scheme, I don't suppose you know of anyone else?"

"No. I know Dawson didn't kill him. He isn't a murderer. He and Harvey were friends. They played golf regularly, and poker on occasion. I've been thinking about who it could be. I even thought maybe Juan Carlos might have killed him so he could have me to himself, but I was with Juan Carlos the night Harvey was shot. Sometimes I blame myself. Had I been here, maybe he wouldn't have been killed."

"Or maybe you'd have a bullet in your head, too," Kari said.

Olivia grimaced and I gave Kari that look again.

"I'm sorry I don't have any helpful information. I'm as anxious to find the murderer as you are." She picked up the cigar cutter again and held it gently in both hands. "Thank you for bringing me his things. I didn't think I would miss him, but I do. He put work before me, but he was still good to me. I know he loved me in his own way." She put her head down. I saw her lips moving in prayer. When she was finished, she picked her head up. "You two are very nice to stop by."

This was our cue to leave. The three of us walked back to the foyer in silence. Maria was coming down the stairs with a large suitcase and sat it next to another one by the door. "Your cosmetic bag is all that's left, Ms. Olivia."

Kari turned to Olivia. "You going somewhere?"

Olivia looked at the bags, then opened her hand and looked again at the cigar cutter. She took a deep breath. "No. I've changed my mind.

Maria, I'm sorry. Would you please take my things back upstairs?"

She turned to look at Kari and me. "You two have opened my eyes. I was trying to stay detached from all this. I thought running back home to Barcelona with Juan Carlos was the best solution. Now I know that's a cop-out. I need to stay here and face the ridicule, face the creditors, and do what I can to help find Harvey's murderer."

"That's a much better plan," I said.

#

"That went differently than I expected," Kari said as we drove back to the office.

"Me, too. I thought she would threaten us with the putter and run us off her porch. I didn't anticipate tea and polite conversation."

"We misjudged her."

"We sure did."

The JFX obliged us once again by moving freely at this hour. We passed a transit bus, and Kari said, "Hey look. It's Delroy." He was seated in his usual position right behind the driver. "You gotta admire his commitment."

My cell phone rang. Kari grabbed it from my purse and looked at the screen. "It's Marty."

"Go ahead and answer it."

"Marty, it's Kari. Jess is driving. What's up? Uhuh… uhuh… that's karma, man. That's a beautiful thing. We're on our way back. Should be there in five minutes. Offer them something to drink, and there are Berger cookies in the cabinet by the refrigerator." She disconnected.

"What'd he say?"

"Remember that minivan family that Milligan was scavenging for at the hospital that day we went to meet Tony? The parents didn't want to wait for Stuart to return from Hilton Head. They walked across the street with their file and asked to meet with you."

"Me? Why me?"

"They like your face. Told Marty you have an honest face. They're waiting for you."

It was happening. It was official. I was a local celebrity ambulance chaser. It wasn't the noblest of legal practices, but being recognized for being honest in the legal community was a rarity.

I was determined to impress the pants off of these clients.

#

My meeting with the parents went well. We talked for a half hour about their claims and the process. They listened intently and signed off on the paperwork without additional questions. They had walked off with the entire contents of Milligan's file, so the transition to our firm would be seamless. The police report was pending, but it looked like a clean case. Easy money for DGA. I thanked them both for coming, made sure they had my card, and told them to call me anytime.

"Well, Jess, how does it feel to have a client ask for you by name?" It was Dawson. He was standing in my doorway with Marty at his side.

"A little surprising, actually. I feel a bit of pressure, like I've put myself out there to be a terrific attorney and now I have to make good on that promise."

"You'll make good on it."

Marty put a hand on Dawson's shoulders. "They grow up so fast don't they?" They looked at me like proud parents, then burst into laughter and high-five'd each other.

#

Brenda Ballister sent the photos of Tyler Martin playing laser tag with his alleged neck and back injury. She included a video clip of him leaping over a barrel, twisting in midair to take a shot, and landing with a graceful tuck and roll. I scheduled an appointment with Tyler without telling him about the offer of $1,500 or the photos. He sat across from me, his shoulder-length blond hair pulled back by a pair of Ray Ban sunglasses perched on his head. He was wearing a Tommy Hilfiger T-shirt, a pair of Calvin Klein Jeans, and a pricey pair of Nikes. This guy didn't shop at Target.

"So, Tyler, we've got a situation here with your claim. The adjuster is not convinced that this fender bender could have caused you any injury and she's playing hardball. She offered $1,500 to settle your case."

"I'm not taking no $1,500. What does she know? She wasn't there. I was hurt when we got hit. So was my buddy. I had to miss work. I couldn't do anything but sit on the couch for weeks. She don't know what she's talking about."

"She and I talked a lot about the accident. We saw the photos of both vehicles and read through Dr. Shon's reports. I'll tell you, Tyler, I'm not impressed either."

He wasn't expecting that. His last claim with DGA was similar to this one and it settled for three times as much. He was expecting a similar windfall. "You don't know what you're doing here. I want to talk to Dawson."

"You can't talk to Dawson. He's not here. But lets you and I try to go through the details again. So, how long would you say you were on the couch?" I put a calendar in front of him and pointed to February 3. "This is the day of the accident. When did you feel well enough to report to work and go about your normal activities?"

He studied the calendar like he was looking at a treasure map. "Well, Dr. Shon said I could go back to work on the tenth." He pointed to Monday the tenth of February. "I went to work and all after that, but I was still in pain and couldn't do nothing else until about here." He pointed to the February 21st. "But even then, I still had a little back pain."

"You were doing nothing but sitting on the couch and muddling through work from the date of the accident through here?" I drew a finger across the days of the calendar from February 3 to February 21.

"That's about right," he said.

I placed a series of photographs in front of him, one after the other like in the interrogation room scenes on *Law & Order*. Each picture showed him playing laser tag with his buddies. The time stamp was Saturday, February 8, five days after the accident.

"Do you recognize the guy in the photo?"

"That ain't me."

"Cut the crap. Of course it's you. It looks like you. Plus, take a look at this." I put another photograph in front of him of the registration log with his name highlighted. "That looks like your name now, doesn't it?"

"So? Maybe it's not my signature." He crossed his arms and leaned back in his chair with a smug look on his face.

"That's bull, Tyler. You're lucky this adjuster is offering you anything."

"I won't settle for $1,500. Can you try to get her to $3,000?"

Irritation pinched my patience.

"No, Tyler. You accept this settlement right now or go find yourself another lawyer. After my fee and Dr. Shon's bills, you'll walk away with $500. That's a gift given the clear evidence that..." I wanted to call him a liar and a thief, but doing so seemed to make me complicit. I waved my hands over the photos and said, "Well, given this."

He paused, then looked up at me like he had it all figured out. "I heard Dawson got himself arrested, so maybe I should get another lawyer."

"Fine. Let me help you with that." I threw one of Stuart Milligan's business cards on top of the pile of incriminating photographs. "This dirtbag is right across the street. Go see if he wants your file."

Tyler looked at me, then at the card, then back at me again. He shifted in his chair and pretended to check his phone. I sat still, waiting for his decision. I figured I couldn't lose here. Either he'd walk out the door with the file and become Stuart's headache, or he'd settle with me and I'd get a small fee. Either way, I was done with him.

I watched as a knowing grin formed on this face. He looked at me, not with the hostility that I expected, but with admiration. "You're okay, Jess. I mean, for a chick in this business, you're pretty tough. You got me beat. I'm gonna take your advice and settle this one. I see the problem. I understand. Tell me where to sign off."

I picked up the trash can by the side of my desk and cleared the photographs from sight. "You're making the right decision, Tyler. I figured you would. You're a smart guy. Sign here." I put the release form and a pen in front of him and explained that by signing it, he agreed to settle this claim for a total of $1,500 and close the matter. He signed, and I pushed a five-hundred-dollar check in front of him.

"That's $500 for you, $500 to Dr. Shon—who took a big cut on his bill for you—and $500 to us. I'm waiving expenses as a courtesy to you."

"Thank you, Jess. It's not what I got last time"—he said looking at the check—"but it's something. Plus, I learned not to be seen playing laser tag after my next accident."

"It's been a learning experience for both us then."

We shook hands like two professional business associates and he left. I was impressed with myself for earning Tyler's respect, which felt odd. I guess I was getting good at this. Better not tell my mother.

CHAPTER TWENTY-TWO

After multiple failed attempts to squeeze money out of Franco, I was beginning to appreciate the simple, mind-numbing redundancy of dealing with insurance adjusters. But I wasn't giving up on Tony's claim because Franco wasn't playing fair. I had another plan. This one also involved Mrs. Bianco who, after recovering from her intestinal episode, remained my best playing card given her relationship with Franco's mother. We had to attempt another ambush.

It would go down at the House of Hair during Franco's monthly pedicure. I'd arrange it so Mrs. Bianco would be getting a pedicure at the same time. He would be a captive audience with his pant legs pulled up past his knees and his feet soaking in a tub of swirling warm water. I would arrive during their pedicures under the pretense of taking Mrs. B to lunch. She would mention the one connection I had with Franco—Tony. Franco would be forced to explain why he wasn't paying the claim and Mrs. B would erupt and threaten to tell Cecelia. The thought of disappointing his mother would cause Franco to crumble and offer up the $15,000. Justice would be served.

Meanwhile, I needed to focus on getting Marshall's exploding-toilet claim started. My earlier research had turned up five defendants. I had to give notice of the claim to each of them. Sue them all. That's what they teach us in law school. It was a colossal waste of time to bring all five of these companies into this, but it would be legal malpractice on my part if I didn't. I contacted the appropriate government agency for each state to obtain the name of the resident attorney for each defendant. I slaved for an hour over the letter that would serve as notice of Marshall's claim. Considering the subject matter, it was an effort to maintain a serious tone. Upon completion, Kari helped me fax, email, and send each letter to the proper party via certified mail.

I called Marshall to check in on his condition. Lucinda answered the phone. "Hello, Mrs. Ball. This is Jessica Snow."

"What's wrong?"

"Nothing's wrong. I'm calling in to check on Marshall. How's he doing?"

"Oh. It's nice of you to call. He's doing fine. Still some pain, but it gets better every day. Do you want to talk to him?"

"Only if I'm not disturbing him."

"You aren't disturbing him. He's watching *The Price is Right*. He can pause it." I heard her hand the phone to Marshall and tell him it was me. I could also hear the cacophony of music, buzzers, and screaming coming from his television. He did not pause it.

"Hello?"

"Hi, Marshall. This is Jessica Snow. I'm calling to check in on you."

"What?"

The volume on the television was too loud. "This is Jessica Snow. I wanted to check in on you!" *You are the winner of a brand new washer and dryer...*

"You have a check for me?" *applause, applause, applause...*

"No, I'm checking in! You know, asking how you are doing?"

"Oh. I'm doing fine." *Come on down...*

Now I couldn't hear him. "What?" *applause, applause, applause...*

"I said I'm doing fine!"

It was clear *The Price is Right* was far more interesting than a phone call from me.

"I can tell you're busy. I'll check up on you in a couple of days."

"Five hundred fifty. Yes!"

I hung up and made a mental note not to call him again during *The Price is Right* hour.

Since I hadn't heard from Ms. Trudy about her toilet-related injury, I called Mrs. Bianco to see if she'd had a chance to talk to Trudy's mother.

"I'm seeing her today at the community center for bridge. It's championship day. There's fifty dollars at stake."

I thanked her for her help and wished her luck.

Next on my agenda was ordering Marshall's medical records. He had been treated and driven to the hospital by ambulance and had a couple of follow-ups with his primary-care doctor. I sent requests for records to all them via fax, email, and certified mail. Having now covered all the bases from my end, it was a waiting game at this point. I could hear from one or all of the defendants within hours, days, or even a week. Everyone played the game differently.

#

That evening, Mrs. Bianco was sharing her porch and her port with two women I didn't recognize.

"Jessica, come join us. This is Theresa and her daughter Trudy. Remember we talked about Trudy's accident?"

This was great news. My second toilet-explosion case. I'd soon be the local expert.

"Hello. I'm so sorry to hear about your accident, Trudy. How're you feeling?"

Trudy was no taller than five feet and weighed about 200 pounds. She was round. She had a small cast covering her left wrist that wrapped around the lower part of her hand and thumb. I guessed it was difficult for her to sit because she remained standing while the other two were seated.

"It's getting a little better each day. It still hurts to sit down." She shifted on her feet and winced at the effort.

I remained standing in deference to her delicate condition. "I have a client who had a similar accident. He has a large abrasion on his torso that we assume was caused by flying porcelain. How did your accident happen?"

"Same thing, I guess. I had cleaned the bathroom, scrubbed the toilet and all. I gave it a flush and started walking out. That's when I heard the explosion and felt the pain, you know, back there." She gestured toward her prodigious posterior.

"And how long ago did this happen?"

"It was Saturday. This past Saturday."

"Did you take pictures of the damage?"

"No! That would be so embarrassing." She poured another dose of port into her cup.

"I mean the damage to the toilet and your bathroom."

"I took some pictures with my cellular phone," her mother said. She reached into her bag and pulled out a smartphone. She showed me several photos. The porcelain carnage was similar to what I had seen in Marshall Ball's bathroom. I used the phone to email the photos to myself and returned it to Theresa.

My attention returned to Trudy. I went to stand by her, patted her on the shoulder, and said, "That must have been a terrifying experience."

"It sure was." She sipped her port. "There's no bigger humiliation than getting a butt wound when you got a butt the size of mine."

"You got a nice butt," Mrs. Bianco said. "It's a Kim Kardashian butt. People pay money for a butt like that."

I was surprised that Mrs. B knew of Kim Kardashian and further surprised that she knew big butts were in vogue.

"Yeah, but now I'll have a big fat scar on my big fat butt." She emptied her glass for the second time since I arrived.

"I know this will make you uncomfortable, but I'm going to need to get a picture of your wound."

By now the booze must have kicked in because, after a brief pause, she said, "Oh what the hell." She turned her back to me, lifted her skirt, and pulled down her granny panties. As I fumbled for my phone, Trudy fell headfirst into Mrs. Bianco's plentiful basil pot and rolled to her side with her bandaged butt exposed. Theresa bounced over and removed the gauze bandage that protected the wound. I angled in for a few more shots. Trudy mumbled something, made a brief attempt to rise, then settled back down to the floor.

"I suppose it wasn't a good idea to mix the painkillers with the port," her mother said.

Mrs. Bianco hustled over with a pillow and tucked it under Trudy's head. Theresa replaced the gauze dressing and adjusted Trudy's skirt to cover her backside. She needed to sleep off the alcohol, but I needed a signed retainer agreement.

"How about I order us some pizza while we wait for Trudy to wake up?"

Mrs. Bianco and Theresa agreed. I jumped over the railing to my house and returned with a bed sheet to cover the prone Trudy, the pizza shop menu, blank retainer form, and a pen.

Trudy awoke an hour later as we were finishing up our meal. Mrs. Bianco went to get her some coffee and I served her up a couple of slices of pepperoni. We all had some nice girl talk and Trudy signed the retainer agreement.

CHAPTER TWENTY-THREE

The morning crawled by as we waited for the allotted time to pull off our ambush at the House of Hair. It was hard to concentrate on work. I reviewed a few files but spent most of the time shopping online.

Kari and I swung by to pick up Mrs. Bianco around one thirty. We parked down the street from the salon. Franco and Mrs. B had two o'clock pedicure appointments, but we wanted him seated and captive before she arrived.

Mrs. B was thrilled to be part of this plan. "Are you sure you don't want me to wear a wire?"

"I'm sure. Plus, I don't have a wire."

She sighed and pulled her cell phone from her purse. It was an old flip phone.

Kari winced when she saw it. "That's your phone? My toaster's smaller than that."

"It's good phone. I have Cecelia on speed dial. I can bring in the heat if Franco give me hard time."

I hoped she left her gun at home.

Franco's town car parked across the street from the House of Hair. "There he is." His personal security detail was not with him today. He stepped from the car and took a look up and down the street. He removed his suit jacket and placed it in the back seat. He took one last look around before entering the House of Hair.

Mrs. Bianco shoved her phone back in her purse and reached for the door. "Time to go."

"We'll be there in five minutes," I said. She marched toward the salon with stoic determination. My plan was underway.

I used the timer feature on my cell phone to pace out the five minutes. "I'm nervous. What if this doesn't work? I'm all out of ideas."

"This plan is rock solid. Don't you be over thinking it. It's all gonna fall right into place. We got karma on our side. We do good by people and good things happen to us. Mrs. B's got this one in the bag."

Upon entering the salon, I was greeted by Paulette. I kept my eyes on her, avoiding looking to the right where I knew Franco and Mrs. B were seated. As rehearsed, Paulette greeted me in a voice that carried throughout the salon. "Jess, your appointment isn't until next week."

"I know. I'm here to pick up Mrs. Bianco. I'm taking her to lunch."

"Over here, Jessica." Mrs. Bianco waved at me. I walked over with my practiced, polite business smile, Kari at my side.

"Look who's here." Mrs. Bianco gestured toward Franco.

I nodded in recognition. "Mr. Giovanni."

He returned the nod. "Ms. Snow."

Mrs. Bianco smiled. "You two have case together, no? With that nice dancer fellow? How's that going?"

I turned toward Franco. He was pretending to be engrossed with the screen on his cell phone and remained silent.

"We seem to have reached a snag." He still had his face in his phone, ignoring us.

"Franco!" Mrs. B said. "Put that phone down. I know your mother taught you better manners than to play with your cell phone in the middle of a conversation."

He cringed like a chastised teenager, closed the phone, and placed it on the molded plastic tray table next to him. "I'm sorry."

"Now that's better," Mrs. Bianco said. "Jess was about to tell me what you did for that poor young man who got hurt in your store." She looked at me.

"I think Mr. Giovanni should address that."

She smiled and turned toward him. "Tell me, Franco."

He shot daggers at me. I gave him a quizzical look and a full-body shrug.

"You see, Mrs. Bianco, the situation is not as simple as it seems."

"What do you mean? Jess, what's he talking about? I thought you told me that the nice young man slipped on water at Mr. Giovanni's store. Isn't that what happened?"

"That's exactly what happened, but none of the witnesses will talk about it. They're all his employees. Kari and I are the only non-employees who witnessed the accident. Mr. Giovanni has declined payment."

Franco was trying to disappear into the pedicure chair, but he couldn't go anywhere. He had one foot in the soaking tub and the other in the clutches of Ming Le, who understood enough English to know Franco was being a bully.

"Franco Benito Mauralis Giovanni! Is this true?"

He refused eye contact and stared at his feet, wincing at Ming Le's indelicate handling of his foot care.

"Yes. It's true. But its business, you see. It's not personal."

"Does your mother know about this?"

These were the six words Franco Giovanni did not want to hear. He flinched. "I don't discuss my business with her."

"I know she raised you better than to take advantage of people. She will not like to hear about this."

Franco's complexion paled. "You're not going to tell her are you?"

She pulled out her toaster-sized cell phone. "I've got her on speed dial." She held her finger over the "send" button.

"Okay, okay. Don't call my mother. We'll work something out."

Mrs. Bianco put the phone away. Ming Le loosened her grasp on Franco's left foot. I exhaled, not realizing that I had been holding my breath.

"You promise you won't tell momma?"

"You pay Jess the money, I won't tell your momma."

The color returned to Franco's face. His composure restored, he locked eyes with me. "Well played, Ms. Snow." Then his stern mouth loosened into a grin. "Well played."

"I don't know what you're talking about. Now let's discuss dollars."

"Before we get into those details, we must agree that there can be no record of this. There will be no signed release, no waiver, nothing. You destroy your file."

I agreed.

"I'll give your client $15,000. Like I offered in the hospital. We will not discuss his lost wages because I happen to know he was not scheduled to work until the following weekend."

"How do you know his work schedule?"

"I just know. Plus, I will give you $5,000 cash for your time and… well, let's call it your inconvenience."

I hadn't expected the additional $5,000. It felt a little dirty. In the strictest sense of the word, I had blackmailed this guy. My conscience was saying, *Don't take the money.* But all my recent legal training was saying, *Take the money! Take the money!*

"You've got a deal." I stepped up to his elevated chair and shook his hand. "You're paying $20,000 in cash, $5,000 of which is my fee. Nobody speaks of this deal, ever, and there is no signed agreement, just our mutual understanding."

"And Mrs. Bianco never speaks to my mom about this."

Mrs. Bianco made a zipper gesture across her lips. "Never."

I had struck a deal with the mob. My mother was never going to hear about this.

After we dropped Mrs. Bianco off at home, Kari and I headed back to the office. I called Tony along the way and relayed the good news.

"Well that was easy," he said.

#

I rushed home to get ready for my date with Mark. First-date stress often kicks in while trying to decide what to wear. Since we were going to be outdoors in the August heat, I was limited to short sleeves or sleeveless top and shorts, but not too short. We'd be sitting in stadium seats and I wanted to avoid upper thigh spread. I settled on a black V-neck, fitted tee and tan Bermuda shorts. The shorts had roomy pockets for my phone, some cash, and my ID. I wore my hair down but wrapped a tie around my wrist in case the heat forced me to pull it up off my neck and shoulders. After swiping on some mascara, I was ready to go. I grabbed a bottle of water from the refrigerator and waited on the front porch for Mark.

Mrs. Bianco worked on a crossword as she swayed on her glider.

"I've got a date tonight, Mrs. B."

She looked at me with a hopeful smile. When she took in my outfit, her mouth turned downward. "You're not wearing that are you?"

"Yeah. We're going to the Orioles game."

"Is it that nice fireman from the other night?"

"Yup. Here he is now." Mark pulled up and double-parked in front of my house. I bounded down the stairs. He got out and came around, opened the passenger door for me, and gave Mrs. Bianco a friendly wave. He was driving a monstrous Dodge Ram pickup. I needed both hands to pull myself up into the cabin.

I settled in, buckled up, and watched Mark do the same. This was the first time I'd seen him in street clothes. He wore a black pocket T-shirt that hugged his muscular chest and arms. It was tucked into tan cargo shorts. This is when I realize that we were wearing identical outfits. He must have seen the look on my face as he took his place behind the wheel.

"Is something wrong?"

"Look at us. We look like twins!"

He eyed my outfit as he put the car in gear. "You look great."

"Thank you, but *we* look ridiculous."

"No one's going to notice. Half the stadium will be wearing black or orange."

I wanted to ask him to turn the car around so I could change, but I didn't want to appear petty. Instead, I did something I know men are suckers for—I complimented his vehicle. "This is nice." I rubbed the leather seat between us. "But why didn't you get the bigger model?"

He responded with a quick laugh. "My buddy Kyle and I have a side business. We buy old homes, fix them up, and sell them. I keep equipment and materials in the back."

"When do you find time for that?"

"We work the same shifts each week at the station We focus our off days on our houses."

His work ethic impressed me. We talked about his current project— a home on a popular street in Hamden that had been abandoned for four years and neglected for several years prior.

Pedestrians and lazy drivers mucked up the flow of traffic as we got closer to the stadium. Mark didn't seem to notice. He maneuvered his truck around them with impressive calm until he slammed the brakes at the intersection of Conway and Sharp. Our bodies lurched forward, catching on the shoulder harnesses. At the same time, there was a thump on the driver's side front. With halted breath and wide eyes, we watched a woman do a slow roll off the side of the truck and sink to the street.

Mark threw the car in park and jumped out to check on the fallen woman. I followed. She was on her back, holding her right knee and mouthing profanities. "You son of a bitch with your big ass truck. You hit me. I think something's broken. I need an ambulance. I need my lawyer."

It was Melinda.

The harsh reality of my profession punched me in the gut. Having witnessed her scam, there was no denying that hustlers like her would continue to find their way to my office hoping for easy money. But I had the power to turn them away.

"You don't need a lawyer, Melinda. You need a conscience."

She looked up at me. "Ms. Snow? That you? How'd you get here so fast?"

I pointed to the truck. "I was in the front seat of the truck you just walked into."

Mark gave me a surprised look. "You know her?"

"I'll explain later," I told him. To Melinda, I said, "I know what you're up to and I want nothing further to do with you."

"Oh," she said, breaking eye contact with me and rising to her feet. "You know what, I think I'm okay after all." She brushed herself off and patted her hair back into place. "Yup, I'm good. Thanks for your time." She made a quick turn and shuffled away.

Without a word, Mark and I hustled back into the truck.

"How did you know she wasn't hurt?"

I explained my recent discovery of Melinda's tendency to walk into cars so she could make some easy cash.

His soft laugh put me at ease. "That's quite a job you have. You must get all kinds of crazies."

"You have no idea."

Dempsey's Brew Pub is built into the iconic warehouse building. It occupies a prime space inside the ballpark. Mark had made a reservation. We were seated at a high-top table right away. We ordered Rain Delay IPAs, one of Dempsey's home brewed beers. The server walked away, and a beautiful blonde stepped up to Mark.

"Hey, Mark." Her shorts were short, revealing long, lean, muscled legs. A capped-sleeved T-shirt stopped a few inches short of the silver stud in her belly button. Her cavernous cleavage beaconed attention, but Mark's eyes didn't fall there. He looked from her eyes to mine, then back to her.

"I haven't seen you around the Power Plant lately," she said. With each word, she seesawed her shoulders. Mark inched away. I was pleased to see that his expression showed polite disinterest.

"No, you haven't."

Maintaining her close proximity, she looked at me and said, "Who're you?"

Indifference having failed, Mark switched his dial to measured, courteous scolding. "Melanie, this is Jess. Jess and I were having a private conversation. I'm sure you understand." She took a step back, and Mark turned his whole body as far sideways as his chair would permit. She reacted with a shrug of her shoulders, headed off to a table occupied by two men, and shimmied her T-shirt at them. I looked at Mark. His eyes asked me if she was gone yet.

"She's gone," I said. "Old girlfriend?" I kept my tone casual, but a jealous pang sat just under the surface.

"Old something, but not girlfriend. I know I may have seemed rude to her, but trust me, she doesn't understand subtle."

I decided our first date was not the time to inquire about his past relationships and picked up the menu. "The pulled pork looks good."

We both ordered pulled pork sandwiches, two more Rain Delay IPAs, and shared a basket of crab fries. The food was terrific, the conversation warm and comfortable. Melanie had the good sense not to return to our table. A few minutes before game time, we worked our way up the maze of escalators to our seats, which were about twenty-five rows up on the first base side. Great seats, but they were in foul ball territory.

"I expect you to protect me if a ball comes this way," I said.

Mark's eyes brightened. "Or we could let it hit you and then sue them."

"Very funny."

We watched the game and cheered along with the crowd. The Orioles lost, but the evening was a winner. Mark took my hand as we walked to the parking lot. The summer air was tempered by a cool, northern breeze. The bluish glow of the city's artificial lights guided us. As we neared his car, we slowed our pace. He opened the passenger door with his free hand, then pulled me close. I felt the warmth of his chest on mine and breathed in the scent of sandalwood cologne. I smiled up at him and he kissed me. His lips parted mine and sent tingles of electricity through to my toes. He must have sneaked in a mint because the kiss tasted like cinnamon. I liked cinnamon.

He drove me home and double-parked in front of my row house. We turned toward each other. After a moment of comfortable silence, I conjured up a teasing tone. "I'm sure glad we got that first-kiss thing over with back there."

He smiled. "Me, too. That's a real stressor."

We both slid toward the console and leaned in toward each other. He put one hand on my upper thigh and the other on the back of my neck and pulled me close. This kiss was deep and long and made my legs go weak. When our lips parted, I opened my eyes. I was more than a little annoyed that he wasn't looking at me. I followed his gaze to Mrs. Bianco's porch. She stood in her housecoat, looking at us with a silly grin. She was clapping.

CHAPTER TWENTY-FOUR

My cell phone woke me. It was Sharlyn. She asked if I could stop by Hal's on my way to work. She had something to show me. I dressed while replaying my date with Mark in my head. It had been a great evening. Mark was smart, funny, and hard working. The kind of guy to bring home to momma.

I was at Hal's by eight. They didn't open until eleven, so Sharlyn was there alone. She led me to a booth in the back where her giant tote bag sat. She reached in, pulled out a notebook, and pushed it in front of me. "What's this?"

"It's Darnell's. When I moved my things out, I gathered everything in a hurry. I had a lot of notebooks there with my recipes. I shoved them all into a box. I was sorting through everything yesterday, and I found that."

It was black ledger with a faux-leather cover. I opened it. It contained a list of names and dollar figures. It appeared to be an index of buyers who owed him money. Darnell ran lines of credit for his customers.

"I don't think he knows it's missing. Everything's marked 'paid.' He must have started another list in a different ledger."

I stared at the ledger with the reverence deserving of the holy scripture. "This is gold."

This was the nail in Darnell's coffin. The ledger had names, dates, quantities of product, and costs. It was indisputable evidence of Darnell's drug dealings. Chip should be able to negotiate a plea bargain with this kind of proof.

I took the ledger and headed to the office to call Chip, hoping that Sharlyn wouldn't have to testify at all.

Before I reached my desk, Franco called. He had a flair for the dramatic. "Look out your window."

His town car was parked right in front of my office window. Elvis and Paulie stood guard, their arms crossed against their massive pectorals.

"I assume you're in the heavily guarded town car outside my window?"

"You assumed correctly. I have something for you."

"I'll be right there."

I marched toward the town car with the confidence of someone who had done this many times.

Elvis and Paulie each took a step in opposite directions as I approached, exposing the rear passenger door. I opened the door and leaned my head inside. Franco was seated in the opposite corner of the spacious town car. It had two seats that ran the width of the interior. Franco was sitting in the forward-facing seats. I positioned myself opposite him. He was wearing his usual tailored silk suit and shiny black shoes. His black socks had some yellow figures on them. He noticed me trying to take a closer look.

"Minions," he said.

"As in *Despicable Me*?"

"Yeah. I love those little guys. I watch the movies with my grandson all the time. My daughter bought me the socks."

"I like them. They show your whimsical side. Makes you seem less scary."

"Then I shouldn't wear them. It seems I don't scare you anymore."

"You scare the hell out of me. I'm just getting better at hiding it."

He made a sudden move mimicking a punch to my throat. I flinched.

"Just making sure I still got it."

He held up a brown grocery bag that was folded at the top and sat it on the seat next to me.

"Is that the money?"

"It ain't lunch." He bugged out his eyes and gave me a slanted smile.

"You're forgetting—this shady business stuff is new to me. I'm used to getting paid by check." I lifted the bag up and down as if measuring its weight. Like I know what $20,000 in cash feels likes. "So, what's appropriate in these situations? Do I peek into the bag? Do I count it?"

"Do you want to offend me?"

"Oh, I definitely don't want to do that." I glanced outside to see Elvis and Paulie still standing guard. I wished Darnell and Mad Dog could see me in the company of Franco Giovanni and his henchmen. Bet they'd stop messing with Sharlyn and me. "What does it cost to have a bodyguard?"

"My arrangement with those two is a little unorthodox and strictly confidential. Why? You need protection?"

I told him about Darnell, the threats from Mad Dog, and the shootings. "They're not part of your organization, are they?"

He shook his head. "No, but I know who they are. They're low-hanging fruit. Darnell's a two-bit drug dealer who acts like he's the head of a cartel. I'm not in the drug business anymore. Not since the O'Mallory bust. But I can tell you that witness intimidation is a common practice with those guys. He's being a punk. I wouldn't worry about it."

"That's what everyone says, but it's hard not to worry when someone points a gun at you."

I grabbed the bag and scooted my butt over toward the door. "Thank you for working with me on this." I jiggled the bag of money. "And thanks for your perspective on my death threats." I got out of the car, stuck my head back in, and said, "Nice doin' bidness witcha."

He laughed at my lame street accent. I closed the car door and bounced back to the office carrying the brown sack of money. I was pleased to have finalized Tony's claim, but all this cash made me nervous.

Kari saw me walk in and eyed the bag. "You got lunch already?" It was ten in the morning.

"No. It's Tony's settlement. Twenty Gs in cash."

"Girl, we gotta get you to the bank." She buzzed into Dawson's office. "Dawson, we need to run to the bank."

Dawson joined us at Kari's desk with a putter in his hand. "What's going on? I got a tee time in thirty minutes." He narrowed in on the bag. "What's that?"

I opened the bag and stuck it under his chin. He let out a whistle. "So, you managed to get some money out of Franco." He patted my shoulder. "Well done. How much?"

"There's $20,000 in here. $5,000 is our fee. The rest is Tony's."

Dawson eyes wandered for a couple of seconds. I knew he was doing the math in his head. "Our fee should be $6,600, right?"

I held firm. "No, this a backroom deal. There's no contract, no documentation at all. Franco could have kept his offer at the original $15,000, but he didn't. He said our fee is $5,000, and that's what it is. Period."

Dawson held up his hands. "Settle down. I was just asking. You two go ahead and get to the bank. I've got too much cash in the safe."

"Don't run off to play golf until we get back," Kari said. "Marty's in court. You're the only one here." She turned to me. "Let's take your car. I'll hold the money."

We were stopped at the corner of Charles and Monument Streets when we saw Delroy strolling towards us with his friend Ronnie. Kari rolled down her window as they approached.

Delroy was holding a manila envelope. "I was on my way to see you guys. I saw Marshall yesterday. He wanted me to drop off these medical bills."

"Go on over to the office. We're going to the bank. Be back in a couple of minutes," Kari said.

The light turned green and I accelerated through the intersection. As I increased the pressure on the gas pedal, I felt movement around my foot. Adrenaline shot through my system when I looked down and saw a black snake moving around the floor.

"Snake!" I screamed and slammed on the brake. But it wasn't the brake. It was the gas pedal. The car lurched forward. I lifted both feet off the floor to avoid contact with the snake.

Kari screamed, too, and jumped up onto her seat. "A snake! Stop the car." Sheer panic had set in. The snake slithered in impossible directions. With neither foot on the gas or the brake and neither of my hands on the steering wheel, the car was on a comically slow, yet uncontrollable path toward a parked Cadillac Escalade. Kari unbuckled her seat belt, squatted in her seat, and reached for the door handle while the car was still rolling. I followed her lead and unbuckled. Before we could eject ourselves, my front bumper made contact with the rear door of the Escalade and came to an abrupt stop. While Kari and I maintained our positions on top of our seats, the snake was still in frenetic motion. Then, for an instant, it froze. I swear it looked right up at me before disappearing under my seat.

"It's under my seat!"

We were still screaming when Delroy came to my side of the car.

"You been drinking, Jess?"

"Snake!" There's a snake in the car."

Kari opened her door and jumped through. I followed her out, closing and locking the door behind me.

Delroy joined us as we stood outside the vehicle at a safe distance. The front of my car was tucked into the rear quarter panel of the black Escalade. It was blocking one lane of travel, causing a hiccup in the flow of traffic.

"Why's there a snake in your car?"

I knew why. It was Darnell. He planted it as another warning. I needed to call Sharlyn and warn her. While I dialed her number, Kari tapped my arm. She stood trance-like, staring at the car. "The money. The bag of money is in the car."

Great. My brown bag of hard earned money was being held hostage by a creepy black snake. I left a quick message for Sharlyn and refocused my attention on the car.

Delroy, quick to pick up on things, said, "You've got a snake AND a bag of money on your car?"

"Yup."

"How much money?"

"A lot," I said.

"You sure you ain't been drinking?"

"No, but I could sure use one."

"Don't worry, Jess. I'll get your money." He bounded over to the car and opened the back door. After pausing to scan the rear interior, he stuck his head in and called back to us. "Are you sure there was just one snake?"

"We only saw one," Kari said.

The upper half of Delroy's body disappeared into the car. "Got it!" He was backing himself out of the car, brown bag of money in hand, when he screamed. "Ahhh! There's more. More snakes! ... Ow!" He banged the top of his head coming up out of the car but kept his grip on the bag. He staggered over to us. "I think we need to call animal control."

I thanked Delroy for his heroics. "How many snakes did you see?"

"Two, but there could have been more."

I took the bag from him and handed it to Kari. "Will you call Dawson and tell him that we have car trouble? Ask him to track down Marty. Maybe he can take you to the bank while I deal with the car."

I was grateful that the owner of the Escalade hadn't shown up. The damage to both cars was minor, but as far as I was concerned, mine wasn't drivable until the snakes were exorcised.

Kari hung up the phone after talking with Dawson. "Marty's on his way."

I dialed 311 and was transferred to a dispassionate woman in the animal control unit. She was unimpressed with my snake-infested car. I supposed they'd seen it all over the years. She said all eligible personnel were currently purging a vacant warehouse of a family of raccoons. The estimated response time for my non-emergency would be about four hours. I told her I would find another way.

I called Bucky at Bucky's Auto Repair. He had a tow truck. Maybe he'd haul my car away and perform a snake-ectomy. He remembered me. "How's that new tire holding up for you?"

"It's fine, but I have another problem." I told him about the snakes and asked if he could help me.

"Sure can. You know this happened last month to another customer of mine. He pissed off some guy—owed him money or something—and the guy put three black snakes in his minivan. Found 'em on the way to little league with four kids in the car."

I was happy to learn that Bucky had experience solving this kind of problem, yet somehow disappointed that my situation wasn't unique. "How soon can you be here? I'm at Charles and Monument."

"Be there in fifteen minutes."

Marty picked up Kari and the brown bag of money. They sped off in the direction of the bank. Delroy remained at my side.

"Thank you for your help. You don't have to stick around. I've got my mechanic coming."

"I ain't got nothing else to do. I'll stick around until he gets here."

Bucky showed up as Kari and Marty returned from the bank. He showed no apprehension about the slithering serpents and retrieved our purses from the car without incident before hooking it up and hauling it way. He promised to have the snakes removed by tomorrow morning.

#

As soon as I returned to the office, I called Chip and told him I had something to show him that may change the direction of Darnell's upcoming trial. We agreed to meet at Oscar's Pub near the Harbor at five thirty. Interesting that he wanted to meet at a bar on a Friday evening. Was this standard Assistant-State's-Attorney procedure? I didn't want to over-think it.

When I arrived, Chip was seated at the bar with a beer in front of him, chatting with the bartender. I saddled up in the stool next to his and placed my briefcase at my feet. "Come here often?"

He turned and locked eyes with me. A genuine smile formed on his face. "I'm glad you could meet me here. It's been a tough couple of days. I thought we could both use a drink."

"You thought right."

Chip signaled the bartender for me. "I'll have a Corona too, please."

"So, what do you have for me?"

Right to business, I see. I didn't want to display my evidence on the open bar. "We should get a booth." I grabbed my briefcase, he took both beers, and we slid into a booth in the rear. I checked the table to make sure it was clean and opened the briefcase enough to slide out the ledger.

He flipped through the pages. I gave him a minute to digest what he saw. He looked up at me with raised eyebrows then looked back at the ledger. I knew it was useless unless I could connect it to Darnell. "Sharlyn found it among her notebooks after she moved out of Darnell's place."

I could see the wheels turning. His eyes scanned the pages. His lips curled into a slanted smile and tapped the ledger. "This is gold. With this evidence, Darnell would be a fool not to plea out."

"I was hoping you'd say that."

He raised his glass. "To putting scumbags away."

I tapped my glass against his.

"So how does this work? Do you think it will get resolved before Sharlyn has to show up for trial?"

"Let's find out." He pulled out his cell phone, punched some numbers, and leaned back into the corner of our booth.

"It would make a world of difference to Sharlyn and me if you could get a truthful statement about the accident from Darnell. You know, as part of the plea."

He held up a finger to silence me and said, "We'll see." His demeanor was casual, like he was ordering a pizza. He took a pull on his beer.

"Billy, it's Chip." He winked at me. "I've got some new evidence that may have you rethinking my plea offer for Darnell Black." I listened in as he explained the contents of the ledger in detail. As he spoke, I realized that this guy was a bit condescending, a bit arrogant, a bit of a cocky bastard. Still, part of me admired his confidence. From what I could hear, he was going to get his plea deal. I continued to study him.

He disconnected. "He was rattled by this. He wants to see it for himself. You did good work, counselor. Ever think of leaving Dawson and coming to work for a real cause?"

A real cause? Was he implying that my work wasn't a real cause? He was a cocky bastard *and* he'd just pissed me off.

"I make a difference where I am, Chip. I'm not going anywhere." I finished my beer in one long gulp and stood to leave.

Chip rose and grabbed my wrist. Regret registered in his eyes. "I'm sorry. I didn't mean to offend you."

"I'm sure you didn't. You just don't know any better." I pulled free and headed for the exit.

CHAPTER TWENTY-FIVE

The Orioles were playing at 7:05. I planned to watch the game with the twins on their front porch.

On my way home, I stopped at Yoder's Liquor store to pick up a twelve-pack of Corona to bring to the viewing party, and a bottle of Mrs. Bianco's favorite port to thank her for her help with Tony's case. Yoder's used to be a homely place with rusty steel strips holding in bulletproof panels covered with faded advertising posters. It was rebuilt after a fire destroyed the building a year ago. The authorities never determined the cause of the fire. The end result was a crisp new storefront in keeping with the recent renewal of the business district near the waterfront. I walked in and was greeted by the same Pakistani man who always worked the register at this hour. He was tearing off a long strip of lottery scratch-off tickets for an elderly woman. She reached for the tickets with one hand while the other gripped her cane.

I grabbed a bottle of port off the shelf and the Corona from the refrigerator and I returned to the front. The Pakistani man and I exchanged pleasantries about the hot weather and the looming thunderstorm that we hoped wouldn't delay the game. I paid for my packaged goods and left the store. The woman who had purchased the scratch-off tickets sat on a bench outside the store. She looked up at me, waved one of the tickets, and said, "You gotta play to win! I won fifteen dollars!"

"Congratulations," I said. Her eyes lingered on me.

"Hey, I know you. You're that lawyer lady. I saw your exploding-toilet commercial when I was watching a rerun of *Judge Judy*. That Judy is a hoot. Anyway, I may have a case for you. You got a card?"

I pulled a card from the dedicated side pocket of my messenger bag, like pulling a gun from a holster. Kari had taught me the importance of the quick draw with a business card.

"Was someone you know injured?"

"My neighbor, Snappy. Well, Snappy's what we call him. His name is Samuel Napi. He's a little embarrassed by the incident. The flying porcelain tore a nasty gash in his hip. I told him to take some pictures, you know. Just in case."

"That was good advice. I hope he took it. I'd like to talk to him. Have him give me a call."

"I will. Your commercial also did some good down at the old Baptist Church and Bingo Hall. The reverend saw it and inspected the toilets there. Turns out one of them, the one in the office, has one of those exploding parts. He shut it down and is having it replaced."

"I'm glad nobody was hurt."

She started to rise. I took her elbow, guided her upward, and held on until she had her cane in place.

"You are very sweet, and pretty, too. You single? I got a nephew about your age."

What is it with everyone trying to get me a date? "No, Ma'am," I lied. "I've got a boyfriend, but thanks anyway."

We said goodbye, and I strolled toward my car. At least the firm was getting some positive attention with our exploding-toilet commercials. Generating business while providing a public service seemed like a win-win to me.

#

The twins had their wide-screen set up on the front porch so that the screen faced my side. Neighbors brought their own chairs and gathered around both our porches. It was an eclectic group of people ranging in age from college students to retired adults, all united by their love for this city and our baseball team.

During the ninth inning, my cell phone rang. I didn't recognize the number.

"Hello."

"Is this Jessica Snow?"

"Yes, who's this?" I stepped off the porch.

"It's Olivia Metzger. Sorry to bother you, but I found something. I need to speak with you privately."

"Can you meet me in my office in the morning?"

"I'd like to talk with you tonight. I'm sorry, I know it's late, but I think this is important." Her breathing was labored and her voice rattled. She was scared. "Can I meet you somewhere? Anywhere that's convenient for you."

I had enjoyed a couple of beers watching the game and didn't want to drive. "I live in Fells Point. Can you come to my house?"

"Yes. That's perfect. Thank you."

I gave her the address and told her to park in any open spot she found on the street. The game had ended, and our porch party was dwindling. After saying proper good nights to the others, I told Mrs. B about the call from Olivia. "She's Harvey Metzger's wife."

"Isn't she a murder suspect?"

"O'Mallory isn't interested in her. I met her yesterday. She seems genuine, and she loved Harvey. I don't think she murdered him. She doesn't think Dawson did it, either. She wants to track down the real killer, so Harvey's life insurance will pay out. As long as she remains a suspect, they're holding the money."

"So she's not some floozy who cheated on her husband?"

"She cheated all right, but she said her marriage with Harvey had stalled and he didn't discourage her seeking affection elsewhere."

"Still, I don't like you being alone with her. What if she did murder her husband and plans to murder you too for sticking your nose in?"

"That's a little dramatic. She's harmless."

Mrs. Bianco reached into her housecoat and handed me her gun. "Take this. You may need it.."

"I can't take that. You know I don't know how to handle a gun."

"Yes. That is why you need me to teach you. Let me sit in on your meeting tonight. You can tell her I'm your secretary."

"Wearing a housecoat?"

"I'm not changing. If you make me change, I'll put on another housecoat."

"I'll let you sit in, but we're telling her the truth. That you're my friend and that Harvey lost your money, too. And that you're packing in case she tries to kill me."

When Olivia arrived, that's what I told her.

Olivia responded with a short, sad laugh. "I'm not a murderer."

"Jessica likes you, but I don't know you well enough to trust you yet. Keep your hands where I can see them." They narrowed their eyes at each other and lowered themselves into the two chairs flanking the coffee table.

"You said on the phone that you found something. What is it?"

"After I unpacked that giant suitcase, I went to store it in the guest-room closet. I noticed an old briefcase of Harvey's. It had been a gift from his first wife. I saw some papers in it. I took a closer look and"— her hands were shaking as she reached into her bag—"I found these."

I took the papers and examined them. A sick awareness took hold of my insides. The documents were identical to the financial statements that Dawson and Mrs. Bianco had shown me. What was unimaginable was the name on the statement and the amount of the initial deposit. The account belonged to Kevin O'Mallory and the deposit was for $300,000. My breathing halted, its pattern disrupted. I forced an inhale.

"What's wrong?" Mrs. Bianco leaned in toward me and scanned the papers. "Who's Kevin O'Mallory?"

"He's the lead detective working on finding Harvey Metzger's murderer."

"How's a detective come up with $300,000 cash?" Mrs. Bianco asked.

Off the top of my head, I could think of a couple of ways. "Maybe he inherited it. Or maybe he sold some real estate."

Olivia added, "Maybe he won it playing craps at the Horseshoe."

"Maybe he's a dirty cop and he stole it," Mrs. Bianco said.

Then it hit me. Why didn't I connect the dots sooner? O'Mallory, the East Side drug bust, the missing money, and the deposit into O'Mallory's account with Harvey. It was all connected somehow. And Franco? Franco's reaction at the trial when O'Mallory said there was only $30,000 found at the drug house. Was it Franco's money that went missing during the bust? The pieces were coming together. But how did O'Mallory's investment elude the authorities? There must have been some evidence in Harvey's office.

"Was O'Mallory there when they searched your house?" I asked Olivia.

"There was no 'they.' O'Mallory was alone. He handed me a warrant and went about searching Harvey's office. He said it was routine. All he took were paper files, Harvey's computer, and his iPad. He said the forensic accountants needed all the information so they could try to track down the money. The next day he called to ask if I was sure there weren't any other files in the house."

We sat immersed in our own thoughts for a while. O'Mallory didn't find what he was looking for during his solo search. He knew Harvey had records of his windfall investment somewhere and he had to find them. They were evidence of theft and murder. He'd need to destroy them. No wonder he had seemed so preoccupied and out of sorts when Helen and I spoke to him.

Olivia pointed to the file. "I can't keep these in my house. He may try to come back and search again."

"You should leave them with Jess," Mrs. Bianco said.

The sight of the documents and their implications turned my stomach. "I don't want them in my house either. If somehow they were found here I could be charged with withholding information pertinent to a murder investigation. I could lose my license."

Mrs. Bianco arranged the documents into a neat pile, folded them, and shoved them into the pocket of her housecoat. "I'll take them."

Olivia was playing with the straps on her Gucci handbag. "Thank you for meeting me here. You can see why I didn't want to call the cops."

"I'm glad you called me. Let's talk again tomorrow after I've had more time to process all this information and figure out the next step."

We stood to end the meeting. Mrs. Bianco looked at Olivia. She put her small, steady hand on Olivia's shoulder and said, "I'm sorry I didn't trust you at first. You're a nice lady. I'll take my hand off my gun, see?" She pulled her empty hand out of her housecoat pocket and waved it in the air.

Olivia located her keys and headed toward the door. "Thank you again for your help. Thank you, both." She gave us each a deliberate look and an affirmative nod and walked out into the night. Mrs. Bianco and I watched from the front porch until she entered her car and drove off.

This was an unlikely turn of events and an unlikely alliance. I had to tell Kari and Helen, but it was late, and I didn't want to discuss this over the phone. It would have to wait until tomorrow.

My sleep was interrupted by the sound of my phone ringing. The bedside clock read 3:15 a.m. This could not be good news.

I sat up in bed and answered. "Hello?"

"My house. My house is on fire." It was Olivia. She spoke through breathless sobs. "I was sleeping when the smoke detector went off. I went downstairs and Harvey's office was on fire."

"Are you okay?"

She ignored my question. "Jess, you know who did this. This is no accident."

I knew it was no accident. O'Mallory had started the fire to assure that his financial statements would never be found. "I'm on my way."

I did a quick change, throwing on a pair of black yoga pants and a dark purple T-shirt with the Ravens' logo on the front and bolted out the door.

Traffic was not an issue as I worked my way through Fells Point and onto the JFX. Three fire trucks and an ambulance were parked on the street in front of Olivia's house. Two TV news crew vans stood watch across the street. The sickening smell of smoke and charred wood filled the air. Olivia stood near the magnolia tree where Kari and I had parked a couple of days ago. She was with a middle-aged couple. The woman had her arm around Olivia and the man stood close by on the other side.

"Olivia, are you all right? I'm so sorry."

"Thank you for coming, Jess. These are my neighbors, the Hendersons. They live across the street." We exchanged perfunctory greetings. Olivia assured them she was OK, and I explained that I would take Olivia home with me. The Hendersons retreated and joined the other neighbors looking onto the tragedy.

"Where's Maria?" I asked.

"She had the night off and is staying with a friend."

The firemen continued to work on the house, but the immediacy of the situation had passed. The house was still standing. Its stone front looked untouched except all the windows were gone, and the frames were covered with soot that was blacker than black. An addition off the side of the house also lost its windows. The plastic siding looked like melted vanilla ice cream. I noticed Mark standing by the truck with John and Kyle, sorting through gear. Kyle recognized me and gave Mark a nudge. I issued a simple wave and he headed in my direction.

Before he could speak, I said, "I'm not stalking you. And I don't have a thing for fires. It's another coincidence. I swear." I gestured toward Olivia. "This is Olivia, the homeowner—a friend of mine."

He turned toward Olivia. "The fire was confined to the north side of the house, but I'm afraid the damage from the smoke is extensive. The investigator is on his way."

Olivia lifted her head. "Thank you."

Mark looked behind him. His pals were still busying themselves with the hoses and equipment. He took my hand. "Can I talk to you for a minute?"

I let Mark guide me away.

"I had fun the other night. I was going to call you yesterday, but didn't want to seem too pushy."

I nodded in agreement. "The 'day after' contact—always a tough call." He squeezed my hand. I shed my teasing tone. "I had a good time, too."

"Think we should try it again?"

"Yeah. I think so too."

We stopped at a place on the sidewalk away from the news people and the onlookers. I turned to him. He must have noticed the concern on my face. "Something wrong?"

"Remember the murder I told you about?"

"The Ponzi scheme guy, right?" So he had been listening.

"That's his widow."

He frowned. "Poor thing. Lost her husband, now her house." And he's sensitive, too.

"You'll think I'm all kinds of crazy for saying this, but I'm afraid the murder and this fire are linked, and I'm pretty sure I know who's responsible."

He looked at me with equal amounts of concern and confusion. I imagine he was trying to determine whether or not I was, in fact, a paranoid lunatic. "Have you talked to the police?"

I leaned into him and whispered, "No." I could smell his aftershave through the smoky scent on his gear. I loved the way he smelled. "The guy I suspect is a cop. I pieced things together a few hours ago. I know it sounds crazy, but I wanted someone else to know. His name's Kevin O'Mallory."

He took both my hands in his, peered down into my eyes, and said, "How can I help?"

My breathing slowed as I focused on his strong hands holding mine. "I'm still trying to process it. Right now, I'm too tired to formulate a plan."

We stood in silence for a few somber moments. Mark decided to lighten the mood. "So you're not stalking me then?"

"I'm not that crazy."

Kyle stood by the fire truck and called to him. "I better go." He gave my hand a gentle squeeze, kissed my forehead, and ran off toward the trucks. I rejoined Olivia. We watched the firemen finish loading the gear before heading for my car. As we drove off, I looked at Olivia's charred house and wondered how her homeowners' insurer would try to get out of paying for the damage.

CHAPTER TWENTY-SIX

Olivia spent the rest of night in my guest room. If the fire was intended to kill her, we had to assume there would be other attempts. It was best she stayed with me rather than a local relative where she might be tracked down. We didn't get back to sleep until about six. At eight, she joined me in the kitchen for coffee. I sent a group text to Dawson, Kari, and Marty that I would be late for work and would explain why later.

Olivia was wearing what she had gone to bed in last night before she escaped the fire—a pair of short, pink pajama bottoms with lace along the hem and a matching short-sleeve button-up top that didn't button all the way up. All her clothes had been ruined in the fire. I had little that would fit her. She was about two inches taller than I was and much better endowed upstairs and in her backyard. She was very fit from her recent obsession with Pilates. I was envious of her tall body and smooth curves.

"I need to get to the office this morning, but I don't want to leave you alone."

"I'll be fine. I've got to make some calls about the insurance on the house, and I need to buy some clothes."

"We can go through my closet."

We eyed each other's frames and laughed. "We can try," she said, patting her curvy hips.

I found a sundress that Olivia managed to squeeze her boobs into. We had the same size feet, so it was easy to outfit her in a pair of strappy sandals. She showered, borrowed my makeup, fussed a bit with her hair, and she was ready to face the day. I had the local news channel on while we got ready. The drive-by media was reporting that the fire had been caused by a faulty water heater.

I phoned Mrs. Bianco and told her what had happened. She hung up the phone and was at my door within thirty seconds. She pushed her way through the front room carrying a foil-wrapped package and headed back toward my kitchen where Olivia was pouring coffee. She unwrapped the foil to reveal her homemade banana bread. I handed her a knife and a cutting board. She sliced as she spoke. "Things tend to get a bit hairy when there's a dirty cop involved. You can't rely on anyone associated with the police department to help you."

I put a handful of napkins next to the bread, and we dove in. "I'm not going to ask for their help," I said with my mouth full. "I'm going to see Franco Giovanni."

"The mob guy?" Olivia asked.

"Alleged mob guy," I said, and wondered why I felt defensive. He's got an interest in O'Mallory, too. I think it has something to do with the drug money that was never recovered from the East Side drug bust. I think O'Mallory stole the money during the raid."

"And then he gave the money to my husband to invest," Olivia said.

"But the money belongs to Franco Giovanni," Mrs. Bianco added. "He's not a forgiving man."

"You know him?" Olivia asked.

"My late husband had some business dealings with him." Mrs. Bianco turned to me. "Franco would be interested to know about the large deposit that O'Mallory made. You go talk to him."

I left Mrs. Bianco and Olivia in my kitchen sipping coffee and eating banana bread.

It was past ten by the time I reached the office. Marty was in the conference room doing a deposition. Kari was stationed at the front desk. She told me Dawson was interviewing another client. It had big-case potential, and he didn't want to be disturbed. I was glad Marty and Dawson were busy because I didn't need them involved in this yet. I wanted to talk to Kari alone.

Kari put the answering service on and joined me in my office.

"What's going on? I don't like that look in your eyes."

"Last night, I got a call from Olivia. She came to my house because she had evidence linking O'Mallory to Harvey's death. O'Mallory was one of Harvey's investors. He made a deposit of $300,000, cash last May."

"How does a cop get hold of $300,000?"

"Exactly. You remember that Helen told us about the undercover work that O'Mallory did and the money that was never recovered? I think O'Mallory took the money and invested it with Harvey Metzger, and I think the money belonged to Franco Giovanni."

"Jesus, Mary, and Joe." Kari made the sign of the cross. "What are we going to do?"

"I'm going to talk to Franco."

"I'm going with you."

"No. You stay here. If Dawson asks where I am, cover for me. Tell him I'm at the courthouse."

"Shouldn't we tell him what's going on with O'Mallory?"

"No, the fewer people who know the better. Besides, Dawson's no good with a secret. We don't want O'Mallory knowing we suspect him."

The front door opened and Chip walked in.

"I've got some good news for you," he said.

"I sure could use some. Is it about Darnell?"

"Yes. He plead out. There's no need for Sharlyn to testify tomorrow."

Relief washed over me. I wanted to hug Chip, but I was still mad at him.

"Wow. That's great news, Chip. Thanks. Sharlyn will be so

relieved."

"It sure is," Kari said. "No more guns, no more snakes."

"Snakes?" Chip asked.

"Yeah. When the bullets didn't scare us off, Darnell set some snakes loose on us."

Chip cringed. "Can I talk to you privately?"

We went into my office and sat opposite each other in my guest chairs.

"I'm pretty sure I offended you last night. I'm sorry."

I wasn't ready to let him off the hook.

"You belittled my job."

"I didn't mean to. I was trying to compliment you. I think you'd make a great Assistant State's Attorney. You're a great personal injury attorney, too. It just came out all wrong. Forgive me?"

He seemed sincere and vulnerable, so I threw him a bone. "Sure. You're forgiven."

"There's something else." He handed me an envelope. I opened it and read the contents of a two-paragraph statement. It contained Darnell Black's notarized signature and the truth about his liability for Sharlyn's injuries.

I smiled as I read it and looked up at Chip. He was like a little boy waiting to be praised.

"Thank you. This is exactly what we needed. Now I could get Sharlyn her money."

He shrugged like it was nothing, but I knew that what he had done for me was a bit unorthodox. He didn't need to do this as part of the plea deal, but he did, and I was grateful.

"Sharlyn will be thrilled. It's what she deserves, you know. She's on a good path now. That money will get her out of that neighborhood and away from Darnell's people."

"I know. That's why I did it."

"I guess I owe you one."

#

I called Franco and told him I had a matter to discuss with him, but didn't want to give him the details over the phone. He told me to meet him at Aldo's at noon for lunch.

There were only a handful of patrons there when I arrived. The bartender recognized me and waived me back toward Franco's rear booth.

The players were assembled like last time. Franco was sitting alone reading the *New York Times*. Elvis and Paulie were in an adjacent booth playing cards.

"Thank you for meeting me."

"I'm intrigued by your need to see me. I hope this is not about our settlement arrangement. We had a deal and deals are to be kept."

"It's not about that. A deal's a deal, like you said, and I will always keep my word. This is a different matter. It's an issue involving theft and murder. I would go to the police, but, you see, I know there is at least one dirty cop involved. I'm coming to you because I think you know this cop and I think it's your money he stole."

Franco peered over his reading glasses at me. His expression gave nothing away. "I like how you get right to the point." He folded his newspaper, slowly and methodically, exacting each crease like a crude origami. I assumed he was processing the bombshell I'd just dropped on him. The silence was torturous. He took his reading glasses off and laid them on top of the paper.

"How do I know you're not wired?"

I hadn't anticipated this question, but I should have. I was indirectly accusing him of being involved in the East Side drug network. "I'm not wired." I nodded to the security twins. "You can have them search me if you want."

Franco turned toward the other table and gave a subtle chin up to his men. Elvis stood. I scooted out from the booth and handed him my messenger bag, which he gave to Paulie. He dumped it on their table and started rooting through it. I held my arms out to the sides like I'd seen in the movies and steeled myself against the personal intrusion. Working from the top, Elvis patted me down with two quick and firm hands. It was over within a few uncomfortable seconds. He gestured for me to take a seat. Paulie finished with my purse and returned it.

"What do you know about the money?" Franco asked.

"You as much as told me by your reaction to O'Mallory's testimony at the trial. I thought you'd burst a vein when O'Mallory said they found thirty grand. I hope you don't play poker. You have a terrible poker face."

"Very perceptive, counselor. What else you got?"

"I haven't figured out how he got away with the money, but I know where it ended up." I retrieved the manila envelope from my bag and handed it to him. It contained the financial documents Olivia had found. Franco opened the envelope, put the papers on the table in front of him, and picked up his reading glasses.

"Where did you get these?"

"Metzger's wife Olivia found them hidden in a closet away from all the other documents. She brought them to me. Obviously, this implicates O'Mallory in Harvey Metzger's murder. It seems to suggest he somehow got hold of your money sometime before, during, or after the East Side bust."

He continued to examine the documents. "It looks like $300,000 in cash was deposited about three weeks after the bust. Where's the rest of it?"

"You mean there was more?"

"At least double that. Which means that O'Mallory is still sitting on a shitload of my cash."

This news unbalanced me. I thought I was on top of the facts. My confidence wiggled, but I stayed focused. "Or he had a partner in crime who has the other half of the money."

"You mean he wasn't alone on this?" Franco spoke between clenched teeth. He leaned across the table, his eyes challenging me.

"I don't know. I'm trying to piece it together. I can't go to the police or DEA. I don't know who I can trust."

His jaw relaxed and a smile formed on his face. "But you can trust me?"

I hadn't thought about that. Could I trust him? He was a reputed mob leader but otherwise appeared to be a fair and savvy businessman. I could trust him as long as I didn't cross him, and I had no intention of doing that.

"Yeah. I trust you."

He gave me a challenging stare.

"Look," I said. "I don't know you well. But what I have learned from our recent business dealing is that you're a fair man. A man who has to watch out and protect his own interests and reputation. You can't let O'Mallory get away with stealing half a million dollars from you, and I can't let him get away with murdering Metzger and hanging it on his wife, or Dawson, or anyone else. So we kinda have similar goals here. Let's figure out a way to get what we both want."

He sat back. He raised a hand to get the server's attention and, without asking me, he ordered us lunch. While we waited for the food, he asked how I liked being a personal injury attorney.

"I like my work," I told him. "Even though it can be distasteful at times."

"Young lady, you don't know from distasteful."

Our food arrived. It was served family style. The server put bowls of pasta, meat sauce, and antipasto salad on our table and repeated the process for the bodyguards. Franco took a plate, filled it with a sampling of everything, and handed it to me. We ate in silence for a couple of minutes.

"So how do we take down O'Mallory?"

Franco's response was rapid and matter-of-fact. "We'll need to snatch O'Mallory off the street, put some pressure on him, and get him to confess."

"Sounds like you've done this kind of thing before."

"Not as often as you'd think, but we're pretty good at it."

It occurred to me that Franco's kind of justice was quite different than mine. Justice for him would be getting hold of the rest of the money that was stolen from him and putting a bullet between O'Mallory's eyes. I couldn't be a part of that.

"Maybe I've seen too many gangster movies, but I can't be part of the torture and murder of a cop."

"We don't murder cops. That brings on too much heat. And we don't have to torture him. You're gonna do that."

I choked on a mouthful of noodles and reached for my napkin. He clarified, "Your kind of torture will be mental, not physical. All you have to do is show him these papers"—he held up the statements—"and tell him that I want to know where the rest of my money is. If he doesn't tell you, he'll get a personal visit from my friends and me."

"How do I know he won't try to kill me?"

"You'll be safe. Make it clear to him that you're under my protection and that if anything were to happen to you, he would find himself missing a few limbs before I toss him into the harbor. You'll have him meet you in your office in the middle of the day and have your coworkers within earshot."

"Why should he confess anything to me?"

"Because you'll make it clear that he can either deal with you and he can take his chances with the judicial system, or he can deal with me and my brand of justice."

"Okay. That's pretty compelling. I got this."

As I was leaving Aldo's, my phone rang. Mark's name appeared on the display. Not for one second did I consider answering it. I couldn't tell him about the plan I had devised with Franco. He'd either try to talk me out of it or insist on being there. I let it go to voicemail. I'd call him later today after it was over.

CHAPTER TWENTY-SEVEN

We decided that Franco and his men would be waiting in their car outside my office. Franco had Paulie hide a microphone on my desk so they could listen to my conversation with O'Mallory, in case something went wrong. Kari was positioned at the front desk. Marty and Dawson were expected to be in court for the rest of the afternoon. Helen Holman was tucked away in the conference room and would join Kari after O'Mallory was in my office and the door was closed.

I conned O'Mallory into making a house call by telling him that I had new information pertaining to Olivia and Juan Carlos that was proof-positive of their involvement in the murder. He hustled right over.

"What's this all about? You said you have another lead on the Metzger murder."

"Yes, I do. Please have a seat." I sat behind my desk. He sat in a chair facing me. I rested my hand on the folder containing Harvey's documents.

"I have to be honest with you. None of us are very impressed with your detective work on this matter."

He sat on the edge of his chair and leaned in towards me. "You've got a lot of nerve. What do you know about investigating a murder?"

I took that as a rhetorical question and continued. "It seemed too easy to focus on Dawson. I couldn't understand why you weren't investigating other investors."

"How do you know I wasn't? I talked to a few who were local."

"But you didn't interview this one." I used the forefinger of my right hand to slide the file toward him, another trick I learned from *Law & Order*. I thought it exuded calm and confidence. I watched as he opened the file and examined its contents. His jaw muscles went rigid and his breathing stalled. A brief stillness followed. He tossed the documents on my desk like they were meaningless. "So what if I was an investor? This doesn't mean I killed Metzger."

"You found out that Metzger lost your money and you shot him."

"You should stick to chasing ambulances." He laughed and rose from his chair. I decided to play the rest of my cards.

"I know where you got the money to invest with Harvey. Where's the rest of it?"

"What're you talking about? Harvey lost it all."

I pressed the intercom button. "Kari, can you please send in Helen."

"Helen?"

"Helen Holman. You know, the investigative reporter who covered your East Side drug bust." His body went rigid again.

Helen glided through the door. "You should sit back down," she told him.

He held the armrest and lowered himself into the chair slowly, like an arthritic senior. His eyes scanned the floor, failing to focus. Kari stayed posted at my door.

Helen took the chair next to O'Mallory and turned it toward him. Leaning in, she said, "This is going to make a great story. A crooked cop, drug money, mob involvement, and murder. It's a reporter's dream. You're in a lot of trouble, mister. I know that there was over half a million dollars in that house the night you raided it. I also know that you gave Harvey Metzger three hundred thousand in cash three weeks after the bust. Now the money you gave Metzger is gone. Where's the rest of it?'

He raised his head, sat up straight, and looked from me to Helen and back again like we were bugs and he had a can of Raid. "Is this a shakedown? Are you two after the rest of the money? This is unbelievable. A lawyer and a reporter. You are both a disgrace to your professions. Why should I tell you where the money is?"

"Because its rightful owner wants it back." I gave him my best 'I got ya' smile.

His blustery indignation gave way to palpable fear.

"It can't be," he said. "You can't be working for Giovanni."

He stood and began to pace the room. His firearm was holstered at his side. Mumbling to himself, he ran his fingers through his hair. A band of sweat framed his hairline. He was trapped, and a trapped man could do anything. I thought this might be a good time to reveal our strength.

"Take a look out the window." I pulled back the curtains. "Do you recognize that town car?" He looked out the window, then pulled back, ducking out of the way.

"Oh shit. What does he want?"

"You know what he wants," Helen said. "He wants the rest of his money, and he wants your head on a platter. But Jess got him to promise that if you tell us where the money is and they can recover it, then he'll lose interest in your head."

He turned to me. "How'd you get him to agree to that?"

"He's a businessman. He's not a bad person," I said. O'Mallory gave me raised eyebrows. "Okay, so he's a little bit of a bad person, but he doesn't like killing people. He wants his money. You're just a messy problem that I told him I would handle."

"Handle? How're you going to handle me?"

"I've got a friend in the State's Attorney's office who'd be very interested in all this. Then Helen's going to write this story and sell it to the highest bidder. You'll be behind bars soon. Your story will make headlines. But at least you won't be dead." I gestured toward the town car.

O'Mallory continued to pace and mumble to himself. After a few quiet moments, he said, "The money is in a storage unit." He fumbled in his pocket and pulled something out. "Here's the key. The key chain has the address. It's building seven." He handed it to me.

I examined the plastic marker attached to the key ring—Easy Access Self Storage in Arbutus, about twenty minutes from here. I opened my office door, handed Kari the key, and asked her to walk it out to the town car. Helen and I went to the window to watch the exchange. O'Mallory peered over our shoulders. Elvis was in the driver's seat and took the key from Kari. Paulie stepped out of the front passenger seat and followed Kari back to our office.

He sat in the reception area and picked up a three-month-old *People* magazine, effectively trapping O'Mallory in my office until we got word that the money was retrieved from the storage unit. Kari went to sit next to him, a little too close.

O'Mallory resumed his seat and sunk into it. His face was pale and shiny from perspiration. "What's Giovanni going to do after he gets the money?"

"He'll call here and let me know his interest in you is over. That's my favor to you. My interest in this is to nail you for murdering Metzger. I want Dawson and Olivia's names cleared."

He sat upright. "I'm telling you. I did not murder him. I may be a crooked cop, but I'm not a murderer. I found out about Harvey's Ponzi scheme along with everyone else, except Dawson. Dawson was the first."

Helen paced behind O'Mallory. "We're convinced you killed Harvey, but let's pretend you didn't. Who do you think did it?"

He shook his head. "I don't know. All my leads were dead ends."

"So, you know it wasn't Dawson."

"He could have returned later to off Metzger, but my gut tells me he didn't."

"Then why did you arrest him?" I asked.

"I had to arrest someone."

"Shit, O'Mallory. You're a real asshole."

Kari came through the door. "They found the money. Franco said the piece of shit can go."

O'Mallory stood up. His eyes were pinned to mine. "Just like that? I can go?"

"You can go, but you won't get far." I picked up the phone on my desk. "I'm calling my friend at the State's Attorney's office. They'll be hunting you down before you hit the JFX."

He bolted, knocked Kari out of the way, then slowed as he passed Paulie. Once he was sure Paulie wasn't going to pop him, he took off through the front door and disappeared into the humid shadows of the city.

I called Chip and told him what I had learned about the missing drug money and O'Mallory's involvement and recent confession. I explained that both Kari and Helen Holman had witnessed the confession and that I had documents that showed he'd invested a windfall of money. This was enough to get Chip's attention.

"We had a feeling it was an inside job," Chip said. "But we didn't get anywhere with our investigation. I'll call the Commissioner. He'll be able to mobilize the other agencies. Send me a copy of the documents so I can justify taking action. I'll keep you posted."

I called Mark next, but it went straight to voicemail. I left a message saying that my hunch about O'Mallory was half right and told him not to worry.

It was super-sleuth work. We had coerced a Baltimore City detective into admitting to stealing gobs of money from the clutches of a mobster. After we passed around our mutual congratulations, there was silence. I realized it was a hollow victory. There had been no arrest and no confession to killing Metzger. Sure we had recovered mob money, but that's not an accomplishment to be shared in polite circles.

"We've still got work to do, ladies," I said. "At this point, we've served Franco's agenda, but not our own. We have O'Mallory dead to rights on the theft charge, but we still haven't caught a murderer. I was naive to think it would be that easy."

"It's only that easy on the cops shows," Kari said. "This real-life shit is tricky."

Helen nodded. "True, but you all did some good work here. You exposed a dirty cop. That's a victory in anyone's book." She headed for the door. "Plus, I got an exclusive. I'm off to write my story."

Chip called back to let me know everything was in place. "We've got our people on notice, as well as the DEA unit that worked on the bust originally. O'Mallory's identity is all over the wires. Every law enforcement officer and TSA agent knows his face. They've flagged his passport. He's not going anywhere."

"That's great, Chip. Thank you."

"I'll keep you posted." He disconnected.

I knew I should have been excited about my part in O'Mallory's impending capture, but the truth was, we were no closer to finding Metzger's murderer. How did I get so off track? I had made too many assumptions about the fact that O'Mallory was one of Metzger's investors. From that fact alone, I concluded he had both stolen the money *and* killed Harvey. It was possible that he was a thief, but not a murderer. I had to consider the possibility that someone else murdered Harvey.

#

The air was heavy with humidity as I cruised toward home. My timing was bad. Another Orioles game had ended, leaving beer-bloated baseball fans to spill onto the crosswalks. They formed an endless swell of orange and black that did not let up for three traffic light rotations. Even though I was anxious to get home and watch the finale of *Next Food Network Star,* I watched them with patience, enjoying the spirit of the city. Devoted baseball and football fans were a united force— part of the charm of Baltimore. I included myself among them. They ambled along inches from my front bumper. Eventually, the green light coincided with a brief ebb of the pedestrian flow and I drove on to the next block, and so on, until finally reaching my neighborhood.

It was late, so parking near my row house was impossible. I circled the block twice before settling on a spot two blocks south. As I walked home, I took stock of where things were and concluded that everything was pretty messed up. For all my efforts, I had nothing. Except for maybe a mob guy who owes me one. I supposed that was something.

I reached my house and noticed Mrs. Bianco's front porch light was off. Her porch swing was vacant. At this hour, I was not surprised that she had turned in, but I was surprised that her porch light wasn't on. I always counted on it to guide me up my own stairs. As I reached for the handrail, I felt a presence behind me and a sudden pressure in my back. I couldn't see him, but I knew it was O'Mallory. He wrapped his fingers around my forearm, squeezing through to the bone. Fear gripped me almost as hard when I felt his gun at my spine.

"Keep moving, counselor. Get up the stairs."

He pushed me forward. The fear turned to anger. Sure I was scared. I was Freddy-Kruger-at-my-door scared. But I'd had enough of O'Mallory. I wasn't going to make it easy for him. I went limp like a rag doll and crumbled to the ground. My legs bent out to my left side, my right hip hit the cement sidewalk, and my head flopped forward. He held his grip on my left arm. My upper arm was parallel to the ground, and my hand and forearm were perpendicular. I must have looked like a life-sized marionette.

"Get the hell up or I'll put a bullet in your head."

The barrel of his gun found its way from the small of my back to the side of my dangling head. I moved my feet in an effort to get them back under my hips so I could stand. Rising, I heard the screechy sound of an MTA bus coming to a stop at the curb. Delroy. Please let Delroy be out for a late-night ride.

O'Mallory heard the bus, too, and tried to look nonchalant. He let go of my left arm and spun me around, so I was facing him. He smiled down at me and brought me into a giant bear hug. My arms hung straight down at my side.

"Don't move a fucking inch."

I managed to turn my head toward the bus. There he was. Delroy! He looked confused to see me standing there in an awkward embrace with this man. O'Mallory held me until he heard the bus pull off. Then he grabbed my right arm with his left hand, spun me around, and pulled me up the steps. I had to signal my distress to Delroy. I put my left hand to the side of my head, my forefinger and thumb forming the classic gun shape, and shot myself in the head with my finger pistol. My last hope was that Delroy saw, and that he would do something to save me.

We reached the top step. I stumbled, fell forward, and pulled down the side table that housed my sole plant, a cactus. It hit the cement floor and shattered. I hated to sacrifice it, but I wanted the sound of breaking ceramic to awaken Mrs. Bianco.

"You're a fucking disaster. Get up." He yanked me to my feet again, and this time he put the gun to my gut. "Find your keys and open the damn door."

Once we were inside, he shoved me into a chair and drew the curtains on the two windows facing the street. He either failed to notice or didn't care that the curtains were merely sheers. At night, with the lights on inside, anyone standing on the sidewalk could make out silhouettes. I pull down the horizontal blinds most evenings, but not tonight. After his careless drawing of my curtain sheers, he took a seat opposite me. His chest was heaving like he'd dragged an elephant inside.

"Don't think I don't know you pulled that shit on purpose. The rag-doll act, tripping up the stairs. I should have put a bullet in you."

"You're supposed to be halfway across the state by now. What the hell are you still doing here? What is it you want from me?"

"You're my insurance, counselor. The feds have blocked all the roads leading out of the city. I'm a wanted man. And I'm not so sure Franco isn't done with me. He's not one to forgive and forget, you know. You got any beer? Whiskey or something?"

"I've got some Corona in the fridge. Help yourself."

He pointed the gun toward me and then toward the kitchen. I rose to my feet and headed for the kitchen with him right behind. I grabbed a beer and handed it to him with shaky hands. We reversed direction and headed back out to the front room, where he motioned with the gun for me to sit.

"So what's your plan?" I asked.

"Don't ask me so many fucking questions." He massaged the area around his eyebrows with his free hand and struggled to keep one eye pinned on me. The gun was hanging heavy in his hand. He was unraveling. Why not help him along?

"It was one question, asshole."

His hand stopped their massaging motion. "Asshole. You're calling me an asshole? You conspire with a mob boss to get me to confess to stealing the drug money. You accuse me of murder. You can't even walk up your own stairs without having me drag you to your feet, and you call me an asshole."

"Okay. Since you're holding the gun, I'll stop calling you an asshole."

We sat in silence for a few minutes while he downed his beer.

"If you didn't kill Harvey, then who did?"

"I told you. I don't fuckin' know. How should I know?"

"Because you're the detective. You must have some idea who did it."

"Look, I went through the motions. I followed a lead or two, but my head wasn't in it. I was killing time until I could grab the money and lose myself in Morocco for a while. Thanks to you, I still have to lose myself, but without the money."

"I didn't mean to uncover your colossal corruption. I was just looking for a murderer. If you had been doing your job then maybe I wouldn't have stumbled on your little secret. So you see, it's all actually your fault."

"Right. It's my fault you're a real pain in the ass."

"I have to use the bathroom."

"Where is it?"

"Some detective you are. We walked past it on our way to the kitchen. It's the open door on the right."

He stood with his gun at his side and walked sideways to the bathroom door. He peeked inside, then waved for me to get up. I stood in the hallway as he looked through the cabinets and drawers of my tiny powder room, all the while with the gun trained on me.

He stepped out of the bathroom and waved me in.

"Keep the door open."

"What the hell.? No way I'm keeping the door open."

"Then there's no way you're taking a leak."

My bladder left me no time to negotiate.

"Fine, but at least position yourself so you can't see in."

He took a step back toward the living room and looked toward the back door. He couldn't see me from that angle. I fumbled with my pants and assumed a position on the commode. I had just finished washing my hands when *ktaashh*. My front windows exploded. Water rushed past the bathroom door through the narrow hall. O'Mallory screamed. I peeked out and saw his feet fly up, sending him headfirst past the bathroom door and into the back door.

A powerful geyser pummeled him, pinned him down, then suddenly stopped. I stepped out. He wasn't moving. My front door crashed open. Mrs. Bianco rushed in brandishing her handgun like she'd been FBI-trained. She spotted me in the bathroom doorway. "Get back, Jess."

I complied and saw her march past me. "Don't move." O'Mallory remained a huddled mass on the floor. He must have lost his gun while he surfed through the hall because he didn't attempt any defense. Mark entered next and rushed toward me. His fellow firefighters, John and Kyle, dashed past him toward Mrs. Bianco and O'Mallory.

Mark took me by my shoulders and pulled me into his soggy arms. "Are you alright?"

I was trembling. "Yes. I'm fine." We turned toward the others. Mrs. Bianco's gun stayed trained on O'Mallory. She did not waiver. She pulled a zip tie out of her housecoat and handed it to Kyle. "Do you always carry one of these with you?" he asked.

"It's smart. Never know when one will come in handy." She reached into her housecoat again. Duct tape, too."

"I don't think we'll need the duct tape," Kyle said. He secured O'Mallory's hands behind his back. "You can put your gun away now.

O'Mallory offered no resistance. He sat mumbling to himself.

I looked up at Mark. "How did you know I was in trouble?"

"It was Delroy." He nodded his head toward the living room. Delroy was standing there, watching me with wide eyes. I peeled myself away from Mark and went to join Delroy. The floor was covered with water. My feet flew up and I landed on my ass. Delroy reached down to give me a hand, but his feet came out from under him, too, and he landed by my side. "Damn Sperry's. These shoes are supposed 'ta be water shoes."

Mark pulled us up, and we patted at our soggy clothes. I turned back to Delroy. "Tell me what you did."

"I knew you needed help, so I called Kari."

"And Kari called me at the firehouse," Mark added. "I knew we couldn't call 911. We had to act fast. John and Kyle were with me at the station. We grabbed the truck and headed over here. Mrs. Bianco was standing on her porch with her finger on the trigger when we arrived. We could see through the curtains that he had a gun on you."

Mrs. Bianco looked at me with concern. "I heard a crash on your porch. I looked out and saw your cactus had fallen, and the pot had broken. You wouldn't have left it there and gone along inside. I knew something was wrong. That asshole is lucky these firefighters showed up when they did because I was seconds away from blowing his head off."

I found my phone and called Chip. After listening to my version of events, he sounded concerned. "Jess, I'm sorry. I had no idea it would come to that. I should have protected you. I should have assigned security."

"Nobody anticipated this. Besides, I'm fine."

Chip said he'd contact the police commissioner to arrange for the transport of O'Mallory. As I hung up, Kari bounded into the house. "I'm late. What'd I miss?" She looked at me. "You okay?" Then she looked at Mark, then back to me again. "Oh yeah, girl. You're okay. Now tell me what happened."

I explained the kidnapping and water rescue to Kari. John and Kyle grabbed O'Mallory and hauled him out to the front porch. He stared at the floor and let the men escort him away.

I surveyed my home. My front window was broken and the living room furniture was tossed about. All of it was drenched. The water took a straight path down the hall and to the kitchen. It was subsiding, but I was concerned about where it was going. Mrs. Bianco opened the basement door, peeked down, closed the door, and said, "I'm going to call my insurance company. Jess, you pack up some things and come stay with me until we get this mess cleaned up." She sloshed out the front door. Delroy started to follow her out.

"Wait, Delroy," I said. I walked toward him and gave him a hug. "Thank you. You saved my life."

"Ah, it was nothing."

Mark approached us and reached out to shake Delroy's hand. "It wasn't nothing. You saw Jess was in trouble and you took action. You're the true hero here."

"Is there a reward?" Delroy asked with pleading eyes. There was a second or two of awkward silence, and then he smiled wide. "Ha! I had ya going there for a minute." He was still laughing as he left.

The police commissioner arrived, and I gave him the play-by-play of events. A pair of DEA guys took O'Mallory into custody. They lowered him into an unmarked sedan. He seemed a shell of a man. I didn't know what would happen to him next.

Mark took me in his arms again. "Why don't you get your things and I'll walk you over to Mrs. Bianco's."

I felt a shallow victory as I headed toward the stairs. I was pleased to have played a part in taking down a dirty cop, but I couldn't be proud. The real murderer was still out there, and I was determined to find him.

CHAPTER TWENTY-EIGHT

I awoke to the smell of sausage browning on the stove and followed my nose to the kitchen.

"Good morning," I said to Mrs. Bianco, who was tending the sausage skillet and scrambling eggs at the same time.

"Ah, Jessica, how you feel this morning?"

"I feel pretty good." And it was true. I felt relieved in a strange way. I guess that's what happens when you get a good night's sleep after your life is threatened and you're saved by your friends.

I helped myself to some coffee. "Thank you for letting me stay here last night. I'm sorry about the water damage next door."

"You did me a favor. I called the insurance company. They are coming out today. It's all covered. We'll get a brand-new wood floor for nothing. I guess I'm on the bright side."

"The saying is 'there's always a bright side.'"

"Ahh. And I'm on it."

Mrs. B and I ate breakfast together. The sausage was crispy and the eggs were loaded with cheese. She was my kind of cook. After we ate, I helped with the dishes and took a shower. I was heading out the door when my mom called. "Hi, Mom."

I had decided not to tell my mother about the kidnapping last night.

It would only fuel her concern for my safety and give her more reason to suggest I find another job. While I was rattled by what happened, I remained calm and confident. I had developed a second family here in the city. I found comfort in it, like I belonged.

"What's up?" I asked her.

"I wanted to let you know the plumber came yesterday and installed the new parts for our toilets. We're safe now. He was a nice young man. Single. Good job. I thought maybe you two would hit it off."

Good grief.

"Thanks, Mom. But I'm kind of seeing someone."

"Why didn't you tell me? When do we get to meet him?"

"It's still new. If things work out, I'll bring him by the house sometime soon."

"Okay, dear. I'd like to hear all about him, but right now your dad and I have to get ready for the funeral."

"What funeral?"

"Mr. Marcone."

"Who's that?"

"You know, the Marcones. You went to school with their daughter, Chantel."

"I went to high school with Chantel Devista."

"Oh, right. She kept her birth father's last name when her mom married Mr. Marcone. Anyway, he lost a long battle with cancer and the service is this morning."

Chantel's dad died? Had I known her father was at death's door, I never would have given her name to the media. I felt terrible having added to her stress. I made a mental note to apologize to her, or at least send a condolence card.

#

A lot had happened, but Harvey's murderer remained elusive. I tracked down Howdy Doody to see where things stood with the investigation.

"We've charged O'Mallory with the murder," he said. "I thought you knew that."

"No, I didn't. I thought he was being charged with grand theft and kidnapping."

"We threw in the murder charge, too."

"Just like that? You're making a mistake. The real murderer is still out there."

Not long after I hung up with the detective, I received a call from O'Mallory's attorney. Now that O'Mallory was on the hot seat for the murder, he'd developed a renewed interest in discovering the real killer. I had the upper hand here. The man who had kidnapped me, assaulted me, and threatened my friends was now seeking my help. I'd be tempted to refuse if it wasn't for my desire to clear Dawson's name and get Olivia her insurance money. So I went to see the scumbag.

The prison was like the ones you see in the movies. An institutional building with pasty-faced guards carrying weapons, drunk on power and trying not to look bored. A pimple-faced guard who looked like he wasn't even old enough to attend prom was posted at the front desk. I glided over, trying to look like I'd done this a dozen times, and signed the clipboard.

"What're you doing? That clipboard's for lawyers. This one's for girlfriends and other visitors." He pointed to a second clipboard.

I reached into my bag for my business card. "I am a lawyer. I'm here to see Kevin O'Mallory."

He studied me, trying to reimagine me as a lawyer. I gave him my billboard smile and recognition registered on his face.

"Oh yeah, I know you. I saw that exploding-toilet commercial you did and checked out my toilets right away. Mine were fine, but my Aunt Mae's was one with the defective part. She was so grateful that we discovered it before her bathroom got blown to pieces."

"I'm glad I was able to help." I handed him my business card. "Keep me in mind if you need legal assistance."

"I'll call for O'Mallory to be transported to the visitors' lounge. You can go wait there." He pointed to a set of barred doors that buzzed as I approached them. I walked through and was met by another guard. "Hey, Larry," my new friend called out to the second guard. "She's going back to see O'Mallory. She's Jessica Snow, that television lawyer." Larry was unimpressed. He greeted me with a cold stare and told me to follow him.

Visitor's lounge was a misnomer. There was nothing lounge-like about it. Toward the back was a row of partitioned desktops with clear Plexiglas fronts that divided a similar set of desktops on the other side. A corded phone was located on the left partition wall of each side. Plastic chairs with metal legs were positioned at each desk. There was only one other visitor. A woman who appeared to be in her sixties was looking through the glass at a young man who could have been her son. They were quiet and somber.

To the right were two glassed-in conference-type rooms. I was guided to one of the conference rooms. The decor was also cold and uncomfortable. The large table had a softball-sized eye-hook that was bolted to the center, and the table legs were bolted to the floor. The eye-hook had a set of handcuffs locked onto it. I took my seat at the table. Larry positioned himself outside the door.

I watched O'Mallory as he was escorted down the hall. He seemed to have aged five years since yesterday. The bright-orange prison jumpsuit he was wearing was a startling sign of how far he had fallen. His hands were cuffed in front of him. Larry intercepted O'Mallory from the other guard, brought him into the room, and secured him to the eye-hook on the table by clamping the two sets of cuffs together. There was silence during this process. Larry left the room and positioned himself outside, staring in.

"You must have told them you were representing me. Otherwise, we wouldn't have been given this room."

"They knew I was a lawyer. I let them assume the rest."

"Well played."

"Look. I'm not going to pretend to be nice to you. I'm still kinda pissed about last night. Why I should help you?"

"You're the only one who wants to know who really killed Metzger. Don't you want to clear your boss's name."

"Okay, tell me what you've held back."

"I was there that night."

"The night Harvey was killed?"

He nodded. "I saw Dawson leave in his Mercedes as I arrived. He didn't see me. I went to have a talk with Metzger, but he wasn't himself. He was nervous and agitated. I assumed it had to do with something he discussed with Dawson. My visit wasn't long. He poured himself a bourbon when I arrived and poured a second one as I was leaving."

"What was it you needed to talk to him about?"

"I heard he was spending a lot of time at the Horseshoe, and I wanted to make sure he wasn't gambling away my money. I didn't realize he had lost it. But here's the important thing. There was someone else there that night. The night Harvey was killed."

"Who?"

"Chantel Devista."

"Stuart Milligan's secretary?"

"Could there be more than one?"

"What was she doing there?"

"I saw her there a couple of times when I was going over my portfolio with Harvey. She entered through the side door to the kitchen as I was leaving out the front. She's dating Maria, the housekeeper."

My mouth fell open. I hadn't seen that coming. "So Dawson was there, and you were there, and Chantel was there. Was Maria there?"

"I didn't see Maria."

"So, let's say Chantel murdered Harvey. What was her motive?"

"I don't know. I didn't have time to follow that angle. Maybe it had nothing to do with the money. Maybe she was protecting Maria. If Maria is illegal, then maybe Harvey found out and threatened to turn her in. Or maybe Harvey had a thing for Maria and threatened Chantel to keep her hands off. I have no idea. That's why I need you to look into it."

Larry came in. "Time's up."

O'Mallory looked at me with desperation in his eyes. "Will you please follow up on that angle? Let me know what you find."

This guy had some nerve calling in a favor. "You're not in a position to ask me for my help." I stood to exercise my freedom to leave.

"But you have to help. You're a lawyer."

That got a laugh out of Larry.

#

Kari was busy updating our computer files when I returned to the office.

"We've never had so many files. Between the stuff you keep bringing in and all the new criminal cases, we're in uncharted territory. I may need an assistant. I was thinking of getting one of them college interns. They work for free, you know."

I had done an internship in college during the Fall of my senior year with the legal department of a real-estate investment company. It served to teach me that I didn't want to work in the legal department of any large company. The lawyers there were strapped to their desks shuffling contracts. There weren't even any field trips to the property sites. All I did was fetch coffee, store files in the basement, retrieve files from the basement, and pick up the vice president's dry cleaning. I liked picking up the dry cleaning because it got me out of the building and the cleaners was next to a Quiznos. I picked up lunch there almost every day. I missed Quiznos.

"I don't have time to think about an intern now. I got a lead on Harvey's murder and I need your help."

"What's up?"

I explained what O'Mallory had told me about Chantel and Maria. I also shared my concern that O'Mallory was still lying, and that he might be trying to pin the murder on someone else. I had several unanswered questions but didn't know where to start.

"We could start here," Kari said. She shuffled through the mess of files on her desk to pull out a large manila envelope. It had been hand-delivered and had no address, just my name. "Helen dropped this off first thing this morning."

I opened the envelope and pulled out a small stack of papers. Kari continued. "She said it's copies of everything that O'Mallory had in his file on Harvey's murder."

I leafed through it, looking for the list of investors, which I considered a list of suspects. I knew I wouldn't find Chantel's name there. She had a secretary's salary. I scanned the list, hoping to see a name I might recognize. My second time through, I saw it. It was the name my mother spoke this morning: Marcone.

"Come on," I said to Kari. "We're going to a funeral."

"Why? I hate funerals."

I explained that Chantel's stepfather had passed away. "Look," I said, pointing to his name. "He invested his money with Harvey."

Kari put the answering service on. I locked the front door and we hustled out the back.

"I'll drive," I said.

"Oh no, you won't. Last time I got in your car, I was attacked by snakes. I'm driving."

I looked up the funeral location on my cell phone. It was at a church on Roland Avenue, a few minutes up the road. As we drove north, I applied logic to the relevant facts surrounding the murder and churned it all around in my head. Nothing cohesive formed. I was on the cusp of something, but there were a few pieces missing. I was hoping to find one of those missing pieces at the funeral. I wanted to see Chantel and her mother, and Maria. Maybe they'd give something away. It was arguable that a funeral was not the place to carry on an investigation, so I hoped my mother wouldn't see me.

By the time we got to the church, the service was in full swing. We took a seat in the rear pew and scanned the crowd. Mr. Marcone had been a popular guy. I recognized many of the parents from our Mount Washington neighborhood. And then I spotted Olivia. It shouldn't have surprised me that she was there. She must have known the Marcones. I could see Chantel up front. Maria and Stuart Milligan sat on either side of her. Where was Mrs. Marcone?

The service dragged on to the point where I needed to get some fresh air. I nudged Kari, who had fallen asleep. She awoke with a loud intake of air. A few heads turned toward us. I signaled for her to follow me. As I pushed the large door open, its metal hinges creaked like a clap of thunder. The music stopped, and this time all heads turned toward us. I caught Olivia's eye gave her an imploring look and motioned to the door. Kari and I found a shady spot under a dogwood tree. Moments later, Olivia joined us.

"You two sure know how to get attention." She laughed. "It's a shame about Mr. Marcone. Poor Chantel." She lowered her head and made the sign of the cross. "To lose both your parents in the same week. So sad."

Both her parents! "What happened to Mrs. Marcone?"

"Oh. You don't know? She's in hospice care. Not expected to make it through the week."

I knew right then that it was, in fact, all about the money. On the night of Harvey's murder, both Marcones were at death's door and Chantel, as their only child, would stand to inherit everything. She found out that night that her inheritance was gone. Harvey had embezzled all of it.

Before I could share this information, Chantel and Maria came around the corner from the rear of the church. They were rushing out toward the street, arguing. The service wasn't over yet. Why was she leaving her own father's funeral?

I signaled for Kari and Olivia to stay put and slinked between cars in the parking lot, moving toward the suspicious duo.

"How could you forget your passport?" Chantel said to Maria.

"It no big deal. We go now. We do smoky smoke, then go to my cousin's house, get passport. It's on the way. Two minutes. Done. Then we fly away."

The phrase "we fly away" caught my attention and made my pulse race. But what did she mean by do "smoky smoke"? It seemed like an odd time to get high, but at least that would slow them down.

Chantel's Acura was parked at the curb. They hopped in. Chantel backed out of her spot. I caught a glimpse of the rear cargo space in her vehicle and counted five suitcases of varying sizes. The Acura took off heading north on Roland Avenue.

Olivia and Kari caught up to me. "What's going on?" Olivia asked.

"Get in the car," I said. "I'll explain on the way." We piled into Kari's car. I told her to follow Chantel's.

We rocketed up Roland Avenue. I brought Olivia up to speed on what we had learned this morning. "I think they're going to Chantel's house to get high, then pick up Maria's passport and head to the airport. The back of her car was loaded with suitcases."

Olivia's voice was soft and fragile, "Maria?" Then it rose. "Maria? My Maria?" Her volume reaching the level of her disbelief. "How could she?"

"We don't know the level of her involvement," I offered in consolation.

Kari shook her head. "What I don't understand is why would they stop to get high if they're on the run?"

"Maria's afraid of flying," Olivia said. "My guess is she's smoking to calm down before the flight."

Kari shrugged. "At least that should buy us some time. We gotta stop them."

I tried to reach Detective Howdy Doody but got his voicemail.

I tried calling Chip. He had the weight of the State's Attorney's office behind him. Maybe he could convince the police that the killers were getting away. I pulled up his number and hit the green button. Damn. I got his voicemail. I left a detailed message and disconnected.

Then I called Helen and explained the situation to her. She said she would keep trying to get through to Detective Jones.

While my heart and mind were racing, our car was crawling along. Traffic on Roland Avenue was heavy. It was the last week in August and the first week back to school. We were caught up in the gridlock that accompanied school dismissal time. I could see Chantel's Acura two cars ahead, stopped at the light.

"This isn't a high-speed chase," Kari said. "We've got time for more calls. Why don't you call 911?"

"Because they won't believe us."

My phone rang. It was Chip. "Hey, Jess. I got your message.

What's up?"

"I know who killed Harvey Metzger. We're following them now. I think they're heading to a house on South Road in Mount Washington, but they won't be there long. We tried to reach Detective Jones, but he didn't answer his cell. I don't know what else to do. We need some authority here soon or they'll be long gone."

"Give me the address and I'll see what I can do."

I relayed the information. "Thanks, Chip."

"Be careful. Wait for the police. Don't try to stop them. If you're right, they killed one person. One more won't make any difference to them."

Chip was right. I couldn't confront them myself, but I couldn't let them leave, either. I needed some muscle. I called Franco.

By way of greeting, he said, "Don't tell me you're suing me again."

"Funny. No, I need your help. This is serious. I found out who killed Harvey. There are two of them. I need them to be detained until I can get the police here. I wondered, you know, since you owe me and all for getting your money back, if you could send Elvis and Paulie to delay their departure until the authorities get here?"

"What you're asking me to do is illegal. It's called false imprisonment."

"Sure. I figured your guys would be good at it."

He laughed, a knowing, appreciative laugh, and asked me for the location.

We had finally inched our way through the school traffic and reached the Northern Parkway intersection. The Acura was in the far left turning lane. We remained out of sight, two car lengths behind, as they continued to travel west across Falls Road and up into the Mount Washington neighborhood. Kari eased up on the gas and fell back a little so they wouldn't spot us. Chantel pulled into her driveway. We parked a few houses down where we could still see the front door.

Helen called. "I keep getting Detective Jones's voicemail. Any luck on your end?"

"Nothing solid. Chip said he'd see what he could do, but that could take a while. I'm not taking any chances. I've got Franco sending his bodyguards over to detain Chantel and Maria until the police get here."

"Give me the address. This is going to make a great news story."

I gave her our location and told her to park away from the house.

"Now what?" Kari asked.

"Now we wait."

We didn't have to wait long. Elvis and Paulie arrived in a black Yukon and pulled up next to my car.

"That was fast," I said.

"We was over at Pimlico," Elvis said. "Paulie likes to play the horses."

"That's the house. Two doors up. The one with the wraparound porch. They're two women in their late twenties. It's possible that one of them is armed, maybe both. So be careful."

"That them?" Elvis asked.

I followed his eyes to the Marcone's front porch. Chantel and Maria were walking down the steps. "Yup. That's them."

"Go wait in your car."

Elvis and Paulie took off and blocked the driveway with their SUV, which dwarfed Chantel's Acura. The rest happened at rapid speed. With weapons drawn casually at their sides, Elvis and Paulie approached opposite car doors and hauled out Chantel and Maria like they were rag dolls. The men spun their captives around, pulled their arms behind their backs, and secured their wrists with zip-ties. Each one was frisked. Paulie used a third zip-tie to shackle them together to the front lamppost.

Once Chantel and Maria were contained, we approached. Chantel was squirming. Her expression was venomous. Maria sat with her head lowered. Her lips were moving in a silent prayer. The sound of sirens perforated the quiet of the neighborhood.

Elvis and Paulie took off before I could thank them. Our two prisoners had opposing reactions to seeing us. "Jess, you bitch lawyer. I'm gonna sue your ass for this," Chantel said.

Maria glanced at Olivia, then lowered her head again. "I'm sorry,

Mrs. Olivia. I'm sorry."

"Jesus, Mary, and Joe, there's smoke." Kari looked toward the house. Black plumes of smoke rose from the rear corner. Chantel's parents' house was on fire.

I was such an idiot. That's what Maria meant by "smokey smoke". They had set the fire. Chantel was desperate for a windfall of money after Harvey lost her inheritance. She must have figured she could torch the house and collect from the homeowner's policy. I gave Chantel a death glare. "Your family home? How could you?"

"Whaddya mean? I didn't do anything," she said.

Detective Jones arrived with a new partner. Now that he was no longer in the shadow of O'Mallory, he looked less like Howdy Doody. I explained everything that I had uncovered about Chantel's plan.

"How'd they get cuffed together to a lamppost?" he asked me.

I couldn't rat on my mobster friends, but I also couldn't lie to the police. A vague answer would suffice. "It wasn't me."

"Some muscle-wrapped guys with guns showed up out of the blue. They tied us up and drove off. That's when this bitch"—Chantel jerked her head in my direction—"showed up."

I shrugged. "My timing was perfect. I have an instinct for these things."

More sirens. Two fire trucks raced up the street toward us.

Detective Jones raised his eyebrows. "And the fire?"

I waved my hand toward Chantel. "She started the fire for the insurance money."

Turning to his partner, Detective Jones said, "Let's get them downtown."

I felt a hand on the small of my back. "Are you okay?" It was Chip.

"I'm fine. Thanks for getting the cavalry here."

With his hand still on my back, he guided me across the street. We watched as the fire trucks pulled up in front of the house. Kari and Olivia followed. Thick black smoke continued to rise from the back of the house, and I could see an occasional flame reach upward. I looked around for Mark but didn't see him.

Helen pulled up and joined us on the sidewalk. I rehashed the events for her, speaking into her recorder. Olivia and Kari chimed in with their own details.

Exhaustion overwhelmed me. I hurried to the end and told Helen to call me to fill in the blanks. Stepping from the curb, I realized Chip was still with me.

He offered to take me home.

"Thanks, but Kari will give me a ride."

He stayed by my side as we walked to Kari's car. "Are you sure you're alright, Jess?"

"I'm fine. Just tired. Now that it's over I realized how much energy this whole thing has sucked out of me."

He reached out for my elbow and turned me toward him. "You know you did a hell of job here. Do you realize that in the last week you helped me put away a drug dealer, nailed O'Mallory for grand theft, survived a kidnapping, and now you caught a couple of murderers?"

"Not bad for an ambulance chaser," I said.

Still holding my elbow, he pulled me toward him and kissed my forehead. "You're way more than that, Jess."

It was an uncomfortably tender moment. I had rid myself of my law-school crush on Chip days ago, and now I sensed the tables had turned. Could I resurrect my feelings for him? What about Mark? I liked Mark, and I was pretty sure Mark liked me.

As I pondered this delicious dilemma, I glanced over Chip's shoulder and saw Mark approaching. I pulled free from Chip. Mark was in street clothes. His Suburban was parked next to Helen's sedan.

"Hey, I guess it's your day off."

He looked at Chip and then at me. "I heard about the fire and thought I'd come by to see if they needed me to suit up. Helen told me what happened. Are you okay?"

"Just another day at the office. Kari was about to take me home."

"I can take you home," he offered. His eyes bounced back to Chip.

I realized I hadn't introduced them. "Mark, this is Chip. Chip is the

State's Attorney I told you about. The one who worked out that plea so Sharlyn didn't have to testify against her ex?"

"Oh right." Mark reached out to shake Chip's hand. "Heard that turned out well for everyone."

They pumped hands while sizing each other up. Then Mark turned to me. "They've got the fire under control. I can take you home if you're ready."

I was ready. I wanted Mark to take me home, but I had declined Chip's offer in favor of Kari giving me a ride. I didn't want to hurt his feelings. As I struggled to find the proper response, there came the distinct sound of tires screeching followed by metal crushing together. Our heads whipped around toward the noise at the intersection. A gray sedan had been T-boned by a black pickup truck. It went eerily quiet for the seconds following the impact. No one moved.

Then my training took over. I pulled out my phone and dialed 911 with one hand. With the other, I grabbed Kari and tugged her with me in the direction of the intersection. "Do you have some of my cards?"

"You know I do, girl."

We set off toward the accident at the intersection in full stride, leaving the men behind to battle over which one of them would drive me home.

Made in the USA
Columbia, SC
05 October 2017